THE NEW MEN

C. P. SNOW

PENGUIN BOOKS

Penguin Books Ltd, Harmondsworth, Middlesex, England
Penguin Books Australia Ltd, Ringwood, Victoria, Australia

—

First published by Macmillan 1954
Published in Penguin Books 1959
Reprinted 1961, 1962, 1963, 1965, 1967

—

—

Made and printed in Great Britain
by Cox and Wyman Ltd,
London, Reading and Fakenham
Set in Monotype Bembo

CONTENTS

CONTENTS

PART ONE

A QUESTION OF POSSIBILITY

CHAPTER I

Argument with a Brother

I HEARD the first rumour in the middle of an argument with my brother, when I was trying to persuade him not to marry, but it did not seem much more than a distraction.

He had brought Irene to lunch with me on a wet, windy morning in late February. The year was 1939, and I was still living in college. As we sat at table in my dining-room the rain slashed against the windows, and once or twice smoke from the open sixteenth-century grate blew across the room. It was so dark outside that I had turned all the sconce lights on, warm against the panelling; in that comfortable light, while the wind thudded against the window-panes, Irene set to work to get me on her side.

I had not met her before, but Martin had mentioned her name enough to make me guess about her. He had first picked her up in London, at one of his richer friends', and I gathered that she had no money but plenty of invitations. This seemed to amuse Martin, but to me she sounded too much like a shabby-smart girl, who thought her best chance was to find an able husband.

The more I heard of her, the more anxious I was for Martin – as a father might be for a son, for there were nine years between us. He was only twenty-five, and while other people saw him as stable and detached, the last man to commit a piece of foolishness, abnormally capable of looking after himself, I could not stop myself worrying.

The day before this luncheon, Martin had asked, without seeming over-eager, whether I would like to meet Irene. Yet I knew, and she knew, that it was a visit of inspection.

She called me by my Christian name in her first greeting: and, as I poured her out a glass of sherry, was saying:

7

'I always imagined you as darker than Martin. You should be dark!'

'You should drink sherry,' I said. She had the kind of impudence which provoked me and which had its attraction.

'Is it always sherry before meals?'

'What else?' I said.

'Fixed tastes!' she cried. 'Now *that* I did expect.'

As we began to eat, she went on teasing. It was the teasing, at once spontaneous and practised, of a young woman who has enjoyed playing for the attention of older men. She had the manner of a mischievous daughter, her laughter high-pitched, disrespectful, sharp with with a kind of constrained glee – and underneath just enough ultimate deference to please.

Yet, despite that manner, she looked older than her age, which was the same as Martin's. She was a tall woman, full-breasted, with a stoop that made one feel that she was self-conscious about her figure; often when she laughed she made a bow which reduced her height still more, which made her seem to be acting like a little girl. The skin of her cheeks looked already worn and high-coloured underneath the make-up.

Her features were not pretty, but one noticed her eyes, narrow, treacle-brown, glinting under the heavy upper lids. For me, in that first meeting, she had some physical charm.

Apart from that, I thought that she was reckless and honest in her own fashion. I could not satisfy myself about what she felt for Martin. She was fond of him, but I did not believe that she loved him; yet she longed to marry him. That was the first thing I was looking for, and within a few minutes I had no doubt. I still wanted to know why she longed for it so much.

She spoke like an adventuress, but this was a curious piece of adventuress-ship. That day she asked us, frankly, inquisitively, about our early life at home. She knew that we had come from the lower-middle-class back-streets of a provincial town, that I had struggled through to a career at the Bar and had then changed to academic law and settled in the college. Following after me, Martin had won a scholarship in natural science there, and I had been able to help pay his way. For nearly three years he had been doing research at the Cavendish.

As we talked, I realized that to Irene it seemed as strange, as exciting, as *different*, a slice of existence as Martin had found hers.

She had drunk more than her share of the wine. She broke out:
'Of course, you two had a better time than I had.'

'It has its disadvantages,' said Martin.

'You hadn't got everyone sitting on your head. Whenever I did anything I wanted to, my poor old father used to say: "Irene, remember you're a Brunskill." Well, that would have been pretty destroying even if the Brunskills had been specially grand. I thought it was too grim altogether when they sent me to school, and the only girl who'd heard the wonderful name thought we were Norwegians.'

I told her of my acquaintance, Lord Boscastle, whose formula of social dismissal was 'Who *is* he? I'm afraid I don't *know* the fellow.' She gave her yelp of laughter.

'That's what I should get,' she said. 'And it's much more dismaying if you've been taught that you may be poverty-stricken but that you are slightly superior.'

In fact, as I discovered later, she was overdoing it, partly because she had a vein of inverted snobbery and was exaggerating her misfortunes in front of us. Her father was living on his pension from the Indian Army, but some of the Brunskills could have been called county. In secret, Irene kept up her interest in the gradations of smartness among her smart friends.

She went on drinking, but, as we sat round the fire for our coffee, she took hold of herself and began questioning me about my plans. Was I going abroad that Easter vacation? When could she and Martin see me again? Wouldn't I meet them in London? Wouldn't I join them for a May Week ball?

'I'm afraid I can't,' I said.

'Do come. Wouldn't you like being seen with me?'

'My wife isn't fit to dance just now,' I said.

'Bring someone else.'

It was obvious that Martin had not told her of my wife's condition. She lived alone in London, and saw no one except me; increasingly those visits were hard to bear.

'I'm sorry,' I said.

'You don't want to dance with me. You're quite right, I'm not much good.'

'It must be seven or eight years since I went to a ball,' I reflected. 'Good Lord, time goes too fast.'

I had said it casually, platitudinously, but a line came between Irene's brows and her voice sharpened.

'That's near the bone,' she said.

'What's the matter?'

'I hate the thought of time.'

Quickly Martin smiled at her and was changing the subject, but she insisted.

'Time's winged chariot,' she said and looked at me. 'Do *you* like the thought of it?'

Soon she cheered up, and decided it was time to leave Martin and me together. She made some excuse; she might as well have invited us to discuss her.

I said goodbye to her in the little passage outside my gyp-cupboard, between the room-door and the oak.

'I'm afraid I've been horribly boring and talked too much,' she said, as she pressed my hand.

I passed it off.

'I always talk too much when I'm nervous.' She opened the outer door. Still she could not leave it alone; she glanced back over her shoulder, and called to me:

'I'm very nervous today, Lewis. Believe me, I am.'

She was begging me not to speak against her. As I turned back into the room a gust of wind crashed the door shut behind me. The smoke had cleared from the fireplace, the coal was cherry-red in the iron wicker of the grate. Across the hearth Martin's face was swept smooth in the unfluctuating glow.

He gave me a smile with his mouth tight and pulled down at one corner; it was a cagey, observant smile that he often wore, and which, together with his open expression and acute eyes, made his mood difficult to read.

His face was a young man's, but one that would not alter much until he was old; the skin would not take lines easily, except round the eyes; he was fair, and the hair curled, crisp and thick, close to his skull. He was shorter than I was, and not more than an inch or two taller than Irene, but his shoulders, neck and wrists were strong.

Without speaking, I sat down opposite to him, then I said:

'Well?'

'Well?' he replied.

His smile had not changed. His tone was easy. It would have been hard to tell how painfully he cared that I should approve of her; but I knew it.

Our sympathy had always been close, and was growing closer as we grew older. Between us there was a bond of trust. But much of our communication was unspoken, and it was rare for us to be direct with each other, especially about our deeper feelings.

It was partly that, like many men who appear spontaneous at a first meeting, we each had a vein of reserve. I sometimes broke loose from mine, but Martin's seemed to be part of his nature, as though he would never cease making elaborate plans to hide his secrets, to over-insure against the chances of life. I was watching him develop into a cautious, subtle and far-sighted man.

It was partly that reserve which kept us from being direct with each other; but much more it was the special restraint and delicacy which is often found in brothers' love.

'I think she's attractive,' I said, 'and distinctly good company.'

'Yes, isn't she?' said Martin.

Already we were fencing.

'Does she have a job of some kind?'

'I believe she's been someone's secretary.'

'Does that give her enough to live on, in London?'

'I've got an idea,' said Martin, with an appearance of elaborate reflection, 'that she shares a flat with another young woman.'

'She must find it pretty hard to keep going,' I said.

Martin agreed. 'I suppose it's genuinely difficult for them to make a living, isn't it?'

He was capable of stonewalling indefinitely. Trying another line, I asked whether he had decided anything about his own future. His research grant ran out by the summer, and, if there were no war (our habitual phrase that year), he would have to find a job. He would get a decent one, but, we both knew by this time, there were three or four contemporaries ahead of him, who would take the plums. His research was sound, so Walter Luke said, who supervised him: but Luke added that, judged by high standards, he was turning out good but not quite good enough.

I was more disappointed than I wanted Martin to see, for I had invested much hope in him, including hopes of my own that had been frustrated. His expectations, however, seemed to be humbler than mine. He was ready to come to terms with his talents, to be sorry they were not greater, but to make the best of them. If he believed that he might surprise us all, he hid it. He accepted Luke's opinion as just. That afternoon he thought the likelihood was that he would get a post in a provincial university.

'If you thought of marrying,' I said, 'you couldn't very well manage on that.'

'I suppose it has been done,' he replied.

Then I asked:

'As a matter of fact, are you intending to marry her?'

There was a pause.

'It's not completely out of the question,' he said.

His tone stayed even, but just for an instant his open, attentive expression broke, and I saw his eyes flash. They were dark blue, hard, transparently bright, of a kind common in our family. As they met mine, I knew in my heart that his resolve was formed. Yet I could not help arguing against it. My temper was fraying; as I tried not to sound clucking and protective, I could hear with dislike the edge in my own voice.

'I must say,' I broke out, 'that I think it would be very unwise.'

'I wondered if you would feel that,' said Martin.

'She'd be a load on you.'

'Why do you think that, particularly?'

He had the interested air of a man discussing the love-affairs of an acquaintance, well-liked, but for whom he had no intimate concern. It was assumed partly to vex me a little; but in part it was a protection against me.

'Do you think that she'd be much good as a professional man's wife?'

'I can see that she would have her disadvantages,' he said reasonably.

'You need someone who'll let you work in peace and for that you couldn't find anyone worse.'

'I think I could get my own way there,' said Martin.

'No, you couldn't. Not if you care for her at all, which I presume you do, otherwise you wouldn't be contemplating this piece of suicide.'

'Yes, I do care for her,' he said.

The coals fell suddenly, leaving a bright and fragile hollow in which the sparks stood still as fireflies. He leaned across to throw on coal. When he had sat back again I said:

'Then imagine what it would be like. She's rackety and you're prudent. She'd have all the time in the world on her hands, and do you think she's the woman to stay still? What do you think you'd find when you got home?'

'It's just possible that I might be able to settle her down.'

I was handling it badly, I knew. I said:

'You know, I'm not a great expert on happy marriages. But on unhappy ones I do know as much as most men.'

Martin gave a friendly, sarcastic smile. I went on. He met each point on the plane of reason. He had reckoned them out himself; no one insured more carefully against the future. I was telling him nothing he did not know. I became angry again.

'She's pretty shallow, you know. I expect her loves are too.'

Martin did not reply.

'She's bright, but she's not very clever.'

'That doesn't matter to me,' he said.

'You'd find her boring in time.'

'I couldn't have done less so up to now,' said Martin.

'Just imagine her being bright – for – ten years. In ten years you'd be sick and tired of her.'

'Ten years,' said Martin. He added: 'If that's the worst that happens!'

'She'd be driving you off your head.'

'If this fission affair works,' said Martin, 'we shall be lucky if we have any heads.'

That was the actual moment at which I first heard the rumour. There was a touch of irritation in Martin's voice, because over his marriage I had pressed him too far.

He was putting me off. He had not spoken with any special weight, for he was thinking about Irene and my opposition; yet something in his tone brought me up sharp, and I had to inquire:

'Is this anything new?'

'Very new,' said Martin. He was still trying to lead my attention away, but also he was half-caught up, as he said: 'It's very new, but I don't know how everyone missed it. I might have seen it myself!' He told me that, within the past fortnight, letters had been published in scientific journals in several countries, and that the Cavendish people and physicists everywhere were talking of nothing else. That I could understand. He then gave me an explanation which I could not understand, although I had heard plenty of the jargon of nuclear physics from him and Luke. 'Fission'. 'Neutrons'. 'Chain reaction'. I could not follow. But I could gather that at last the sources of nuclear energy were in principle open to be set loose; and that it might be possible to make an explosive such as no one had realistically imagined.

'Scientists always exaggerate,' I said.

'This isn't exaggerated,' said Martin. 'If it happens, one of these bombs would blow up Cambridge. I mean, there'd be *nothing* left.'

'Will it happen?'

'It seems to be about an even chance.'

I had stood up, as I attempted to follow his explanation. Then I walked across the room and looked out of the window into the court, where the rain was blowing before the wind, forming great driven puddles along the verges of the grass; in a moment I returned to where Martin was still sitting by the fire. We were both sobered, but to me this piece of news, though it hung over us as we faced each other, seemed nothing but a red-herring.

I came back, more gently now, to the prospect of his marriage. Had he really thought what, in terms of day-to-day living, it might mean? He was once more polite, sensible, brotherly. He would admit the force of any one of my doubts: he would say yes to each criticism. Although underneath I could feel his intention, embedded right in the core of his will, nevertheless he was ready to make any other concession to my worry.

Nothing said in anger would be remembered, he was as good as saying, with his good-natured, sarcastic smile. In fact, even in the bitterest moment of the quarrel, I had taken that for granted. It did not enter my mind that anything could touch the confidence between us.

CHAPTER 2

A Code Name

MARTIN married Irene that autumn, but I could not visit them for some time afterwards. For the war had started: he was working at

Rosyth in one of the first degaussing parties, and, as for me, I was already a temporary civil servant in London.

As the early months of war went by, I heard nothing, and thought little, about my brother's marriage; but the piece of scientific news which, when I was trying to turn him against Irene, he had used as a false trail, came several times into my office-work.

It happened so through some personal coincidences. It was because the Minister knew me that I went into his department, and it was because of his own singular position that we saw the minutes of the scientific committees. His name was Thomas Bevill, and he was a second cousin of Lord Boscastle. He had been a professional politician all his life without making much of a mark in public; in private, in any government milieu he was one of the most trusted of men. He had the unusual gift of being both familiar and discreet; forty years before, when he began his career, he had set himself never to give away a secret, and never to allow himself the bright remark that makes a needless enemy. So by 1939 he had become such a link as all governments needed, particularly at the beginning of a war, before the forms of administration had settled down: they needed a man like Thomas Bevill as the chairman of confidential committees, the man to be kept informed of what was going on, the supreme post-office.

Just before war began, he asked me to join him as one of his personal assistants. He had met me two or three times with the Boscastles, which was a virtue in his eyes, and I had been trained as a lawyer, which was another. He thought I was suitable raw material to learn discretion. Gradually, in the first autumn of the war, he let me item by item into his confidential files. That was why, one autumn afternoon, he sent word that he would like a 'little talk' with Hector Rose and me.

The Minister's room was only two doors from mine, and both, relics of the eighteenth-century Treasury, looked out over Whitehall itself, brilliant that afternoon with autumn sun that blazed from the windows opposite ours. The Minister was not in the room, but Sir Hector Rose was already sitting by the side of the coal-fire. He was a man in the early forties, stocky, powerful, and youthful-looking, his official black coat and striped trousers cut to conceal his heavy muscles. The flesh of his cheeks shone as though untouched, and his face, hair, and eyes had the same lightness. He greeted me with his usual excessive politeness. Then he said:

'I suppose you have no idea what our master is going to occupy us with?'

I said no, and it was clear that he had none.

'Has anyone else been summoned, do you know, Eliot?'

I did not think so. Rose said: 'That makes us a very cosy little party.'

He spoke with a flick of the tongue, but he did not mean that it was strange for him, the Permanent Secretary, to be invited along with someone many rungs lower (I had started as what the Civil Service called a principal). Rose was too confident a man to bother about trivialities like that; he was himself formal, but he only objected to informality in others when it interfered with his administrative power.

The Minister came in, carrying a coal-scuttle, on his hand a grimy cloth glove. He knelt by the grate, picked out lumps of coal and built up the fire. He was naturally familiar and unobtrusive in manner, but sometimes I thought he had developed it into an act. When people called on him in Whitehall, he would take their hats and coats and stow them punctiliously away in his cupboard. Kneeling by the fire, he looked thin-shouldered, wispy, like an elderly clerk.

'I just wanted to have a word with you two,' he said, still bending down.

'An old boy came in to see me a day or two ago,' he went on, as he pulled up a chair between us, round the fire. The 'old boy' was an eminent physicist, not more than sixty, that is, ten years Bevill's junior. And the visit had taken place a week before: Bevill had been thinking things out.

'I think I ought to put you two in the swim,' he said. 'Though, as you may have gathered, I'm a great believer in no one knowing more than he's got to know to do his job. And I don't mind telling you that I've wondered whether either of you have got to know this time. But Eliot must, if he's going to be much use to me, and there may be some action for you, Rose, not now, perhaps in a year or so's time.'

'If you think it wiser that I shouldn't know till then, Minister,' said Rose. Underneath the courtesy, he was irked by Bevill's talent for using two words where one would do. I thought that he underrated the old man, particularly when, as now, he settled down comfortably to another Polonius-like discourse on security. The first thing, said the Minister, was to forget all about the official hierarchy, the next was to forget that you had any relatives. If you possess a secret, he said, your secretary may have to know: but not your second-in-command: and not your wife.

'If you decide to leave me out at this stage, I shall perfectly well understand,' said Rose, getting back to relevance.

'No, my dear chap. It wouldn't be practical,' said the Minister. 'I shouldn't be able to pull the wool over your ears.'

The Minister sometimes got his idioms mixed up. Rose went on watching him with pale, heavy-lidded eyes, which met the old man's frank, ingenuous, blue ones. With the same simple frank expression, Bevill said:

'As a matter of fact, some of these scientists believe they can present us with a great big bang. Like thousands of tons of T.N.T. *That* would be a futurist war, *if* you like. That old boy the other day said we ought to be ready to put some money on it.'

It sounded like the gossip I had heard in Cambridge, and I said so.

'Ought you to have heard?' said Bevill, who thought of science in nothing but military terms. 'These chaps will talk. Whatever you do, you can't stop them talking. But they're pushing on with it. I've collected three appreciations already. Forget all I tell you until you have to remember – that's what I do. But the stuff to watch is what they call a uranium isotope.'

He said the words slowly as though separating the syllables for children to spell. 'U. 235,' he added, as though domesticating a foreign name. To each of the three of us, the words and symbols might as well have been in Hittite, though Rose and I would have been regarded as highly educated men.

The Minister went on to say that, though the scientists 'as usual' were disagreeing among themselves, some of them believed that making a 'superbomb' was now only a matter of a series of techniques. They also believed that whichever side got the weapon first would win the war.

'These people always think that it's easier to win wars than I do,' he added imperturbably.

'How soon before it's a feasible proposition?' Rose asked him.

'Not tomorrow,' said Bevill. 'Anything up to ten years.'

'That's a very long-term prospect,' said Rose.

'I'm not an optimist,' the Minister replied. 'It may be a very long-term war. But I agree with you, my dear chap, it doesn't sound like business for this time. Still it won't do any harm to watch out and keep our powder dry.'

'Many thanks for giving me the warning, Minister,' said Rose, deciding there was nothing more of use to be learned that afternoon. 'Many, many thanks.'

But before Rose could get away, Bevill showed us his private dossier of the uranium project. We must not refer to it again by that name, he said: as with all other projects of high secrecy, he copied out the 'appreciations' in his own hand, keeping no copies: the documents were then mounted in a loose-leaf cover, on which he printed a pet name.

'I'm going to show you my name for this new stunt,' he said, with a smile that was frank, shy and eager. And into that smile there crept the almost salacious pleasure that many men show as they talk of secrets.

He turned over the cover, and we saw, painted in bold capitals, the words:

MR TOAD

'That's what we'll call it here, if you don't mind,' he added.

CHAPTER 3

What might have been Foresight

IT still did not seem significant. That winter, one or two of us who were in the secret discussed it, but, although we looked round the room before we spoke, it did not catch hold of us as something real.

Once Francis Getliffe, whom I had known longer than the other scientists, said to me:

'I hope it's *never* possible.'

But even he, though he did not want any men anywhere to possess this power, spoke without heaviness, as if it were a danger of the future, a piece of science-fiction, like the earth running into a comet's path.

All the arrangements of those first months of Mr Toad were on the pettiest scale – a handful of scientists, nearly all of them working part-time, scattered round three or four university laboratories: a professor wondering whether he might spend three hundred and fifty pounds for some extra help: an improvised committee, meeting once a month, sending its minutes to the Minister in longhand.

In the summer of 1940, on one of those mornings of steady, in-different sunshine that left upon some of us, for years afterwards, an inescapable memory, I was walking down Piccadilly and noticed half a dozen men coming out of the Royal Society's door in Burlington House. I knew most of them by sight. They were scientists, nearly all youngish men: one or two were carrying continental briefcases; they might have been coming from an examiners' meeting. In fact, they were the committee, and the sight of them brought back the Minister's pet name, which, with the war news dragging like an illness, did not seem much of a joke.

Soon afterwards, in the Minister's office we received intelligence that the Germans were working on the bomb. Although we had all assumed it, the news was sharp: it added another fear. Also it rough-ened the tongues of those who were crusading for the project. Step by step they won for it a little more attention. By the spring of 1941 they obtained sanction for a research establishment – not a grand establishment like those working on radio and the immediate weapons of war, but one with perhaps a hundred scientists to their thousands. For a site, they picked on a place called Barford – which I had not heard of, but found to be a village in Warwickshire, a few miles from Stratford-on-Avon.

It became one of my duties to help them collect staff. I could hardly have had a more niggling job, for almost all scientists were by this time caught up in the war. Even for projects of high priority it was difficult enough to extract them, and so far as priority was concerned, the Barford project still had none at all. The only good scientists not yet employed were refugees, and it was clear that they would have to form the nucleus of Barford.

Accepting those facts, the Barford superintendent and his backers still made a claim, a modest claim, for at least one or two of the better young Englishmen. It was thus that I was asked to sound Walter Luke; if we could get him released from his radio work, would he be willing to move to Barford?

Then I wondered about Martin. I had heard little from him. I should have heard, if things had been going well, if, like a good many scientists of his age, he had fallen on his feet. For eighteen months he had been doing a piece of technical routine. He seemed to be doing it just as competently, neither less nor more, than a hundred other young men in the naval ports. From a distance I had been watching, without being able to help.

I could not say much about Barford; in any case I knew that in this matter his temperament would work like mine; we said yes, but we did not like to be managed. Nevertheless, I could drop a hint. He could see for himself that it might give him a chance.

Later, my memory tended to cheat; it made me look as though I had the gift of foresight. That was quite untrue. In the spring of 1941, there were several other projects on Bevill's files which seemed to me of a different order of importance from Mr Toad. As for Barford, I did not believe that anything would come of it, and my chief interest was that it might give Martin a better chance.

CHAPTER 4

Result of a Manoeuvre

IT was some weeks before either Luke or Martin could get to London, but then I arranged to see them both on the same afternoon in May.

Martin was the first to arrive. It was over a year since we had met, and, as we enquired about each other, there was the sense of well-being, the wiping-away of anxiety's fret, that one only gets with those who have become part of the deep habit of one's life.

Soon I asked:

'How is Irene?'

'Very well,' said Martin, looking straight into my eyes, giving nothing away.

He walked round my office, admiring the Regency mantelpiece and the view over Whitehall. He was rejoicing that I was having something of a success – for, entirely through the Minister's backing, I had just been promoted. In a section of the war, I now had my bit of subfusc power. I was for shrugging it off; but Martin, however, set more store by official honours than I did.

'Are you sure you're making the most of it?' he said, with a proprietorial, insistent air.

He was delighted, and in his delight there was no envy. Yet suddenly he was sounding knowledgeable and worldly; it was strange, out of the haze of family memories, to see him standing there, a calculating man. If he had a success himself, I thought, he would have all the tricks ready to exploit it.

Actually, he had nothing to exploit. I listened to him saying that, as far as his job went, there was still nothing whatever to report. No change. I was full of irritation, for, when you hope for someone as I did for him, you blame them for their own misfortunes.

'So far as there's been any luck in the family,' I said, 'I've had it.'

'I don't believe in luck to that extent,' said Martin, without complaint.

'You've had none,' I said.

Then Martin smiled, and brought out a phrase which would have been meaningless to any but us two. 'You've got someone to live up to.' It was a phrase of our mother's, holding me up before him as an example, for I had been her favourite son. I recalled her as she lay dying, instructing me sternly not to think too little of Martin. No injunction could ever have been less called-for; but later I believed that she was making amends to herself for not having loved him more.

Martin was talking of her when, an hour before I expected him, Walter Luke came in. Ever since I had known him as a younger man – he was still not thirty – he had thrown the whole of his nature into everything he felt. I had seen him triumphant with every cell of his body, as a human integer of flesh and bone: and I had seen him angry. That afternoon he was ashamed of himself, and it was not possible for a man to throw more of his force into being ashamed.

'Hello, Lewis. Hallo, Martin,' he said. 'I've just been ticked off. I deserved it, and I got it, and I'm beginning to wonder when I shall manage to grow up.'

He slumped on to a chair, immersed in his dejection. His backbone, usually so straight in his thick energetic frame, curved disconsolately against the leather; yet he exuded vigour, and both Martin and I were smiling at him. His cheeks were not as ruddy as when I first saw him at high table, five years before. In the last two years he had carried responsibility, and even on his physique the strain had told. Now he looked his age; there were grey hairs at his temples; but his voice remained eager, rich and youthful, still bearing a rumble from the Plymouth dockyard where he was brought up.

He had just come from one of the radio committees, where he had been arguing with someone he called a 'stuffed shirt' (and who was highly placed). The stuffed shirt had been canvassing his favourite idea, 'and I tell you,' said Luke, 'If I'd been asked to think of something bloody silly, I couldn't have thought up anything so fantastically bloody silly as that.' Luke had apparently proceeded to say so, using his peculiar resources of eloquence. The chairman, who was even more highly placed than the stuffed shirt, had told him this was not the right spirit: he was thinking of his own ideas, and didn't want the other's to work.

'The old bleeder was perfectly right,' said Luke with simplicity. He went on:

'I never know whether I've got cross because some imbecile is talking balderdash or whether my own precious ego is getting trampled on. I wish one of you shrewd chaps would teach me.'

Walter Luke was neither pretending nor laughing at himself; he was contrite. Then, with the same freshness and resilience, he had finished with his contrition. He sat up straight in his chair, and asked what I wanted to see him about.

I said we had better have a word alone. Luke said:

'Why have we got to turf Martin out?'

'Lewis is right,' said Martin, getting ready to go.

'It depends which surprise-packet he's going to pull out of the bag,' said Luke, with a broad, fresh grin. He looked at me: 'Barford?'

I was taken off guard.

'Teach your grandmother to suck eggs,' said Luke. 'We know all about *that*.'

Martin was smiling, as Luke began to talk to him. It was clear that Martin, though he was discreet, knew enough to horrify the Minister; as for Luke, he knew as much as anyone I had heard.

For anyone used to Bevill's precautions, this was startling to listen to. In terms of sense, it should not have been such a surprise. Word was going round among nuclear physicists, and Luke, young as he was, was one of the best of them. He had already been consulted on a scientific point; he could guess the rest.

I had to accept it. There was also an advantage in speaking in front of Martin; it might be the most natural way to draw him in.

At that moment, he was listening to Luke with a tucked-in, sarcastic smile, as though he were half-admiring Luke's gifts, half-amused by him as a man.

'Well,' I said to Luke, 'as you know so much, you probably know what I've been told to ask.'

'I hadn't heard anything,' he replied, 'but they must be after me.'

'Would you be ready to go?'

Luke did not answer, but said: 'Who else have they got?'

For the first time that afternoon, I was able to tell him something. The Superintendent, Drawbell, the engineering heads –

'Good God alive,' Luke interrupted, 'Lewis, *who are these uncles?*'

A list of names of refugees – and then I mentioned Arthur Mounteney.

'I'm glad they've got hold of one scientist, anyway,' said Luke 'He did some nice work once. He's just about finished, of course.'

'Do you feel like going in?' I asked.

Luke would not reply.

'Why don't they get hold of Martin?' he said. 'He's wasted where he is.'

'They're not likely to ask for me,' said Martin.

'Your name keeps cropping up,' I said to Luke.

Usually, when I had seen men offered jobs, they had decided within three minutes, even though they concealed it from themselves, even though they managed to prolong the pleasure of deciding. Just for once, it was not so.

'It's all very well,' said Luke. 'I just don't know where I can be most use.' He was not used to hesitating; he did not like it; he tried to explain himself. If he stayed where he was, he could promise us a 'bit of hardware' in eighteen months. Whereas, if he joined this 'new party' there was no guarantee that anything would happen for years.

There was nothing exaggerated in Luke's tone just then. I was used to the rowdiness with which he judged his colleagues, especially his seniors; it was the same with most of the rising scientists; they had none of the convention of politeness that bureaucrats like Sir Hector

Rose were trained to, and often Rose and his friends disliked them accordingly. Listening to Luke that afternoon, no one would have thought, for instance, that the poor old derelict Mounteney was in fact a Nobel prizewinner aged about forty. But on his own value Luke was neither boastful nor modest. He was a good scientist; good scientists counted in the war, and he was not going to see himself wasted. He had lost that tincture of the absurd which had made Martin smile. He spoke without nonsense, with the directness of a man who knows what he can and cannot do.

'I wish some of you wise old men would settle it for me,' he said to me.

I shook my head. I had put Bevill's request, but that was as far as I felt justified in going. For what my judgement of the war was worth, I thought on balance that Luke should stay where he was.

He could not make up his mind. As the three of us walked across the Park towards my flat in Dolphin Square, he fell first into a spell of abstraction and then broke out suddenly into a kind of argument with himself, telling us of a new device in what we than called R.D.F. and were later to call Radar. The evening was bright. A cool wind blew from the east, bringing the rubble dust to our nostrils, although it was some days since the last raid. Under our feet the grass was dust-greyed and dry. I was worried about the war that evening; I could see no end to it; it was a comfort to be with those two, in their different fashions steady-hearted and robust.

On the way home, and all the evening, Martin kept putting questions to Luke, steering him back to nuclear fission. I could feel, though, that he was waiting for Luke to leave. He had something to say to me in private

At last we took Luke to the bus stop, and Martin and I turned back towards St George's Square. The full moon shone down on the light-less blind-faced streets, and the shadows were dark indigo. Flecks of cloud, as though scanning the short syllables in a line of verse, stood against the impenetrable sky. Under the moon, the roofs of Pimlico shone blue as steel. The wind had fallen. It was a silent, beautiful wartime night.

'By the way –' said Martin, with constraint in his voice.

'Yes?'

'I'd be grateful if you could get me in to this project somehow.'

I had never known him ask a favour of this kind before. He had not once come to me for official help, either at Cambridge or since. Now he was driven – scruple, pride, made his voice stiff, but he was driven.

'I was going to suggest it,' I said. 'Of course, I'll – '

'I really would be grateful.'

My manoeuvre had come off, but as he spoke I felt no pleasure. I had taken it on myself to interfere; from now on I should have some responsibility for what happened to him.

Now the trigger had been touched, he was intent on going: why it meant so much, I could not tell. His career? – something of that, perhaps, but he was not reckoning the chances that night. Concern about his wife? – he would not volunteer anything. No: simple though the explanation might seem for a man like Martin, it was the science itself that drew him. Though he might have no great talent, nuclear physics had obsessed him since he was a boy. He did not know, that night, what he could add at Barford; he only knew that he wanted to be there.

He admitted as much: but he had more practical matters to deal with. Having swallowed his pride, he did not intend to prostrate himself for nothing.

'You're sure that you can get me in? I should have thought the first move was to persuade someone else to suggest me. Walter Luke would do . . .' Could I write to Luke that night? Could I, as an insurance, remind Mounteney that Martin and I were brothers?

It was late before we went to bed; by that time Martin had written out an aide memoire of the people I was to see, write to, and telephone next day.

CHAPTER 5

Advice from a Man in Trouble

MARTIN's transfer went through smoothly, and he had begun work at Barford by June. With Luke, it took months longer.

In November I paid them an official visit. The Superintendent was still demanding men, and some of his sponsors in Whitehall had become more active; they even began to say that one of the schemes at Barford might give results within two years.

Francis Getliffe and the other scientific statesmen were sceptical. They were so discouraging that the Minister did not feel it worth while to inspect Barford himself; but, with his usual desire to keep all doors open, he sent me down instead.

I spent a morning and afternoon walking round laboratories listening to explanations I only one-tenth comprehended, listening also to the clicking, like one-fingered typewriting, of Geiger counters. But I comprehended one thing clearly. There were two main lines at Barford – one which Luke had set up on his own, with a few assistants, and the other led by a man called Rudd. Rudd was the second-in-command of the establishment; his line was, in principle, to separate the isotope, and they were attempting several methods; it was one of these, on which Martin and a team of scientists were working, which Rudd was trying to sell. As an official, I had been exposed to a good deal of salesmanship, but this, for unremitting obsessive concentration, was in a class by itself.

It was having an effect on me. Next morning I was due for a conference with the Superintendent, and I needed to clear my head. So, as an excuse, I went off by myself to call on Luke.

It meant a walk through a country lane leading from the mansion, which had been turned into the administrative headquarters, to the airfield. The hedges were brittle and dark with the coming winter, the only touch of brightness was the green of the ivy flowers. At the top of the rise the mist was shredding away, and suddenly, on the plateau, the huts, hangars, half-built brick ranges, stood out in the light of the cold and silvery sun.

Inside Luke's hangar, the vista was desolate. A quarter of the roof was open to the sky, and a piece of canvas was hanging down like a velarium. The only construction in sight was a cube of concrete, about six feet high, with a small door in it standing slightly ajar, through which a beam of light escaped. The afternoon had turned cold, and in the half-light, lit only by that beam on the wet floor and a naked bulb on the side of the hangar, the chill struck like the breath of a cave. No place looked less like an engine-room of the scientific future; it might have been the relic of a civilization far gone in decay.

There was not a person in sight. In a moment, as though he had

26

heard me, Luke came out of the cube-door, muttering to someone within. He was wearing a windjacket, which made him seem more than ever square, like an Eskimo, like a Polar explorer. He beat his arms across his chest and blew on his fingers.

'Hello, Lewis,' he said. 'It's bloody cold, and this blasted experiment won't go, and I want to run away and cry.'

I was interrupting him, he was fretting to get back to work; a voice from inside the tube asked about the next move. For minutes together, Luke gave orders for a new start the following day. 'What shall we do tonight?' came the voice.

Luke considered. For once he did not find the words. At last he said:

'*We'll just go home.*'

I walked back with him, for he and his wife had invited some of my old acquaintances to meet me at their house that evening. He was so dejected that I did not like to press him, and yet I had to confirm what everyone was telling me – that he was getting nowhere. Even so, my own question sounded flat in the bitter air.

'How is it going, Walter?'

Luke swore. 'How do *you* think it's going?'

'Is it going to come out?'

'Does it look like it?' he replied.

I told him that I should be talking next morning to Drawbell, that nothing I could say would signify much, but it all helped to form opinion.

'You didn't do much good bringing me here, did you?'

Then he corrected himself, though his tone was still dejected. 'That's not fair,' he said.

I asked more about his method (which aimed at plutonium, not the isotope).

'I'm not promising anything,' said Luke.

'Will it work in time?'

'I can't see the way tonight,' he said, with another curse.

'Shall you?'

He said, half depressed, half boastful:

'What do you think I'm here for?'

But that was his only burst of arrogance, and in the party at his house he sat preoccupied. So did Martin, for a different reason: for

Irene had arranged to meet him there, and, when everyone else had arrived, still did not come.

Each time the door opened Martin looked round, only to see the Mounteneys enter, then the Puchweins. And yet, though he was saying little and Luke brooded as he went round filling glasses from a jug of beer, the evening was a cosy one. Out of doors, the countryside was freezing. It was a winter night, the fields stretching in frosted silence. Outside was the war, but within our voices and the light of the fire. It was a night on which one felt lapped in safeness to the finger-tips.

Ideas, hopes, floated in the domestic air. For the first time at Barford, I heard an argument about something other than the project. After science, in those wartime nights, men like Puchwein and Mounteney had a second favourite subject. They argued as naturally as most of us drink, I was thinking, feeling an obscure fondness for them as I listened to them getting down to their second subject, which was politics.

For Puchwein, in fact, I had the peculiar fondness one bears someone to whom one has done a good turn. A close friend of mine called Roy Calvert had taken risks to smuggle Puchwein out of Berlin in 1938, and several of us had helped support him. But Puchwein was not in the least got down by having to accept charity. His manner remained patriarchal, it was he who dispensed the patronage. He had a reputation as a chemist. He was a very big man, bald and grey, though still under forty. When he took off his spectacles his eyes slanted downward, so that he always seemed about to weep. Actually, he was cheerful, kind, and so uxorious that his wife was showing lines of temper. But he forgot her, he was immersed, as he and she and Mounteney, and sometimes Nora Luke and I, threw the political phrases to and fro in front of the fire.

Some of those phrases, as used by both Puchweins and Mounteney but by no one else in the room, would have given me a clue if I had not known already. 'The party' for the Communist Party, 'Soviet' as an adjective for Russian, 'Fascists' as a collective term to include National-Socialists, 'The Daily' for the *Daily Worker*, 'social democrats' to describe members of the Labour Party such as Luke, or even unorthodox liberals such as Martin and me – all those were shibboleths, and meant, if one had ever listened to the dialect of intellectual communism, that those who used them were not far from the party line.

Neither Puchwein nor Mounteney concealed it. Throughout the thirties it had been nothing to conceal. They did not hold party tickets, so far as anyone knew; but they were in sympathy, Mounteney in slightly irregular sympathy. None of us was surprised or concerned that it should be so, certainly not in that November of 1941, when not only to the Puchweins but to conservative-minded Englishmen, it seemed self-evident that the war was being won or lost on Russian land.

Just then Luke went round with the beer again, the argument suddenly quietened, and I heard Emma Mounteney whispering to Hanna Puchwein with a glance in Martin's direction:

'Where is our wandering girl tonight?'

Hanna looked away, but Emma was hard to stop.

'I wonder,' she whispered, 'if T—' (a man I scarcely knew) 'is on his lonesome.'

Martin was on the other side of the fire. I thought that he could not have heard. Nevertheless, before Puchwein began again, Martin apologized for Irene. She was finishing some work, he said; it must have taken longer than she reckoned, and it looked as though she might not get there at all. His composure was complete. I had once known a similar situation, but I had not summoned up half his self-command. Yet, as the talk clattered on, his eyes often gazed into the fire, and he was still listening for a ring at the door.

Martin had not spoken since his apology for her, and I wanted to shield him from going home with the Mounteneys, whose house (at Barford the scientists and their families were crammed on top of each other, as in a frontier town) he shared. So I invented a pretext for us to walk home together.

In the village street, all was quiet. A pencil of light edged the top of a blacked-out window-frame. Otherwise the village was sleeping as it might have done on a Jacobean night, when some of these houses were built. Martin's footsteps, slower and heavier than mine although he was the lighter man, seemed loud on the frosty road. I left him to break the silence. Our steps remained the only noise, until he remarked, as though casually:

'Walter Luke didn't say much tonight, did he?'

I agreed.

'He must have had something in his mind. His experiment, I suppose.' And that was all he said.

Martin was doing what we have all done, refer to ourselves, half apologize, half confide, by pretending an interest in another. If I had been an intimate friend but not a brother, perhaps even if I had been a stranger, I thought that just at that moment he would have unburdened himself. Often it is the reserved who, when a pain, or even more, a humiliation, has lived inside them too long, suddenly break out into a confidence to someone they scarcely know. But I was the last person to whom he could let go.

As we both showed when we first talked of his engagement, there was a delicacy in our kind of brothers' love; and the closer we came to our sexual lives, the more that delicacy made us speak in terms of generalization and sarcasm. We knew each other very well by instinct. We could guess which women would attract the other, and often it was an attraction that we shared. Yet I had never told him any detail either of my married life or of a love-affair. I should have felt it, not so much embarrassing to speak, though that would also have been true, but worse than embarrassing to force him to listen. It was the same from him to me. He could not tell me whom he suspected she went to bed with; he could not tell me what she was like in his own bed; and so it was no relief to speak at all.

At the cross-roads he asked if I minded walking a few yards to the bridge; it was as though he wanted an excuse for not returning home (or was it superstition, as though, if he did not hurry back, all would be well?'). It was a moonless night, and the stars were faint, but there was a glimmer on the river. All of a sudden a November meteorite scorched its way across the sky, and then another.

'More energy there than we shall make,' said Martin, nodding in the direction of the establishment.

Now that my eyes were accustomed to the light I could make out the expression on his face. It was set and sad – and yet he was controlling his voice, he was beginning to speak seriously, about the project.

'By the way,' he said, 'I suppose the people here are putting some pressure on you?'

I said yes.

'They want you to invest in this place in a big way?'

Again I said yes.

'As long as you all realize that *nothing* here is within years of being tested –' He broke off, and then said:

'It would be very nice for me if Rudd's show came off. I should get some reflected glory, which I could do with.'

For a moment his voice was chilled, as though his secret thoughts were too strong: but I understood.

'You don't think it *will* come off?'

He paused.

'I haven't got the grasp some of these people have, you know, and most of them believe in it.' Then he added: 'But I shouldn't like you to plump for it too far.'

'What's the matter with it?'

'I think your own reputation will look nicer,' he said, 'if you go fairly slow this time.'

It was not until we were walking towards his house that he said:

'I can't explain why I'm not convinced. I wish I were better at this game, then perhaps I could.'

When we had mounted to his landing above the Mounteneys, there was no light under the door. As soon as we were inside the room Martin said, and for an instant his voice had become unrecognizable:

'I detest living in other people's houses.'

In that instant his face was white with temper. Was he thinking that Emma Mounteney would know the exact time that Irene climbed up the stairs? Then he spoke, once more calmly:

'I think I'd better wait up for her. I don't think she's taken a key.'

CHAPTER 6

Morning Before the Office

NEXT morning I woke out of heavy sleep, and was dragged at by a memory of muttering (it might have been a dream, or else something heard in the distance) from the bedroom next door. When I got up and went into breakfast, Irene told me that Martin had already left for the laboratory. She was wearing a dressing-gown, her voice was quiet but tight; without her make-up, she looked both drabber and younger.

In silence I ate the toast and jam of a wartime breakfast. Looking down from the window into the sunny morning, I could see the river flash through the elm-branches. I was aware that her gaze was fixed on me.

Suddenly she cried out:

'Why do you dislike me so?'

'I don't,' I said.

'I can't bear not to be liked.'

Very quickly, almost as though she had been rehearsing it, she told me a story of how, when she was twelve, she went to stay with a 'glamorous' schoolfriend, and how the other girl had been asked by an aunt. 'Who is your best friend? Is Irene your best friend?' And the answer had come, polite and putting-off, 'Oh, Irene has so many friends.'

'I couldn't face her again,' said Irene, and then: 'I wish *you* would like me.'

'It doesn't matter to either of us.'

'I want you to.' Her tone was at the same time penitent, shameless, provocative; it was easy to imagine how she spoke to her husband. I had to rouse myself.

'You want it both ways, you know,' I said.

'What have I done against you?' she burst out defiantly.

'Nothing.'

'Then why can't we get on?'

'You know as well as I do. Do you expect me to approve of you as my brother's wife?'

'So that's it,' she said.

'Don't pretend that's news,' I said. 'Why have you started this – *this morning*?'

She had crossed over to the window-seat, and was watching me with sharp eyes, which were beginning to fill with tears.

'You've taken against me, just because I couldn't stand the very thought of those people last night.'

'You know perfectly well that's not all.'

'Would you like me to tell you what I was really doing?'

I shook my head. 'You're not a fool. You must realize that you're damaging him –'

'I suppose my *dear* friends were wondering who I'd taken to bed, weren't they?'

'Of course.'

'Who did they think?'

I would not reply.

'Whose name did you hear?' she cried.

Impatiently I repeated Emma's question about T——. She gave a yelp of laughter. She was for an instant in high spirits, nothing but amused.

'They *can't* think that!'

She stared at me: the tears had gone.

'You won't believe me, but they're wrong. It wasn't him, it wasn't anyone. I just couldn't stand their faces any more, I had to get out on my own. They're hopelessly wrong. Please believe me!'

I said:

'Whether they're right or wrong – in a place like this you mustn't given anyone an excuse to gossip, it doesn't matter whether it's justified or not.'

'How often I've heard that,' she said with a glint in her eyes.

'When?'

'All night long. Do you think you're the *first* to scold me?' She looked at me, and went on: 'He was specially angry because *you* were here to see.'

After a moment, I said: 'That's neither here nor there.'

'Isn't it?' said Irene.

'The only thing I've got a right to talk about,' I said, 'are the practical consequences. Unless you want to damage his career, the least you can do for Martin is behave yourself on the outside.'

'I promised him that this morning,' she said in a thin voice.

'Can you keep your promise?'

'You needn't worry.' Her voice was thinner still.

Then she stood up, shook herself, went to the looking-glass and remained there, studying her reflection.

'We ought to be moving soon,' she said, her voice full again, brisk, and matter-of-fact. 'These people aren't altogether wrong about me. I may as well tell you that, though I expect you know.'

I was getting up, but she said no, and sat down opposite me.

R—B

'They've got the idea right, but it's my past coming back on me.' She added, without emotion: 'I've been a bad girl. I've had some men.'

Yes, she would have liked to be an adventuress: but somehow she hadn't managed it. 'Perhaps you've got to be cooler than I am to bring it off,' she said, half-mystified.

It was she who had been used, not her lovers; and there was one who, when she thought of him, still had power over her.

'Martin knew about him before we married,' she said. 'Have you heard of Edgar Hankins?'

I had not only heard of him, but ten years before had known him fairly well.

'I loved him very much,' she said. She went on: 'I ought to have made him marry me.'

'Was it a matter of will?' I said, feeling more tender to her.

'No,' said Irene, 'I've got the will, but I can't trust my nerves.'

Then I asked why she had married Martin. She began not by answering the question, but by saying: 'You shouldn't worry too much about Martin.'

'Why not?'

'I fancy he's a harder man than you are.'

She said it as though she were praising him. Reverting to her businesslike manner, she went on about her reasons for the marriage. She had found some of her friends competing for him, she said; and that provoked her. But most of all she wanted safety.

'I was getting notorious,' she said. 'When people heard my name, they were beginning to say "Oh, her".'

Curiously, by this time she and I were on easy terms. Nevertheless, I did not know how much to believe. She was anxious not to give herself the benefit of the doubt, she was putting herself in the coldest light. Nearly always, I thought, there was something men or women were protecting, when deliberately, and with pride, almost with conceit, they showed you their most callous side.

All of a sudden she looked at me with her eyes narrowed and frightened.

'Why did you ask me – about marrying him?'

I tried to put her off.

'Do you want him to leave me?'

'That's not my business,' I said.

'Are you trying to take him away?' Her tone had been brittle, the tears had been near again, and she sighed.

Then she threw her head back, and put on her matey, hard-baked smile. 'You can try anything you like,' she said. 'Nothing will have any effect on him, you ought to know that by now.'

Within ten minutes we were walking along the footpath to the laboratories, Irene's face groomed as though nothing were more impossible than tears or anger, both of us talking as though there had been no scene between us. Just once, she referred back to it, when she commented out of the blue:

'Mornings before the office.'

It was her phrase for any kind of morning drama: it was a phrase that only had meaning if your working life was disciplined, as all of ours had by this time become. Whatever was left behind at home, the files were waiting. As we walked along the country footpath, I was myself sorting out my official thoughts, collecting what I could safely say to Drawbell.

Before I called on Drawbell, I said goodbye to Martin. He was standing in his laboratory, looking at one of the counters: tiny neon lamps, the size of buttons, flickered in and out, the noise tapped on, on the indicator the figures moved like a taxi register.

'Any progress?' I asked.

'Nothing new,' said Martin patiently. He and others had already explained to me that what was true of pure scientific research was truer still of this: that the days of crisis were few: that it was only after long periods of preparation, measured in months, not days, that they came to a 'result' – one day of excitement, and afterwards another period of building, routine, long-drawn-out suspense.

In the office where Drawbell's secretaries worked, I was kept waiting among the typing stools and dictaphones before I could see him. I suspected that he was doing it on purpose, as I went on chatting to Hanna Puchwein and her assistant, Mary Pearson, the wife of one of the chief engineers, a young woman who at that first impression seemed just spectacled and flushing. At last the bell trilled on Hanna's desk, and she took me in.

Drawbell's office had in the past been the main drawing-room of the Barford house. On the high walls, where the white paint was chipping from the panels, were pinned charts, tables of organization, graphs, diagrams. The room was so long that there was time to notice my footsteps on the parquet as I went towards Drawbell's desk. He sat, steadily regarding me, watching me come towards him without changing his expression or making a sound.

All this was put on. I had met him several times, in that office as well as in London. He was not an academic, and Luke and the others said, with their usual boisterous lack of respect, that he was not a scientist at all. In peacetime he had been head of another government station. Though I knew that he was not unformidable, I knew also that he was a bit of a humbug and a bit of a clown.

He remained silent. I sat down in an armchair by his desk. He went on gazing at me, with an unwinking inflexible stare from his right eye: the other had little vision and turned blankly off at forty-five degrees. He was bald: square-jowled: podgy-nosed: wide-mouthed, with upturning melon-lips. I studied him, also without speaking.

'Eliot,' he said at last, 'I'm not satisfied with the support that we're receiving.'

I said that this was what I had come to talk about.

'Now you've had an opportunity to see what we're doing.'

I said yes.

'I hope you've made the most of it. I hope you are beginning to realize that this place may be – I don't say that it is, I say *may be* – the most important institution in the entire world. And I'm going to ask you straight out: what help am I to expect from headquarters?'

I hesitated.

'Naturally, I expect some positive results from you,' said Drawbell.

I was the wrong man for this opening, but I had to be patient. I had two problems on my mind. What was going to happen? I had not much doubt of the answer – but how frankly should I tell it to Drawbell?

I knew in cold blood what was bound to happen. Even if Rudd's scheme worked (perhaps Martin was under-estimating its chances), it would take years. All the scientists they wanted were working elsewhere, most of them on R.D.F., on work that would pay dividends in one year or two, not in the remote future: no one in authority could take the risk of moving them; even if the Barford result was certain, instead of uncertain, no one at that stage of the war could do much more.

If I were to be any use as an administrator to Barford, I had to get them to trust me: so I decided to be open with Drawbell. I said that no one could spend any time with his scientists without becoming infected with their faith. He nodded his head. I should report that to Hector Rose and the Minister, for what it was worth: but Drawbell must not expect too much.

'Why not?'

I told him what I had been thinking to myself. He was up against the facts of war. Whatever I reported to the Minister, or the Minister represented to his committees, or the committees recommended on their own, would make little difference. Barford would get buildings and equipment without any serious trouble, but could only hope for a few extra scientists. However much faith anyone had, the men just did not exist.

'Strip the country,' said Drawbell.

I told him any set of responsible persons would have to say no. We couldn't weaken ourselves in 1943 or 1944 for the sake of a gigantic gamble.

'I won't tolerate the word gamble,' said Drawbell, in a loud monotonous voice, speaking like a man trying to hold back his anger.

I had expected him to be reasonable; I had misjudged him.

He would not listen to my case. He shouted me down. He tried cajoling me, saying that I was the only man in the Minister's entourage with any imagination. He tried threatening me, asking how I should feel when the Germans dropped the first uranium bomb on London.

I was used, like any official who has had to carry bad news, to being blamed for it, but it was an effort to keep my temper.

'Quite frankly,' said Drawbell, meaning by that phrase that something unpleasant was coming, 'I hoped that you were going to be less obstructive.'

He went on:

'Of course, I shan't be able to hide it from your *superiors* that we've been disappointed by your visit.'

I said that was up to him.

'If your superiors take the same hopeless attitude as you do, Eliot, it will be a black day for this country.'

'You must tell them so.'

Suddenly Drawbell gave a surprisingly sweet smile. 'I've told them already, Eliot, and I shall go on telling them.'

He behaved as though it were no use abusing me further, and began to talk in a realistic manner.

'Well,' he said, 'assuming that you're right to be hopeless – how many scientists shall I get?'

I had not replied before Drawbell put on a grin, half coaxing, half jeering:

'Come on. Just between you and me.'

So all that display of indignation had been an act; he was ready to use his own moods, my comfort, anything or anyone else, for the sake of Barford.

This time I was cautious. I said that another establishment, doing work of the highest war priority, had just been allowed to search for thirty scientists of reputation. If the Minister and the committees made out the strongest case for Barford, they might get ten to twenty.

'Well, if it's only ten,' said Drawbell, surprisingly reasonable, 'that's better than a slap in the belly with a wet fish.'

He regarded me with good nature, as though I had, through no special fault of my own but for a higher purpose, been roughly handled. It was amiably that he inquired:

'Would you like to know what I shall do with them?'

I expected him to say – they will go to Rudd.

Drawbell made a theatrical pause, and said: '*I shall put them where they are most needed.*'

I asked, impatient at this new turn, where that would be.

'Rudd thinks he will get them all,' said Drawbell.

'Will he?'

'Not on your life. It's not good for anyone to think they're the only runners in the field.'

He gave a cheerful, malevolent chuckle. One could tell how he enjoyed using his power, keeping his assistants down to their proper level, dividing and ruling.

To complete the surprise, he was proposing to reinforce Luke whom he disliked, whom he had heard disparaged for weeks.

'It doesn't matter who brings it off,' he said, 'so long as someone does.'

He nodded, for once quite natural: 'I don't know whether you pray

38

much, Eliot, but I pray God that my people here will get it first. Pray God we get it.'

CHAPTER 7

Voice from a Bath

LOOKING back, I re-examined all I could remember of those early conversations at Barford, searching for any sign of troubled consciences. I was tempted to antedate the conflict which later caused some of them suffering. But it would have been quite untrue.

There was a simple reason why it should be so. All of them knew that the enemy was trying to make a fission bomb. For those who had a qualm of doubt, that was a complete ethical solvent. I had not yet heard from any of the scientists, nor from my friends in government, a single speculation as to whether the bomb should be used. It was just necessary to possess it.

When Drawbell prayed that the Barford project might succeed, he was not speaking lightly; he happened to have kept intact his religious faith. In different words, Puchwein and the fellow-travellers, for just then there was no political divide, would have uttered the same prayer, and so should I.

When I first heard the fission bomb discussed in the Minister's room, my response had been the same as Francis Getliffe's, that is, to hope it would prove physically impossible to make. But in the middle of events, close to Martin and Luke and the others, I could not keep that up. Imperceptibly my hopes had become the same as theirs, that we should get it, that we should get it first. To myself I added a personal one: that Martin would play a part in the success.

During my November visit to Barford my emotions about the project were as simple as that, and they remained so for a long time.

Yet, soon after that visit, I was further from expecting a result even than I had been before. Within quite a short time, a few weeks, the wave of optimism, which had been stirred up by Drawbell, died away; others began to accept what Martin had warned me of by the Barford bridge. It was nothing so dramatic as a failure or even a mistake; it was simply that men realized they had under-estimated the number of men, the amount of chemical plant, the new kinds of engineering, the number of years, before any of the methods under Rudd could produce an ounce of metal.

Then America came into the war, and within a few weeks had assigned several thousand scientists to the job. The Barford people learned of it with relief, but also with envy and a touch of resentment. There seemed nothing left for them to do. A good many of them were sent across to join the American projects. The Minister, whose own post had become shaky, was being pushed into letting others go.

By the early summer of 1942, the argument had begun as to whether or not Barford should be disbanded.

Just as that argument was starting, we heard the first rumours of Luke's idea. Could the Canadians be persuaded to set up a heavy-water plant? the Minister was asked. If so, Luke saw his way through the rest.

No one believed it. The estimates came in, both of money and men. They were modest. No one thought they were realistic. Nearly all the senior scientists, though not Francis Getliffe, thought the idea 'long-haired'.

Following suit, Hector Rose was coming down against it, and deciding that the sensible thing was to send the Barford scientists to America. High officials like Rose had been forced to learn how much their country's power (by the side of America's) had shrunk; Rose was a proud man, and the lesson bit into his pride, but he was too cool-minded not to act on it.

I did not believe that Luke's idea would come to anything. I did not know whether anything could be saved of Barford. As for Martin, I was angry with him again because his luck was so bad.

I was wondering if I could help find him another job, when in July I received a message that he urgently wished to talk to me and would be waiting at my flat.

It was a hot afternoon, and the Minister kept me late. When I arrived at Dolphin Square, I could see no sign of Martin, except his case: tired, out of temper, I began to read the evening paper, comfortless with the grey war news. While I was reading, I heard a splash of water from the bath, and I realized that Martin must be there. I did not call out. There would be time enough for the bleak conversation in front of us.

Then I heard another sound, inexplicable, like a series of metallic taps, not rhythmical but nearly so, as though someone with no sense of time were beating out a very slow tattoo on the bathroom wall. Inexorably it went on, until I cried out, mystified, irritated:

'What *are* you doing?'

'Trying to lodge the pumice-stone on the top of the shaving-cupboard.'

It was one of the more unexpected replies. From his tone, I knew at once that he was lit up with happiness. And I knew just what he was doing. He kept his happiness private, as he did his miseries; and in secret he had his own celebrations. I had watched him, after a success at Cambridge, stand for many minutes throwing an india-rubber up to the cornice, seeing if he could make it perch.

'What have you been up to?' My own tone had quite changed.

'I moved into Luke's outfit a few weeks ago.'

'What?'

'I've got in on the ground floor.'

It was a phrase quite out of character – but I did not care about that. I had ceased to respond to his joy, I was anxious for him again, cross that I had not been consulted.

'Was that wise?' I called.

'I should think so.'

'It must have meant quarrelling with your boss' (I meant Rudd).

'I'm sorry about that.'

'What about Drawbell? Have you got across him?'

'I thought it out' – he seemed amused that I should be accusing him of rashness ' – before I moved.'

'I doubt if Luke's scheme will ever see the light of day,' I cried.

'It must.'

'How many people believe in it?'

'*It's the way to do it.*'

There was a pause. Once more, there came a tinkle on the bathroom floor, meaning that he had missed his aim again.

'Do you really think that?' I said.

'I'm sure.'

'How long have you been sure?'

'I was more sure when I got into this bath than I've ever been.'

'What do you mean?'

'It came to me. *It was all right.*'

Without altering his tone, still relaxed and joyful, he announced that he was going to leave off his efforts with the pumice; he would get out and join me soon. As I waited, although I was trying to think out ways-and-means, although I had a professional's anxiety (how could we manoeuvre Luke's scheme through?), although I could not keep my protectiveness down, yet I was infused with hope. Already I was expecting more for him than he did himself.

I passed as a realistic man. In some senses it was true. But down at the springs of my life I hoped too easily and too much. As an official I could control it; but not always as I imagined my own future, even though by now I knew what had happened to me, I knew where I was weak. Least of all could I control it when I thought of Martin: with myself, I could not help remembering my weaknesses, but I could forget his. So, given the least excuse, as after listening to his voice from the bath, I imagined more glittering triumphs for him than ever, even fifteen years before, I had imagined for myself.

He came in wearing a dressing-gown of mine, and at once I was given enough excuse to hope as much as I could manage. As with most guarded faces, his did not lose its guard in moments of elation – that is, the lines of the mouth, the controlled expression, stayed the same; but his whole face, almost like one of the turnip masks that we used to make as children, seemed to be illuminated from within by a lamp of joy.

We did not begin at once to discuss tactics, for which he had come to London. Sometime that night we should have to; but just for this brief space we put the tactics out of our minds, we gave ourselves the satisfaction of letting it ride.

Martin had been visited by an experience which might not come to him again. So far as I could distinguish, there were two kinds of scientific experience, and a scientist was lucky if he was blessed by a visitation of either just once in his working life. The kind which most of them, certainly Martin, would have judged the higher was not the one he had just known: instead, the higher kind was more like (it was in my view the same as) the experience that the mystics had described so often, the sense of communion with all-being. Martin's was quite different, not so free from self, more active: as though, instead of being one with the world, he held the world in the palm of his

42

hand; as though he had, in his moment of insight, seen the trick by which he could toss it about. It did not matter that the trick had been invented by another; this was a pure experience, without self-regard, so pure that it brought to Martin's smile, as well as joy, a trace of sarcastic surprise – 'Why has this happened to *me*?'

He told me as much, for that evening there was complete confidence between us. Suddenly, he began to laugh outright.

I asked what was the matter.

'I just thought what an absurdly suitable place it was, to feel like this.'

I was at a loss.

'What was?'

'Your bath.'

Then I remembered the legend of Archimedes.

'*He* must have had the feeling often enough,' said Martin.

With a smile, sharp-edged, still elated, now eager for the point of action, he added:

'The trouble is, the old man was a better scientist than I am.'

PART TWO

THE EXPERIMENT

CHAPTER 8

Gambling by a Cautious Man

SOON after Martin's visit, people in the secret began to become partisans about Luke's scheme, either for or against. A decision could not be stalled off for long. Luke had managed to arouse passionate opposition; most of the senior scientists as well as Hector Rose, and his colleagues, wanted to kill the idea and despatch Luke and the others to America. But Francis Getliffe and a few other scientists were being passionate on the other side. And I also was totally committed, and, while they argued for Luke in the committee rooms, did what little I could elsewhere.

I made Hector Rose listen to the whole Luke case. Although we had come to dislike each other, he gave me a full hearing, but I did not shift him.

I did better with the Minister, who had in any case felt a sneaking sympathy with the scheme all the time. The difficulty was that he was losing his influence, and was above all concerned for his own job. While I was trying to persuade him to pay a visit to Barford, he was on edge for a telephone call from Downing Street, which, if it came, meant the end.

However, he agreed to pay the visit.

'If I can see those prima donnas together, I might get some sense out of them,' he said to Rose.

Rose politely agreed – but he was speculating on how many more weeks Bevill would stay in office. Rose had seen ministers come and go before, and he wanted all tidy in case there was a change.

Lesser functionaries than the Minister could have travelled down to Barford by government car; Hector Rose, who himself had no taste for show, would at least have reserved a compartment for the party so that he could talk and work. Bevill did neither. He sat in a crowded train, reading a set of papers of no importance, exactly like a conscientious clerk on the way to Birmingham.

The train trickled on in the sunshine; troops yobbed out on to the little platforms, and once or twice a station flower garden which had been left intact gave out the hot mid-summer scents. There was no dining car on the train; after several hours of travelling the Minister pulled out a bag, and with his sly, gratified smile offered it first to Rose and then to me. It contained grey oatmeal cakes.

'Bikkies,' explained the Minister.

When Drawbell received us in his office, he did not spend any time on me, and not much (in which he was dead wrong) on Hector Rose. Drawbell had no illusions about the dangers to Barford. His single purpose was to get the Minister on his side; but his manner did not overdo it. It was firm, at times bantering and only obscurely deferential.

'I've done one thing you could never do,' he said to the Minister.

The Minister looked mild and surprised.

'Just before the war,' Drawbell went on, 'I saw *you* on *my* television set.'

The Minister gave a happy innocent smile. He knew precisely what was going on, and what Drawbell wanted; he was used to flattery in its most bizarre forms, and, incidentally, always enjoyed it.

But Bevill knew exactly what he intended to do that afternoon. Drawbell's plans for him he side-stepped; he did not want Rose or me; he had come down for a series of private talks with the scientists, and he was determined to have them.

It was not until half past five that Martin came out of the meeting, and then he had Mounteney with him, so that we could not exchange a private word. Old Bevill was still there talking to Rudd, and Mounteney was irritated.

'This is sheer waste of time,' he said to me as we began to walk towards their house, as though his disapproval of old Bevill included me. Although at Cambridge we had been somewhere between acquaintances and friends, he did at that moment disapprove of me.

He was tall and very thin, with a long face and cavernous eye-sockets. It was a kind of face and body one often sees in those with a gift for conceptual thought; and Mounteney's gift was a major one.

He was a man of intense purity of feeling, a man quite unpadded either physically or mentally; and he had an almost total inability to say a softening word.

'It would have been more honest if you had all come here in uniform,' he said to me.

He meant that the government was favouring the forces at the expense of science, in particular at the expense of Barford. It seemed to him obvious – and obvious to any one whose intelligence was higher than an ape's – that government policy was wrong. He was holding me responsible for it. All other facts were irrelevant, including the fact that he knew me moderately well. It was shining clear to him that government policy was moronic, and probably ill-disposed. Here was I: the first thing was to tell me so.

I gathered that the Minister had talked to them both privately and in a group. Luke had been eloquent: his opponents had attacked him: Martin had spoken his mind. The discussion had been rambling, outspoken and inconclusive. Mounteney, although in theory above the battle, was not pleased.

'Luke *is* quite bright,' he said in a tone of surprise and injury, as though it was unreasonable to force him to give praise.

He then returned to denouncing me by proxy. Bevill had said what wonderful work they had done at Barford. Actually, said Mounteney, they had done nothing: the old man knew it; they knew it; they knew he knew it.

'Why *will* you people say these things?' asked Mounteney.

Irene was sitting in a deck-chair in what had once been the garden behind their house, though by this time it was running wild. The bindweed was strangling the last of the phlox, the last ragged pansies; the paths were overgrown with weed. When Mounteney went in to his children, Martin and I sat beside her, on the parched grass, which was hot against the hand. At last Martin was free to give a grim smile.

'Well,' he said to me, 'you'd better see that Luke's scheme goes through.'

'What have you been doing?' she asked.

Martin was still smiling. 'Not only for patriotic reasons,' he went on.

'What *have* you been doing?' She sounded, for the moment, as she might have done if accusing him of some amatory adventure, her voice touched with mock reprobation and a secret pride.

'Something that may not do us any good,' he said, and let us hear the story. He had told Bevill, in front of Drawbell and Rudd, that he and the other young scientists were agreed: either they ought to concentrate on Luke's scheme, or else shut Barford down.

'If I had to do it, it was no use doing it half heartedly,' he said.

'*I'm glad you did it*,' she said, excited by the risk. The teasing air had faded; there was a high flush under her eyes.

'Wait until we see whether it was worth while,' said Martin.

'Never mind that,' she said, and turned to me. 'Aren't you glad he did it?'

Before I answered Martin looked at her and said:

'We may not get our way, you know.'

'I don't care.'

'It would be an odd time to move.'

They were glancing at each other with eyes half challenging, half salacious.

'Why would it be so odd?' I asked, but did not need an answer.

'You can tell Lewis,' said Martin.

'I am going to have a child, dear,' she said.

For the first time since their marriage, I felt nothing but warmth towards her, as I went to her chair and kissed her. Martin's face was softened with delight. If he had not been my brother I should have envied him, for my marriage had been childless, and there were times, increasing as the years passed, when the deprivation nagged at me. And, buried deep within both Martin and me, there was a strong family sense, so that it was natural for him to say:

'I'm glad there'll be another generation.'

As he went indoors to fetch something to drink in celebration, Irene said to me:

'If it's a boy we'll call it after you, Lewis dear. Even though you don't approve of its mother.'

She added: 'He is pleased, isn't he? I did want to do something for him.'

'It's very good news,' I said, as she got up from her chair in the low sunlight, and began to walk about the patch of derelict garden. The evening scents were growing stronger, mint and wormwood mingled in the scorched aromatic tang of the August night. Irene came to a clearing in the long grass, where a group of autumn crocuses shone out, amethyst and solitary, flowers that in my childhood I had heard called 'naked ladies'. Irene bent and picked one, and then stood erect, as though she were no longer concealing the curve of her breast.

'When I was a little girl,' she said, 'I always thought I should have a brood of children.'

'Should you like them?' I asked.

'Time is going on,' she said: but, in the smoothing amber light, she looked younger than I had seen her.

After Martin returned, and we sat there in the dipping sun, the three of us were at peace together as we had not been before. Our content was so strong that Martin did not disturb it when he began speculating again about transferring to Luke, and speaking out that afternoon; he did not disturb it in us, least of all in himself.

'I don't see what else I could have done,' he said.

Martin went on with his thoughts. It was going to be a near thing whether Luke got his head: wasn't that true? So if one could do anything to bring it about, one had to.

'I should have been more sorry if I hadn't spoken.'

If the luck went wrong, it meant a dim job for the rest of the war and probably after. If the luck went right, no one could tell – Martin smiled, his eyes glinted, and he said:

'I'm not sorry that I've gone in with Luke.'

We all took it for granted that he was the most prudent of men, always reckoning out the future, not willing to allow himself a rash word, let alone a rash action. Even I assumed that as part of his flesh and bone. In a sense it was true. And yet none of us had made a wilder marriage, and now, over Barford and his career, he was gambling again.

CHAPTER 9

View of a True Marriage

FROM Martin's I went off to an evening party at Drawbell's. Mrs Drawbell had set herself to catch old Bevill for a social engagement; he had refused tea or dinner, and insisted on returning to London that

49

night, but he had not been able to elude this last invitation, a 'little party' before we caught the train.

Most of the senior Barford staff were already there, and I found my way to a corner next to Walter Luke. From near the window we looked into the centre of the room, where upon the hearthrug Mrs Drawbell, a heavy woman, massive as a monument upon the rug, waited for the Minister.

'Where is this uncle?' said Luke.

'He'll come,' I said. The Minister has not been known to break a social engagement.

Luke's thoughts became canalized once more.

'Does he believe in Jojo?' (Luke's proposal already had a name.)

He corrected himself.

'I don't care whether he believes in it or not. The point is, will he do anything useful about it?'

I said that I thought he was well disposed, but would not find it easy to put through.

'There are times,' said Luke, 'when I get sick and tired of you wise old men.'

Whole hearted and surgent, he said:

'Well, I suppose I'd better mobilize some of the chaps who really know against all you stuffed shirts.'

I was warning him to go carefully (he would still listen to me, even when he was regarding me as a 'wise old man') when the Minister entered. With his unobtrusive trip Bevill went towards Mrs Drawbell.

'I am sorry I haven't been able to get out of the clutches of these fellows,' he said, smiling innocently.

'I am glad you were able to come to my party, Mr Bevill,' she replied. Her voice was deep, her expression dense, gratified, and confident. She had looked forward to having him there; he had come. And now – she had nothing to say.

The Minister said, what a nice room. She agreed. He said, how refreshing to have a drink after a hot, tiring day. She was glad he liked it. He said, it was hard work, walking round the laboratories, especially hard work if you weren't a scientist and didn't understand much. She smiled, heavily, without comment. She had nothing to say to him.

It did not seem to depress her. She had him in her house, the grandson of the last Lord Boscastle but one (his being in the Cabinet had its own virtue, but did not give her the same collector's joy). To her this visit was a prize which she would hoard.

She kept him to herself, standing together on the rug. It was not until she was forced to greet a new arrival that her eyes were distracted, and the Minister could slip away towards the window. He beckoned to us, so that we could make a circle round him, Luke, me, a couple of young scientists whom I did not know by name, Mary Pearson. He caught sight of Mary Pearson's husband, and beckoned also to him.

I had had business talks with Pearson before, for he was one of the top men at Barford and was said to be their best electrical engineer. In those talks I had found him too pleased with himself to give more than a minimum reply. He was a man in the early thirties with a cowlick over his forehead and a wide lazy-looking mouth.

As Bevill crooked his finger, Pearson gave a relaxed smile and came unconcernedly into the ring.

'Now, my friends, we can talk seriously, can't we?' said the Minister.

He basked in the company of the young, and felt quite natural with them. But, as often when he was natural, he was also mildly eccentric; with the intellectual young, he felt most completely at ease, and satisfied with himself, in discussing what he called 'philosophy'. He took it for granted that this was their conception of serious conversation, too; and so the old man, so shrewd and cunning in practice, dug out his relics of idealist speculation, garbled from the philosophers of his youth, F. H. Bradley and McTaggart, and talked proudly on, forcing the young men to attend – while all they wanted, that night of all nights, was to cut the cackle and hear his intentions about Barford and Luke's scheme.

'I don't know about you chaps' – the Minister, who had been ambling on for some time, looked out of the window towards the west – 'but whenever I see a beautiful sunset, I wonder whether there isn't an Ideal Sunset outside Space and Time.'

His audience were getting impatient. But he thought they were taking a point.

'Perhaps you'll say, the Phenomenon is enough. Is the Phenomenon enough? I know it sometimes seems so, to all of us doesn't it? – when you see a beloved woman and see from her smile that she loves you back. I know it seems enough,' said Bevill earnestly and cheerfully.

All of a sudden, only half listening, for I had heard the Minister showing off his philosophy before, I saw the flush on Mary Pearson's face, I saw the smile on Pearson's as he glanced at her. I had not often seen a man so changed. When I met him, he had filled me with antipathy; it came as a shock to see his face radiant. Somewhere Bevill's bumbling words had touched the trigger. The conceit had vanished the indifference about whether he pleased: it was just a face lit up by a mutual love. And so was hers. Her skin was flushed down to the neck of her dress, behind her spectacles her eyes were moist with joy.

Anyone watching as I was would have had no doubt: those two must be sharing erotic bliss. You can share erotic bliss with someone and still not be suffused by love as those two were, but the converse does not hold, and no husband and wife could be so melted by each other's smile without the memory of bliss, and the certainty that it would soon be theirs again. I guessed that their physical happiness was out of the common run. It had been worth listening to the Minister's philosophizing to see it shine.

I was not the only one who saw it shine, for, a few minutes afterwards, as the Minister was saying his goodbyes before we left for the railway station, Luke and I strolled in the lane outside and he said:

'Funny what people see in each other.'

'Is it?'

'It's lucky those two think each other wonderful, because I'm damned if anyone else would.'

He added, with a thoughtful, truculent grin:

'Of course, they might say the same of me and Nora.'

As he walked beside me his whole bearing was jaunty, and many women, at a glance, would have judged him virile. Yet he was sexually a genuinely humble man. He did not believe that women noticed him, it would not have occurred to him to believe it.

'I envy you, you know!' he broke out.

'Whatever for?'

'You know that I am an innocent sort of chap. Why are you making me talk?'

For once, he had forgotten about the project. Like me, he had been stirred by the Pearsons' smile. With his usual immoderation, he was bursting to confide. Confide he did, insisting often that I was pumping him.

'I've kept myself out of things when I ought to have rushed in. I thought I couldn't spare the time from science. It wasn't ambition, I just felt I had to get on. And I didn't know what I was missing. So now I'm batting about trying to make up my mind on problems which you must have coped with when you were twenty. I'm frightened of them, and I don't like being frightened.'

I said that he had not done badly: he had made a happier marriage than most, while mine had been miserable.

'But you know your way about. So does your brother Martin. Neither of you feel like some little brat with his nose up against the shop window and wondering what he has got to do to get inside.'

Totally immersed, he went on:

'I can't bear being left out of things. There are times when I want to see all the places and read all the books and fornicate with all the women. Now you're certain where you stand about all that, you've had your share. What I want to know is, how do I get mine without hurting anyone else?'

I thought, in a way he was right about himself: how young he was. But it was more than calendar youth (at that time he was thirty-one), it was more than a life blinkered and concentrated by his vocation. Perhaps he would never lose his sense of being deprived, of being left out of the party – of being outside in the road, of seeing the lights of houses, homes of voluptuous delight denied to him.

'I suppose I shall get my share in the long run,' said Luke. 'Somehow I must manage it. I'm damned well not going to die feeling I was too frightened to discover what it was all about.' He was looking towards the establishment, and the energy seemed to be pulsing within him, so that in the softening light his sanguine colour became deeper, even his hair seemed to have more sheen.

'Wait till I've got this scheme to go. There's a time for everything,' he said, 'when we've tied this up!'

CHAPTER 10

A Night at Pratt's

BACK in Whitehall, the Minister plumped in on Luke's side. It was gallant for a man whose job was tottering, for it meant opposing those in power. It meant acting against Bevill's own maxims – if those above had it in for you, never make a nuisance of yourself and never go away. For once in his life he disregarded them.

No one could understand why. With Bevill, everyone looked for some cunning political motive. I believed that, just this once, there was none. Underneath the politics, the old man had a vein of narrow, rigid, aristocratic patriotism. He had been convinced that Luke's scheme might be good for the country; that may have been a reason why Bevill made enemies in order to give Luke his head.

A minister likely to be out of office next month had, however, not many cards to play. Probably his single effort in self-sacrifice did not count much either way; what was more decisive was Francis Getliffe's conversation with Hector Rose. I was not present, but within a short time of that conversation, Rose, against his preconceived opinion, against most of his prejudices, changed his mind. He had concluded that the other side's case, in particular Getliffe's case, was stronger than his own. I wondered with some shame – for I could not like him – whether in his place I should have been so fair.

So the dispatch boxes went round, Rose lunched with his colleagues at the Athenaeum, the committees sat: on a night early in November, the Minister went off to a meeting. It was not a cabinet, but a sub-committee of ministers; he believed that, one way or the other, this would settle it. I remained in my office, waiting for him to return.

It was half past eight; in the pool of light from the reading lamp, the foolscap on my desk shone with a blue luminescence; I was too restless to work. I went across the passage to the little room where my new personal assistant was sitting. I had told her to go hours before, but she was over-conscientious; she was a young widow called Vera Allen, comely but reserved, too diffident to chat, stiff at being alone in the building with a man.

I heard the Minister scamper up the stairs, with the light trotting steps that sounded so youthful. I returned to my room. He put his head in, without taking off his bowler hat.

'Still at it?' he said.

He went on:

'I think it's all right, Eliot.'

I exclaimed with relief.

Bevill was flushed, looking curiously boyish in his triumph. He tipped his hat back on his thin grey hair.

'We mustn't count our eggs before they're hatched, but I think it's in the bag,' he said.

In jubilation, he asked if I had eaten and took me off to Pratt's.

He had taken me there before, when he was pleased. He only did it because he had a soft spot for me. For business, for talks with Rose, he went elsewhere; Pratt's was reserved for friends, it was his fortress, his favourite club.

When he first took me inside, I had thought – it seemed strange – of my mother. She had been brought up in a game-keeper's cottage on a Lincolnshire estate; she was proud and snobbish and had great ambitions for me; she was dead years since, she had not seen what happened to me – but just the sight of me with Thomas Bevill, in his most jealously guarded club, eating with men whose names she had read in the papers, would have made her rejoice that her life was not in vain.

Yet if she could have seen me there, she would have been a little puzzled to observe that we were sitting with some discomfort in rooms remarkably like the cottage where she was born. A basement: a living room with a common table and a check cloth: a smoking kitchen with an open hearth: in fact, a landowner's idea of his own gamekeeper's quarters. That was the place to which Thomas Bevill went whenever he wanted to be sure of meeting no one but his aristocratic friends.

Looking at him after our meal, as he sat by the kitchen hearth, drinking a glass of port, I thought that unless one had the chance to see him so, one might be quite misled. People called him unassuming, unsnobbish, realistic, gentle. Unassuming: yes, that was genuine. Unsnobbish, realistic; that was genuine too; unlike his cousin, Lord Boscastle, he did not take refuge, as society evened itself out, in a fantastic and comic snobbery; yet in secret, he did take refuge with his friends here, in a cave-of-the-past, in a feeling, blended of fear, foresight and contempt, that he could preserve bits of his past and make them last his time. Gentle, a bit of an old woman; that was not genuine in the slightest; he was kind to his friends, but the deeper you dug into him the tougher and more impervious he became.

'Well, if they're going to sack me, Eliot,' he said, 'I've left them a nice kettle of fish.' He was simmering in his triumph over Barford. He ordered more glasses of port.

'One of these days,' he said, 'those chaps will blow us all up, and that will be the end of the story.'

The firelight winked in his glass; he held it up to admire the effect, brought it down carefully and looked into it from above.

'It's funny about those chaps,' he reflected. 'I used to think scientists were supermen. But they're not supermen, are they? Some of them are brilliant, I grant you that. But between you and me, Eliot, a good many of them are like garage hands. Those are the chaps who are going to blow us all up.'

I said, for I was not speaking like a subordinate, that a good many of them had more imagination than his colleagues.

Bevill agreed, with cheerful indifference.

'Our fellows can't make much difference to the world, and those chaps can. Do you think it will be a better world, when they've finished with it?'

I thought it might. Not for him, probably not for me and my kind: but for ninety per cent of the human race.

'I don't trust them,' said Thomas Bevill.

Then he said:

'By the by, I like the look of your brother, Eliot.'

It was partly his good manners, having caught himself in a sweeping statement. But he said it as though he meant it.

'He put the cat among the pigeons, you know, that afternoon down there. It's just as well he did, or Master Drawbell mightn't have seen the red light in time, and if they'd all gone on crabbing Luke I couldn't have saved the situation.'

He began laughing, his curious, internal, happy laugh, as though he were smothering a dirty joke.

'Those Drawbells! Between them they'd do anything to get a K, wouldn't they?'

He meant a knighthood. He was constantly amused at the manoeuvres men engaged in to win titles, and no one understood them better.

'Never mind, Eliot,' he said. 'We saved the situation, and now it's up to those chaps not to let us down.'

It was his own uniquely flat expression of delight: but his face was rosy, he did not look like a man of seventy-three, he was revelling in his victory, the hot room, the mildly drunken night.

'If this country gets a super bomb,' he said cheerfully, 'no one will remember me.'

He swung his legs under his chair.

'It's funny about the bomb,' he said. 'If we manage to get it, what do we do with it then?'

This was not the first time that I heard the question: once or twice recently people at Barford had raised it. It was too far away for the scientists to speculate much, even the controversialists like Mounteney, but several of them agreed that we should simply notify the enemy that we possessed the bomb, and give some evidence: that would be enough to end the war. I repeated this view to Bevill.

'I wonder,' he said.

'I wonder,' he repeated. 'Has there ever been a weapon that someone did not want to let off?'

I said, though the issue seemed remote, that this was different in kind. We had both seen the current estimate, that one fission bomb would kill three hundred thousand people at a go.

'Oh, I don't know,' said Bevill. 'Think of what we're trying to do with bombing. We're trying to kill men, women, and children. It's worse than anything Genghiz Khan ever did.'

He said it without relish, without blame, with neutrality.

Soon the room grew warmer, the port went round again, as men came in from a late night meeting. A couple of them were Ministers, and Bevill looked towards them with a politician's insatiable hope. Had they any news for him? He could not help hoping. He was old, he had made such reputation as he could, if he stayed in office he would not add a syllable to it; he knew how irretrievably he was out of favour, and he did not expect to last three months; yet still, on that happy night, he wondered if he might not hear of a reprieve, if he might not hear that he was being kept on, perhaps in an obscurer post.

I saw that his flicker of hope did not last long. From their manner he knew they had nothing to tell him. It did not weigh him down, he was pleased with himself that night. And they brought other news: the invasion fleet was safely out of Gibraltar, and all looked well for the North African landing.

A little later, Bevill and I went out into St James's Street. He twirled his umbrella, a slight little figure in a bowler hat, under the full moon; an old man, slightly drunk, expecting the sack, and full of well being. He said to me with an extra sweep of his umbrella:

'Isn't it nice to be winning?'

I was not sure whether he was talking about Barford, or the war. He repeated it, resoundingly, to the empty street:

'Isn't it nice to be winning?'

CHAPTER II

Two Kinds of Danger

AFTER the Minister's night of victory, there was for months nothing I could do for Luke and Martin. I had to set myself to wait, picking up any rumour from Barford, any straw in the wind. Because I could do nothing, the suspense nagged at me more.

That was the reason I started into anxiety, the instant Hanna Puchwein inquired about Martin's fate.

I was having dinner with the Puchweins at the Connaught, at the farewell party they gave me before Kurt Puchwein left for Chicago. They were standing me a lavish treat; as I sat by Hanna's side, with her husband opposite, in the corner near the door, lights flashed on glass and sank cosily into the rosewood, and I was reflecting, if you were used to English fellow travellers, how incongruous Hanna Puchwein seemed. There was nothing of the self-abnegation of the English radical about her, none of the attempts, so common among other acquaintances of mine, to imitate the manners of the working class. Hanna's glossy head gleamed trimly in our corner, and she was the best groomed woman in the room. She was in her early thirties. She had a small head, narrowing catlike to a pointed chin. Her forehead was white, bland, unlined; but her eyes flashed as she talked, and she had an air that was, I thought, at the same time cultivated and farouche.

Meanwhile Kurt was presenting me with gifts: he was a man who found it delectable to give, though not to receive. He liked doing good turns and letting one know it; but that had always seemed to me more amiable than not liking to do good turns at all. He gave me wine. He gave me his opinion that, out of Luke's project, he and Martin would 'do themselves good in the long run'.

Yet, although he was expending himself to make me cheerful, his own mood was overcast. He and Hanna spoke little to each other; and it occurred to me that probably in an unexacting friendship, such as he felt for me, one saw the best of him. In a closer relation, he could be violent, spoiled, bad tempered.

That night he went to bed early, leaving me and Hanna together, on the excuse that he had some last letters to write. He spun out his goodbye to me, pressing my hand.

'It may be a long time before we meet again, my friend,' he said. He was flying the Atlantic within forty-eight hours. I looked at him – his great prow of a nose, his mouth pinched in, as though with press studs, that night.

'Ah, well,' he said. 'We shall meet once again in the world.'

As soon as he had gone, I spoke to Hanna. Once or twice before I had talked to her intimately, as I had never done with Kurt. I asked, outright:

'Why is Kurt so anxious to go to America?'

He could have stayed at Barford. Apart from Luke's project, some others, including Rudd's, had been left in being. Nothing official ever got closed down flat, old Bevill used to say.

Hanna stared at me, first with a blank, washed, open look (her temper was as formidable as his), then with an expression I could not read.

'Why ask me?' she said. Then quickly:

'Why didn't you persuade your brother to go also?'

It was then I started. She went on:

'Wouldn't it have been better for him?'

I said, at once hyper-sensitive, on the defensive:

'It depends whether Luke's scheme comes off – but a good many of them believe in it. You heard what Kurt said.'

Hanna said:

'Oh that! You're a most single-minded man.'

Her smile had an edge.

'I didn't mean that at all,' she said.

'What did you mean?'

'If he went to America,' she said, 'he might be able to escape from that woman.'

'I don't know whether he wants to escape,' I said.

'I know that he ought to,' said Hanna.

She reminded me that geographical distance, like time, helped one to recover from unhappy love. Three thousand miles could be as good as the passage of six months. Hanna's eyes were flashing with impatience, in which there was, however, a trace of the pleasure with which a man and a woman, not attached but not totally unaware of each other, spread out before them the platitudes and generalizations of love.

I said that I hoped the child might heal their marriage.

'Have you never known women have a child and leave their husbands flat?'

She went on:

'With women like her, children break marriages more often than they save them.'

'Well,' I said, 'if she did leave him, you wouldn't break your heart.'

'Unless he's got free of her first,' she said, 'he might break his.'

I was frowning, and she said:

'I suppose you know that he's been passionately in love with her? And may be still?'

'I think I did know that,' I said.

'She is quite useless to him,' she said. 'If he isn't lucky and doesn't get away, she will destroy a great part of his life.'

I was thinking: when I worried about the danger of Martin's marriage, it had been for cruder reasons than these, it had been because Irene might do him 'practical' harm in terms of money and worldly standing and jobs. I had almost deliberately shut my eyes to what he felt for her: and it was left for Hanna, herself someone whom I had always thought a selfish woman, to show the consideration, the imaginative sympathy, in which I had failed.

It was partly that our loves are entirely serious only to ourselves; years of my own life had been corroded by a passion more wretched than Martin's, and yet, as a spectator of his, I felt as my friends used to feel about mine. We would 'get over it', it was irritating to watch a man dulled by his own infatuation, it seemed, certainly not tragic, scarcely even pathetic, almost his own fault. In fact, all loves but one's own have an element of the tiresome: and from the way I behaved about Martin's until that evening when Hanna forced me to face it, I came to think that was even more true of a brother's unhappy love than of a friend's.

'She gives him nothing he couldn't get from any woman he picked up,' she said. 'And in self-defence he has learned to give nothing back.'

'I think he can bear it,' I said.

'Of course he can bear it. But sometimes it is a greater danger to bear it than not to bear it.'

She went on:

'One can stand so much that one gets frightened of anything better. Isn't that true of you?'

'There's something in that,' I said.

'It isn't noble,' Hanna said. 'It is just that one has become too frightened to choose, and then one goes on standing it. Well, I want to see Martin stop suffering patiently. I want to see him take himself in hand and make his choice.'

As I listened to her, speaking with the bite that sounded at the same time intimate and cross, I felt a touch of concern – for her. It was disturbing to hear her talk so intently of another – not through tenderness for Martin, though she had a little, not even because she was putting me off from talking of her husband, though that was also true. It was disturbing because she was really talking of herself. She was behaving like Martin that night when he and I walked towards his empty house, she was unable to say outright that she too was coming near a choice. About her there clung the desperation, the fragility, of a woman who still looks young but no longer feels it to herself – or rather who, still feeling young, becomes self-conscious that others are marking off the years – and who has become obsessed that she has only one choice to make, one, no more, before she is old.

CHAPTER 12

A Routine Interview

THOSE in the secret did not talk easily with each other, and as the months passed and Luke's 'pile' went up, it was hard to judge how many believed in him. In committee heads were shaken, not much was said, yet feelings ran high. Luke was one of those figures who have the knack, often surprising to themselves, of stirring up controversy; people who did not know him, who had no conception of his surgent, exuberant, often simple-hearted character, grew excited about him, as someone who would benefit the country or as a scandalous trifler with public money, almost as a crook.

Of his supporters, the most highly placed of all was lost in the April of 1943, when Bevill was at last told that his job was wanted for another.

Now that his suspense had ended, I was astonished by the old man's resilience. He moved his papers from Whitehall the same day. Briskly he said goodbye to his staff and made a speech with a remarkable, indeed an excessive, lack of sentimentality. He was not thinking of his years in the old office; he was thinking of nothing but the future. Without any procrastination at all he refused a peerage. If he accepted it, he was accepting the fact that he was out of politics for good: at the age of seventy-four, he was, with the occupational hope of politicians, as difficult to kill as the hope of a consumptive, reckoning his chances of getting back again.

As soon as he left, my own personal influence diminished; I could intervene no more than other civil servants of my rank (in his last month of office, Bevill had got me promoted again, which Rose thought excessive). All I did had to go through Rose, and we were more than ever uneasy with each other.

Nevertheless, Rose intended not to waste my inside knowledge of Barford. He merely requested as a favour that I should report to him any 'point of interest' I picked up on my visits there.

Each of us was being punctilious. When I next went down to Barford, a month or two after Bevill's dismissal, for the christening of Martin's son, I set out to obey Rose to the letter. I held back one incident only and I did so because neither of us would have thought it worth our while.

It was a morning late in May, the sky bright and pale, with an east wind that took the scent out of the wistaria, when I went into the hangar with Martin, in order to see the pile going up before we went to church. The tarpaulins in the roof, still not repaired, flapped in the wind. In the hangar it was cold; I had not known it anything else; but, instead of the dripping floor of winter, it had suddenly gone dusty, and grit blew about in the spring air. Labourers, wearing jerseys, were working in the bleak half light; they were laying bricks for an outer wall, while farther away one could see a kind of box, about eight feet each way; outside was another wall, the first part of the concrete case. Farther down still, Luke's experimental structure lay deserted. Between stood some tables, one or two screened off, packed with radio valves and circuits; on others, as though abandoned, were strewn metal tubing and tea cups. There was no sign of busyness. Labourers padded on, muttering among themselves. The foreman had his hand on the concrete shield, and was listening to Luke.

The paradox was that, as they worked against time, as they studied the German intelligence reports or heard gossip from America (news had come through that the Chicago pile had already run, in the previous December), Luke had nothing like enough to do.

Once he had had his idea, there was no more room for flair or scientific imagination for months, perhaps years to come: the rest was a matter of getting the machine built. It was a matter of organization, extreme attention to detail, knowing when a contractor could not work faster and when he could be pressed. It was a matter of organization that differed only in scale and in what depended on it, but not at all in kind, from being the Clerk of Works to some new public baths. Any competent man could do it, and Martin was there to do it as efficiently as Luke and with less fuss. Luke, who was as lavish with praise as abuse, admitted this. But he could not keep his hands off. Engineers, going as fast as men could within the human limits, heard his swear words over the telephone. They did no great harm. It meant an expense of temper. It meant that, for the most critical months of Luke's working life, he still had nothing to do.

When he came across to speak to me, I noticed that the colour of his face had gone more sallow and that, although the skin under his eyes was fresh and full, without the roughness of true anxiety, it had taken on a bruised, a faint purple tint. He was restless on the balls of his feet. He did not offer to come to church. When he left us, I asked Martin what Luke was going off to do. Martin gave an amused, half indulgent smile.

'He's going to play the piano,' he said.

'What?'

'Just now,' said Martin, 'he plays the piano all day. Five or six hours a day, at least, except when he's having a row.'

'Does he play well?'

'Oh, no,' Martin replied. 'He never learned after he was ten. He plays his old Associated Board pieces.'

In church, with a beam of early afternoon sun falling across the font, a beam in which the motes spun and jiggled and in which Martin's hair was turned to silver gilt, I thought he was standing the strain better than Luke. He smiled at the child with a love more open than he ever showed for his wife.

Just for a moment, though, Martin's smile altered. The parson and Irene and the baby had already left the church, and Martin and I were following, when an old woman entered with a busy air. Martin asked what she was doing, and she replied, full of well-being:

'There's a corpse coming in here soon, sir, and I just wanted to see that everything was nice for him.'

Martin smiled at me, and we followed the others into the sunlight. He did not need to explain; we both had a superstitious sense. He smiled at the thought of the old woman, and did not like it.

It was in the afternoon that I attended to the piece of business which seemed just routine, not interesting enough to discuss with Rose. Drawbell had invited me to what they called an 'allocation meeting' at which they interviewed some of that year's intake of young men. His motive was to demonstrate how few and poor they were, but worn-out argument could get no further. He sat behind a table with his heads of sections on each side; Rudd was there, Mounteney, a couple of Jewish refugees and Martin, deputizing for Luke. Increasingly Luke left the chores to Martin. I could understand it. I could remember being underworked and over anxious, doing so little that one needed to do less.

As the interviews went on, the only flicker of interest for me was that one of the young men came from the same town as Martin and myself and had attended the same grammar school. His family had lived not far from ours in the red-brick streets, and Martin could recall him as a small boy. His name, which was Eric Sawbridge, had a flat, comfortable Midland note.

As he answered questions, he spoke with the faintly aggressive, reproving tone that one often heard at interviews. He was twenty-four, large, heavy, mature, with a single thick line across his forehead; he was a lighter blond than Martin, and might have been a Scandinavian sailor. He had got his First three years before, and had gone on to research. His answers sounded competent, not over gracious; Martin made a reference to school-days and Sawbridge's expression was, for a second, less suspicious. Then Drawbell took the general questioning out of Martin's hands.

'Have you any outside interests?'

'I don't know what you mean.'

'Did you belong to any societies at the university?'

'One or two.' He mentioned a film society in wartime Oxford.

'Do you play any games?'

'I *prefer* the cycle.'

'Do you read anything?'

'I haven't had much time.'

The scientists smiled. These non-technical questions and answers were perfunctory on both sides of the table. Anything outside science was a frippery. That was all. As soon as Sawbridge went out of the room, he was being competed for. Perhaps he was the ablest on view: but Rudd wanted him because he was English, after a Pole, two German Jews, an Irishman. An argument blew up, Rudd suddenly violent. Rudd wanted him: Mounteney wanted him: but Martin got him.

It was a piece of domestic routine, and I felt I could have spent the three hours better. I should have been astonished to know that, two years later, I was forcing my memory to recall that interview with Sawbridge. When it actually happened, I wrote it off. On the other hand, I could not dismiss the conversation I had with Mounteney and Martin late that night.

CHAPTER 13

Beside the Smooth Water

AFTER the interviews, Mounteney had come away intransigent. He was irritated because he had lost over Sawbridge, and could not understand just where Martin had been more adroit. He also could not understand why Martin, like himself an unbeliever, had allowed his son to be baptized.

'Rain making!' said Mounteney. He went on denouncing Martin: if traditions led to decent men telling lies ('what else have you been doing except tell lies?') then they made us all mentally corrupt.

His affection for Martin did not soften Mounteney's remarks, nor, when we returned to the house, did his wife's gaze, at once cocky and longing for a transformation, as though she expected him to give up controversy and say that he had come home in search of her. In fact, he and Martin and I drove in by ourselves to Stratford, where, since there was no room for me in Martin's house, I was staying the night. There all of a sudden Mounteney became gentler.

The three of us had had dinner, and walked down past the theatre to the river's edge. There was little light in the sky, and over towards Clopton Bridge the dim shapes of swans moved upon the dark water. Under the willows, the river smell brought back a night, not here, but in Cambridge: I had been thinking of Cambridge all through dinner, after Martin had mentioned a friend of mine who had been killed that spring.

On our way past the dark theatre, I heard Mounteney whisper to Martin: to my astonishment he seemed to be asking what was the matter with me. At any rate, as we stood by the river, he tried, with a curious brusque delicacy, to distract me: that was how the conversation began.

So awkwardly that he did not sound kind, Mounteney asked me if I were satisfied with the way I had spent my life – and at once started off saying that recently he had been examining his own. What had made him a scientist? How would he justify it? Ought his son and Martin's to be scientists, too?

Soon we were talking intimately. Science, said Mounteney, had been the one permanent source of happiness in his life; and really the happiness was a private, if you like a selfish, one. It was just the happiness he deprived from seeing how nature worked; it would not have lost its strength if nothing he had done added sixpence to practical human betterment. Martin agreed. That was the obscure link between them, who seemed as different as men could be. Deep down, they were contemplatives, utterly unlike Luke, who was as fine a scientist as Mounteney and right out of Martin's reach. For Luke, contemplation was a means, not a joy in itself; *his* happiness was to 'make Mother Nature sit up and beg'. He wanted power over nature so that human beings had a better time.

Both Mounteney and Martin wished that they shared Luke's pleasure. For by this time, their own was beginning to seem too private, not enough justification for a life. Mounteney would have liked to say, as he might have done in less austere times, that science was good in itself; he felt it so; but in the long run he had to fall back on the justification for himself and other scientists, that their work and science in general did practical good to human lives.

'I suppose it *has* done more practical good than harm to human lives?' I said.

Mounteney's dialectic was not scathing that night. Everyone asked these questions in wartime, he said, but whatever the appearance there was no doubt about the answer. It was true that science was responsible for killing a certain number in war – Mounteney broke off and apologized: 'I am sorry to bring this up.'

The friend we had talked of, Roy Calvert, had been killed flying.

'Go on,' I said.

We got the numbers out of proportion, he said. Science killed a certain number: it kept alive a much larger number, something of a quite different order. Taking into account war-danger, now and in the future, this child of Martin's had an actuarial expectation of life of at least sixty-five years. In the eighteenth century, before organized science got going, it would have been about twenty-five. That was the major practical effect of science.

'It's such a big thing,' said Mounteney, 'that it makes minor grumbles insignificant. It will go on *whatever happens*.'

It was then that I mentioned the fission bomb.

'If you people bring that off –'

'I've done nothing useful towards it,' said Mounteney counter-suggestibly.

'If someone possesses the bomb,' I said, 'mightn't *that* make a difference?'

There was a pause.

'It could,' said Mounteney.

'Yes, it could,' said Martin, looking up from the water.

The river-smell was astringent in the darkened air. Somewhere down the stream, a swan unfolded its wings and flapped noisily for a moment before settling again and sailing away.

'If those bombs were used in war,' said Mounteney, 'they might be as lethal as an epidemic.' He added: 'but that won't happen.'

'It mustn't happen,' said Martin.

I told them how, in my conversation with old Bevill at Pratt's, he did not think it incredible that the bomb would be used.

'What else do you expect,' said Mounteney, 'of a broken down reactionary politician?'

'He wasn't approving,' I said. 'He was just saying what might happen.'

'Do you believe it could?'

I was thinking of what the Third Reich had done, and said so.

'That's why we're fighting them,' said Mounteney.

Mounteney had brought some buns for his family. Martin begged one and scattered crumbs on the water, so that swans sailed towards him out of the dark, from the bridge, from down the Avon where it was too dark to make out the church; they moved with a lapping sound, the bow waves catching glimmers of light like scratches on a mirror.

Did I believe it would be used?

'Do you believe it?' Mounteney returned to the question.

'Assuming that it's our side which gets it –'

'Of course,' said Mounteney.

'If anyone gets it,' said Martin, touching wood. It was his turn to ask me:

'You don't believe that we could use it?'

I took some time to answer.

'I find it almost incredible,' I said.

'I'm glad to hear it,' said Mounteney. 'Particularly as you're a pessimistic man.'

'I think it is incredible,' said Martin.

His voice was harsh. He was more moved than Mounteney who, despite his cantankerousness, was a gentle man, to whom any kind of cruelty seemed like a visitation from another planet. Mounteney had never had to struggle with a sadic strain in his own nature. It is men who have had to struggle so who hate cruelty most. Suddenly, listening to the revulsion in Martin's voice, I knew he was one of them.

Sternly, he went on speaking:

'But we ought to take a few sensible steps, just to make sure. I suppose they can be taught to realize what dropping one bomb means.'

We all knew the estimates of deaths the bomb would cause: we knew also the manner of those deaths.

'We can teach them,' said Mounteney. 'We'd better see that the scientists are ready to assert themselves in case there is any whisper of nonsense.'

I said: 'Why scientists specially?'

Mounteney answered: 'Because no one could do it if they could imagine the consequences. The scientists can imagine the consequences.' He gave an ironic smile, unfamiliar on him. 'After all, scientists are no worse than other men.'

Martin smiled. It all seemed far in the future, the shadow of horror passed away.

Suddenly Martin exclaimed. 'It's a mistake to be absent-minded,' he said. We asked him what the matter was.

The swan was stretching his neck, asking for more. 'I've just given him a piece from the palm of my hand,' Martin remarked. 'I'm glad he left my fingers on.'

He threw the last piece of bun into the water, then stood up.

'It wouldn't do any harm,' he said, returning to the discussion, but only out of his habit of precaution, 'to drop a word in high quarters if we get a chance.'

CHAPTER 14

Unexpected Encouragement

I DECIDED to report that conversation about the use of the bomb to Hector Rose. To him it seemed almost unbelievably academic.

'I fancy our masters will cross that bridge when they come to it,' he said. He was as impatient as he ever allowed himself to be. Scientists talked too much; here they were, speculating about ethical dilemmas which might never arise, as though they were back in their student days. 'But I'm grateful to you for keeping me in the picture, my dear Eliot, many, many thanks.'

To Rose, Barford did not present any problems for decision, either then or for months to come. The pile was going up, the first instalment of heavy water had arrived; so far, so good. He was immune to the excitement that had infected me, and, as 1943 went on, I had nothing new to tell him. On my visits, I could see no change. Luke paid a visit to Canada, but otherwise was still fretting his nerves away, unoccupied, playing his piano. Martin spent much time on the hangar floor, watching the builders putting up the frame inch by inch, correct to a thousandth, making a progress perceptible to them and himself, but not to me.

By this time he was showing the strain – though in a fashion opposite to Luke's. Instead of blowing and cursing, Martin sank into a kind of frozen quietness. He was more capable of pretending than Luke, and was still reasonable company. He and Irene seemed friendly when I saw them together; she was a better mother than many people were willing to believe, and the scandal about her had died down. At Barford her name was mentioned without malicious gossip, and in consequence with disappointment, lack of tone and interest.

Often, alone with Martin, I wondered how much in those months of waiting and semi-idleness, he harassed himself about her. How right was Hanna? Was he living with that suspense, as well as the public one?

Even the public one he kept clamped down, but occasionally he was remote, as though thinking of nothing but the day when they would test the pile.

70

I was beginning to feel confident for him, even confident enough to ask Pearson's opinion, the most certain of all to be discouraging, when he called at my flat one evening that autumn.

He was just leaving for Los Alamos, and had come to fetch some papers. I had not been into the office that day, because of an attack of lumbago: Pearson had no more taste for conversation than usual, and intended to take the documents and depart without the unnecessary intermediate stage of sitting down. But, as he was glancing the papers over, the sirens blew, and we heard gunfire in the distance: it sounded like the start of one of the short, sharp air raids that were becoming common that November.

'I think you'd better stay a little while,' I said.

'I might as well,' said Pearson.

He sat down, without having taken off his mackintosh. He sat as though he were quite comfortable; he did not speak until we heard the crunch of bombs, probably some way the other side of the river. Pearson looked at me through glasses which magnified his calm eyes.

'How old is this house?'

That summer I had moved from the Dolphin block into a square close by. As I told Pearson, the houses must be about a hundred years old, run up when Pimlico was a new residential district, now left with the stucco peeling off the porticos.

'A bit too old to stand up well,' said Pearson.

We heard the whine of a bomb, then the jar and rumble. The light bulbs swung, and flecks of plaster fell on to the carpet.

'About a quarter of a mile away,' said Pearson, after a second's consideration. He picked a spicule of plaster off his lapel.

I said I often wish that I had not moved from the steel and concrete of Dolphin Square.

Twice we heard the whine of bombs.

'What floor was yours?' asked Pearson, with impassive interest.

'The fourth.'

'The factor of safety was about eight times what you've got here.'

I was frightened, as I was whenever bombs fell; I could not get used to it. I disliked being frightened in the presence of Pearson, who happened to be brave.

Four bombs: one, Pearson guessed, nearer than a quarter of a mile:

then the gunfire slackened overhead and we could hear it tailing away down the estuary.

'If I were you,' he remarked, 'and they began to drop them near this house, I should get a bit nervous.'

Soon he got up.

'That's all for tonight,' he said.

But even Pearson felt a touch of the elation which came to one after an air raid. He was not quite unaffected; because bombs had been dropping near us, he was a little warmer to me. When I suggested that I should walk part of the way to Victoria, he said, more considerately than I had heard him speak:

'Of course, if you feel up to it.'

In the square the night was misty, but illuminated across the river by a pillar of fire, rose and lilac round an inner tongue of gold, peacefully beautiful. It seemed to be near Nine Elms, but might have been a little farther off, perhaps at Battersea.

'It's silly, trying to knock towns out by high explosive,' said Pearson, as we turned our backs to the blaze and walked towards Belgrave Road. 'It just can't be done,' he said.

I had never known him so communicative, and I took advantage of it.

'What about the other bomb?'

He turned his face towards me, and in the light of another, smaller fire, I saw his eyes, lazy, half suspicious.

'What about it?' he said.

'What's going to happen?'

After a pause, he did not mind answering:

'We're going to get it.'

'Who is?'

'Who do you think?' He meant, of course, the American party he was working in. As with most of the scientists, nationalism in its restricted sense touched him very little – when he said 'we', he thought of nothing but his own group.

'You're sure?' I asked, but he was always sure.

'It stands to reason.'

Then I asked, expecting a flat answer:

'So you don't think anything will come of Luke's affair?' I was prepared for the flat answer; what I actually heard sounded too good to be true.

'I shouldn't like to go as far as that,' he replied, looking in front of him indifferently.

'You believe it might work?' I said.

'When he started talking about it, I thought he'd do himself a bit of no good.' He gave a contented, contemptuous grin. 'But it doesn't seem to have been all hot air.'

'You really think they'll pull it off?'

'I'm not a prophet.'

I asked him again.

'Oh, well,' said Pearson, 'in time Master Luke might show a bit of return for his money. Though' – he gave the same contemptuous grin again – 'he won't do it as soon as he thinks he will.'

I did not receive any greater assurance until the spring, when, in March, I received a note from Luke himself. It said:

The balloon is due to go up on the 22nd. The machine ought to work some time that afternoon, though I can't tell you correct to the nearest hour. We want you to come and see the exhibition. . . .

I had no doubt that Martin did not know of the letter; it would have seemed to him tempting fate. For myself, I felt the same kind of superstition, even a misgiving about going down to watch. If I were not there, all would happen according to plan, Luke triumph, Martin get some fame. If I sat by and watched – yet, of course, I should have to go.

CHAPTER 15

Sister-in-Law

THE twenty-second was only a week away when, one evening just as I was leaving the office, Martin rang me up. He was at Barford; he sounded elaborate, round-about, as though he had something to ask.

'I suppose you don't happen to be free tonight?'

But I could not help interrupting:

'Nothing wrong with the pile?'

(Although, over the telephone, I used a code word.)

'Not that I know of.'

'Everything fixed for next week?'

'I hope so.'

For the first time, I was letting myself wonder what Martin would do with his success.

'Shall you be in your flat tonight?' He had come round to his question.

'I could be,' I said.

'I wish you'd look after Irene a bit, if she comes in.'

'Why should she?'

'I think she will.' He went on: 'She's in rather a state.'

I said I would do anything I could. I asked: 'Is it serious?'

'I'd rather you formed your own opinion.'

I had heard little emotion in his voice – maybe he was past it, I thought. But he apologized for inflicting this on me, and he was relieved to have someone to look after her.

Later that night, I was reading in my sitting-room when the bell rang. I went to open the door, and out of the darkness, into the blue-lit hall, came Irene.

'I'm not popular, am I?' she said, but her laugh was put on.

Without speaking, I led her in.

'This room makes an enemy of me,' she said, still trying to brazen it out. Then she said, not with her childish make believe but without any pretence:

'I couldn't come to anyone but you. Martin knows about it.'

For a few moments I thought she had left him; as she went on speaking I realized it was not so simple. First she asked, as though the prosaic question drove out all others:

'Have you got a telephone?'

She looked round the room, her pupils dilated, her eyes taking in nothing but the telephone she could not see.

'Yes,' I said, trying to soothe her. It stood in the passage.

'Can I use it?'

I said, of course.

Immediately, her eyes still blind, she went out, leaving the door open. I heard her dial, slowly because in the wartime glimmer she could hardly make out the figures. Then her voice: 'Mrs Whelan, it's me again. Is Mr Hankins back yet?'

A mutter from the instrument.

'Not yet?' Irene's voice was high.

Another mutter.

'Listen,' said Irene, 'I've got a telephone number where he can get me now.'

I heard her strike a match and give the Victoria number on my telephone.

Another mutter.

'I'll be here a couple of hours at least,' replied Irene into the telephone. 'Even if he's late, tell him I'll be here till one.'

She came back into my room.

'Is that all right?' she asked, her eyes brighter now, focused on me. I said yes.

'It's for him,' she said. 'It's not for me. He wants to speak to me urgently, and there's nowhere else I can safely wait.'

She stared at me.

'I think he wants me back.'

I tried to steady her: 'What can you tell him?'

'What can I tell him?' she cried, and added, half crying, half hysterical: 'Can I tell him *I'm defeated*?'

The phrase sounded strange, I was mystified: and yet it was at this point I knew that she was not leaving Martin out of hand.

On the other hand, I knew also that she was reading in Hankins's intentions just what she wanted to read. Did he truly want her back? Above all, she would like to believe that.

Perhaps it was commonplace. Did she, like so many other unfaithful wives, want the supreme satisfaction of coming to the crisis and then staying with her husband and turning her lover down?

For all her faults, I did not think she was as commonplace as that. Looking at her, as she sat on my sofa, breathing shortly and shallowly as she listened for the telephone, I did not feel that she was just enjoying the game of love. She was febrile: that proved nothing, she could have been febrile in a flirtation. Her heart was pounding with emotion; I had seen other women so, taking a last fervent goodbye of a lover, on their way back to the marriage bed. But she was also genuinely, wildly unhappy, unhappy because her life was being driven by forces she could not govern or even understand, and unhappy also for the most primal of reasons, because the telephone did not ring and she could not hear his voice.

I tried to comfort her. I spoke of the time, ten years before, when I knew Hankins. It was strange that he, I was thinking, should have been her grand passion, her infatuation, her romantic love—people gave it different names, according to how they judged her. Why should he be the one to get under the skin of this fickle, reckless woman?

No, that did not soothe her. I made a better shot when I talked of her and Martin. I assumed there was something left for both of them, which was what she wanted to hear. We talked of the child, which she fiercely loved.

I recalled the reason she had given, at her breakfast table, for marrying him. 'Tell me,' I said, 'why did *he* marry *you*?'

'Oh, that's simple,' said Irene, 'he just liked the look of me.'

For once that night she spoke with zest, something like triumph.

Soon her anxiety came back. She asked: Should we hear the telephone bell through the wall? Several times she started up, thinking it was beginning to ring. Twice it did ring, and twice she went to the receiver. One call was for me, one a wrong number. The minutes passed, the half hours. Midnight came, one o'clock. She had ceased trying to keep up any conversation long since.

It was not in me to condemn her. I scarcely thought of her as my brother's wife. Faced with the sight of her nervous expectant face, pinched to the point where anxiety is turning into the dread of deprivation, I felt for her just the animal comradeship of those who have been driven to wait for news by telephone, to wait in fear of the post because there may not be a letter, to walk the streets at night waiting for a bedroom light to go out before they can go to sleep. To have lived, even for a time, helpless in the deep undertow of passionate love – at moments one thought that one must come home to it, even if it was a dreadful home, and anyone moving to that same home, as Irene was, seemed at such moments a sister among the others, among all the untroubled strangers going to their neater homes.

At half past two I persuaded her to go to bed. The next morning there was still no message; she wanted to ring up again, but some relic of pride, perhaps my presence and what she had said to me, prevented her. She put on her smart, brazen air to keep her courage up, and with a quip about having spent the night alone with me in my flat, took a taxi to Paddington and the next train back to Barford, waving with spirit till she was out of sight up Lupus Street.

Neither that morning, nor the previous night, had I wished, as I had often wished in the past, that Martin was rid of her.

CHAPTER 16

Points on a Graph

MOST people I met, even on the technical committees, were still ignorant about the whole uranium project. But some could not resist letting one know that they were in the secret too. In the lavatory of the Athenaeum a bald bland head turned to me from the adjacent stall.

'*March 22nd*,' came the whisper and a finger rose to the lips.

On the evening of the twenty-first, just as I was leaving to catch the last train to Barford, Hector Rose gave his ceremonious knock and came into my office.

'Very best wishes, Eliot,' he said. He was awkward; he was for once excited, and tried to hide it.

'This may be a mildly historic occasion,' he said. 'We may all qualify for a footnote to history, which would be somewhat peculiar, don't you think?'

Next morning, sitting opposite to Mrs Drawbell at the breakfast table, I thought there was one person at least immune from the excitement. Drawbell had left for the laboratory, so full of animation that he let the diablerie show through: 'If I were giving honours, Eliot, I shouldn't give them to the prima donnas – no, just to the people who do the good, hard, slogging work.' He gave his melon-lipped grin; he was thinking of his own rewards to come; more than ever, he felt the resentment of a middle man for those who make his fortune. When he went out, the psychological temperature fell.

Mrs Drawbell watched me, heavy and confident in her silence. She said: 'I hope you are enjoying your kipper,' and returned to impassivity again. I said:

'Everyone will be glad when today is over, won't they?'

The women at Barford had had to be told that an experiment was taking place that day; Mrs Drawbell did not know what it was, but she knew this was a crisis. Nevertheless, mine seemed a new idea.

'Perhaps they will,' said Mrs Drawbell.

'It's going to be a strain,' I said.

She gave an opaque smile.

'It's a strain on your husband,' I said.

'He's used to it,' said Mrs Drawbell.

Had she any feeling for him, I wondered? She was his ally; in her immobile fashion, she tried to help him on: it was she who, finding that Martin and Irene had no room to spare, had invited me to stay. Yet she spoke of him with less tenderness than many women speak of their doctors.

Then she talked of Mary Pearson's children; Mrs Drawbell was looking after them for the day. She was confident that their mother's treatment was wrong and her own right. Densely, confidently, with a curious air of being about to offer affection, she pressed her case upon me and was demanding my moral support. I could not help remembering her on my way to the hangar, irritated as I was in any period of suspense that other lives should be going on, with their own egotisms, claiming one's attention, intruding their desires.

I felt my suspense about that day's experiment increase, having been forced to think of something else. When I saw Mary Pearson, sitting at a bench close to the pile, I was short to her; her skin flushed, her eyes clouded behind her spectacles. I made some sort of apology. I could not explain that I felt more keyed up because her name had distracted me.

The hangar was noisy that morning, like a cathedral echoing a party of soldiers. Workmen, mechanics, young scientists, went in and out through the door in the pile's outer wall; Luke was shouting to someone on top of the pile; Martin and a couple of assistants were disentangling the wire from an electrical apparatus on the floor. There were at least twenty men in the hangar, and Mary Pearson was the only woman. And in the middle, white-walled, about three times the height of a man, stood – catching our eyes as though it were a sacred stone – the pile.

Luke greeted me. He was wearing a windjacket tucked into his grey flannel trousers.

'Well, Lewis,' he shouted, 'we're in the hell of a mess.'

'It will be all right on the night,' said someone. There was a burst of laughter, laughter noisy, exultant, with just a prickle of nerves.

The 'pipery' (Luke meant the pipes, but his scientific idiom was getting richer as he grew more triumphant) had 'stood up to' all tests. The uranium slugs were in place. In the past week, Martin had put in a dribble of heavy water, and a test sample had picked up no impurities. But there was one 'bloody last-minute snag' like finding just at the critical moment that you have forgotten – Luke produced a bedroom simile. Most of the 'circuitry', like the pipery, was in order: there was trouble with one switch of the control rods.

'We can't start without them,' said Luke. Martin joined us: I did not wish to ask questions, any question seemed to delay the issue, but they told me how the control rods worked. 'If the pile gets too hot, then they automatically shut the whole thing off,' said Luke.

'Otherwise,' said Martin, 'there is a finite danger that the reaction would be uncontrollable.'

That meant – I knew enough to follow – the pile might turn into something like a nuclear bomb.

Both Luke and Martin were themselves working on the circuits. A couple of radio engineers wanted Luke to let them improvise a switch.

'Think again,' said Luke. 'That cut-off is going to work as we intended it to work, if it means plugging away at the circuits until this time tomorrow.'

Someone went on arguing.

'Curtains,' said Luke.

As Martin returned to the labyrinth of wires, both he and Luke ready to finger valves for hours to come, I wished I had stayed away or that they had a job for me. All I could do was drag up a chair to Mary Pearson's bench. She was self-conscious, perhaps because I had been brusque, perhaps because, with her husband away, she was uncomfortable in the presence of men. Already that morning I had seen some of the youths, gauche but virile, eyeing her. When I sat beside her, though she was not comfortable herself, it was in her nature to try to make me so.

In front of her were instruments which she had been taught to read; she was a competent girl, I thought, she would have made an admirable nurse. There was one of the counters whose ticking I had come to expect in any Barford laboratory; there was a logarithmic amplifier, a DC amplifier, with faces like speedometers, which would give a measure – she had picked up some of the jargon – of the 'neutron flux'.

On the bench was pinned a sheet of graph paper and it was there that she was to plot the course of the experiment. As the heavy water was poured in, the neutron flux would rise: the points on the graph would lead down to a spot where the pile had started to run, where the chain reaction had begun:

'That's going to be the great moment,' said Mary.

The tap and rattle, the curses and argument, the flashes of light, went on round us. I continued to talk to Mary, lowering my voice – though there was no need, for the scientists were shouting. Once or twice she contradicted me, her kind mouth showed a touch of sexual obstinacy. She was totally faithful to Pearson; like many passionate women she was chaste; but she was not chaste because she did not know the temptation; she could have made many men happy, and been happy herself with many men. She would stay faithful to her husband, however long he was kept away, and she was edgy when her eyes brightened in his absence. Again like many happy, passionate, good-natured women, she had just a trace more than her fair share of self regard. The morning ticked on, midday, the early afternoon, none of us had spoken of eating. It must have been after two o'clock when one of the refugees discovered the fault.

At once a conference sprang up, between Mary Pearson's bench and the pile. If they wanted a 'permanent solution', so that they need not worry about the control rods for the next year, it would take twenty-four hours: on the other hand it would be very little risk to patch up a circuit for a trial run, and that could be ready by evening.

Luke stood by himself, square, toeing the floor, his lips chewed in.

'No,' he said loudly, 'there are some risks you have got to take and there are some you haven't. A week might possibly matter, but a day damned well can't. We'll get it right before we start.'

A voice complained: 'We said we should be running on the twenty-second.'

Luke said: 'Well, we now say that we shall be running on the twenty-third.'

He was right. They all knew it. It was only Martin, who, as he and Luke came out of the scrimmage towards me, said, in a tone that the others could not hear:

'It's a pity for the sake of public relations.'

'You'd better look after them,' said Luke. For a moment, his energy had left him. Everyone who was working there trusted him, because they felt (as his seniors did not) that underneath his brashness there was a bedrock of sense. But for Luke himself, it took an effort for the sense to win.

'Tell them we've called it a day,' said Luke with fatigue. 'They can see the fireworks about teatime tomorrow.'

'Not earlier than eight tomorrow night,' said Martin.

For an hour, Martin went off to play politics: explaining to the senior men at Barford, Drawbell, Mounteney, and the rest, who were expected to come to the 'opening' that night, the reason for the delay: telephoning Rose and others in London. I offered to get the news through to Rose myself, but Martin chose to do it all.

Mary Pearson left to fetch sandwiches, voices blew about the hangar, Luke and his team were stripping a lead on top of the pile, and I was able to slip away.

Out of duty, I visited Irene and the child, who was just a year old. Irene said nothing of our last meeting, but as I was playing with the baby she remarked, all of a sudden:

'Lewis, you'd rather be alone, wouldn't you?'

I asked what she meant.

'You and Martin are very much alike, you know. You'd like to hide until this thing is settled, wouldn't you?'

With her eyes fixed on me, I admitted it.

'So would he,' said Irene.

With the half malicious understanding that was springing up between us, she sent me off on my own. I did not want to speak to anyone I knew at Barford, not Mounteney, not Luke, Martin least of all. I made an excuse to Mrs Drawbell that some old acquaintance had asked me out to dinner, but in fact I took the bus to Warwick and spent the evening in a public house.

There I saw only one person from Barford – young Sawbridge, whom we had interviewed twelve months before. Somehow I was driven to be friendly, to get some response of goodwill out of him, as though he were a mascot for the following night.

I stood him a drink, and said something about our native town.

'I've not got much use for it,' said Sawbridge.

It would have soothed me to be sentimental that night. I mentioned some of my friends of the twenties – George Passant – no, Sawbridge had never heard of him.

I kept affectionate memories of the town then, and said so.

'You just lump it down anywhere in America,' said Sawbridge with anger, 'and no one could tell the difference.'

I gave it up, and asked him to have another drink.

'I don't mind if I do,' said Sawbridge.

The next day I got through the hours in the same fashion, sitting in the library, walking by the riverside. The afternoon was quiet, there was no wind; it would have been pleasant to be strolling so, waiting for nothing, with that night's result behind me. The elm twigs were thickening, the twigs in the hedges were dense and black, but there were no leaves anywhere. All was dusky, just before the break of the leaf – except for a patch where the blackthorn shone white, solid, and bare, standing out before the sullen promise of the hedgerow.

I went straight from the blackthorn blossom and the leafless hedge back to the hangar, where the shadow of the pile lay black on the geometrically levelled floor. Martin and Luke were drinking tea on a littered bench close to Mary's and someone was calling instructions by numbers.

They told me that all was ready 'bar the juice'. The juice was heavy water, and it took the next hour to carry it into the hangar. I went with some of the scientists in the first carrying party; they walked among the huts in the spring evening laughing like students on their way back from the laboratory. The heavy-water depot stood on the edge of the airfield, a red brick cube with two sentries at the door; there was a hiatus, then, because the young men had no sense of form but the storekeeper had. He was an old warrant officer with protruding eyes; his instructions said that he could not deliver heavy water except on certain signatures. Against curses, against the rational, nagging, contentious, scientific argument, he just pointed to his rubric, and Martin had to be fetched. He was polite with the storekeeper; to me, he smiled, the only smile of detachment on his face in those two days. The scientists followed into the depot one by one, and came out with what looked like enormous Thermos flasks, which were the containers of heavy water.

Casually the young men joggled back, the silver flasks flashing in the cold green twilight. About it all there was an overwhelming air of jauntiness and youth; it might have been a party of hikers carrying bottles of beer. It was a scene that, even as it took place, I felt obliged to remember – the file in sweaters and grey flannel trousers, swinging the silver flasks, the faces young, thin, disrespectful, masculine.

'Each of those flasks cost God knows what,' said Martin as we watched. He did some mental arithmetic. 'About two thousand pounds.'

By seven o'clock some hundreds of flasks were standing behind the pile. When I discovered that the heavy water from those flasks was going to be poured in by hand, it did not strike me as foreign. It was like much that I had picked up in the air at Cambridge and which Luke and Mounteney and Martin had carried with them. The pile, engineered to a thousandth of an inch; the metals, analytically pure as metals had not been pure before; the whole structure, the most perfect example of the quantitative accuracy of the age; and then Martin and his men were going to slop in the heavy water as though filling up a bath with buckets. They did not mind being slapdash when it did not matter; they took a certain pride in it, like the older generation of Cambridge scientists; the next pile they made, they conceded, they would have the 'juice' syphoned in.

'All set, I think,' said Martin to Luke. Mary Pearson was sitting at her bench, an assistant watching another instrument at her side. Martin's team formed a knot by the pile door. The wall close by was filling with the rest of Luke's staff, for word had gone round that the experiment was due to begin. Drawbell was also there and – it seemed a gallant gesture – Rudd. Mounteney had sent a message that he would come 'as soon as things got significant' (all knew that, for an hour or so, till the pile was half full of heavy water, no one could tell whether it was about to 'run').

Drawbell and the security officers had thought it unrealistic to keep the experiment secret within the establishment. Anyone was allowed in the hangar who would normally have been let in there in the course of business – so that several of the wives, employed in the Barford offices, came in.

The women in the hangar were wearing jerseys and overcoats to guard against the sharp night. Among the blur of faces I saw Hanna Puchwein's glossy head close to young Sawbridge's. Nora Luke, her hair piled up in a bun, had gone pallid with the months of tension which had not lined, but puffed out, her face.

At half past seven there were about seventy people in the hangar, perhaps a third of them spectators. They occupied a crescent that left the pile and the instrument tables free, encroached nowhere near the ranks of heavy-water flasks and the filling station, and which marked out a kind of quarter deck where Luke could walk to and fro, from the pile to Mary Pearson's graph.

He was there alone, now that Martin had gone to the filling place. Luke had slept three hours the night before, he was still wearing the windjacket and crumpled trousers, but he made the quick exercising movements of a man about to start a long-distance race.

'Anything stopping you?' he called to Martin.

'Nothing at all,' said Martin.

'*Then let her go.*'

For an hour it was anti-climax. We could not see much of it, just the scurry of Martin and the others behind the pile, pouring in flask after flask. 'A quarter full,' Martin said at eight o'clock.

Mary Pearson read the flux and made a point on the graph. Luke and Martin nodded; all was as it should be. Martin said: 'My turn to do some more pouring.'

'Glug glug,' said Luke.

As the level of heavy water rose, they poured more slowly. At last: 'Half full.' Mary scrutinized the indicator and inked in another point. Did she know, I was thinking, exactly where those points should fall to mean success? Luke looked over her shoulder.

'There or thereabouts,' he said quietly to Mounteney, who had come in a quarter of an hour before.

Although he had spoken in a low tone, somehow the crowd picked up the first intimation of good news. The excitement was sharper, they were quiet, they were on edge for something to cheer. Once more Martin came round and also studied the graph. 'Not so bad,' he whispered to Luke, raising an eyebrow, and then called out to the man at the filling place: 'Slowly now. Only when I say.'

Flask by flask, the level went up from half way. Mary was reading the flux each minute now. To the first points after half way, neither Luke nor Martin paid much attention. Then, as the minutes went on, they both stood by her watching each point. No one else went near the instrument. The excitement stayed, they were ready for Luke to say – 'In — minutes from now the chain reaction will begin.'

Luke and Martin were staring down at the graph. I could not see their faces. I had almost no fears left. Certainly I did not watch Mary's hand as the level went up to 0·55 inserting a point as though her fingers were weighed down. As her pen stopped above the next point, Luke and Martin straightened themselves and looked at each other. Still the mood round me, the expectancy and elation, had not changed. Luke's glance at Martin might have told me nothing; but Martin's at Luke in one instant let me know the worst.

CHAPTER 17

Quarrel at First Light

As Martin and Luke looked at each other, no one round realized what the graph had told them. Someone threw in a scientific jibe about 'cooking' and Luke replied. He said to the men at the filling place: 'Hold it for a minute.' Even then, no one, not even Mounteney suspected.

He left Mary's bench, pushed through the crowd, and, his stiff strong back straight, walked rapidly to his little office at the hangar side. That was nothing startling; he had done so three times since the experiment began. Martin remained on the 'quarter deck' space, strolled over to the pile and back to Mary's instrument bench, then, with an air of casualness, as it were absent-mindedly, followed Luke. The scientists were chattering round me, relaxed until Luke came back; I did not attract attention, when in a moment I also followed.

In the office Martin was sitting on a chair, his arms rigid by his sides, while Luke paced from the window to the door, three stamping steps, turned, three steps to the window, like a wild dog in the zoo.

As I went in, Martin did not move, greeted me only with his eyes.

'Hello,' he said.

'If only I'd made the whole thing bigger!' Luke was saying, in a grinding voice.

'In fact we didn't,' said Martin.

'How bad is it?' I had to ask.

'It's pretty bad,' said Martin.

Luke cried:

'If only I'd made the thing fifty per cent bigger. Then whatever's gone wrong, it would still have worked!'

'I can't blame ourselves for *that*,' said Martin. His tone was bitter.

'What do you blame us for?' Luke stopped and rounded on him.

'We spoke too soon,' said Martin.

'You mean,' said Luke, 'that I never know when to keep my mouth shut.'

'It doesn't matter what caused it,' said Martin, and his temper for once was ready to match Luke's. 'We've got to take the consequences.'

'Yes,' Luke broke out, 'you're going to look a fool because of me.'

They both felt the fury of collaborators. The fabric of businesslike affection opened, and one saw – Martin's anger at having been led astray, his dislike of trusting his leader too far, perhaps his dislike of having a leader at all, perhaps a flicker of the obscure, destructive satisfaction that comes to a junior partner in a failure for which he is not to blame. One saw Luke's resentment at the partner to whom he had done harm, the ferocious resentment of the leader to someone he has led into failure. Luke was a responsible, confident man, he knew Martin had served him with complete loyalty: in disaster he was choked with anger at the sight of Martin's face.

But those feelings were not their deepest. Each was face to face with his own disaster. Each was taking it in his own fashion. I did not know which was being hurt more.

Martin said: 'It will give some simple pleasure in various quarters.'

He had tried to teach himself not to be proud, he had set out to be sensible, calculating, prepared to risk snubs, but there was a nerve of pride hidden beneath. Now he was preparing himself for a humiliation. He had tried to be content with little, but this time he had believed that what he wanted was in his hands; he was composing himself again to expect nothing.

To Luke, even to me, his stoicism seemed enviable. To himself, it was like an invalid pretending to feel better for the benefit of his visitors and then sinking down when they had gone.

Luke made no attempt at stoicism, less than most men. He assumed that he was the more wretched, that he would jib more at the humiliation.

'Why are the wise old jaw-bacons always right?' he cried, repeating criticisms that had been made of him, dwelling on them, sometimes agreeing with them. 'When shall I learn not to make a mess of things? If ever the jaw-bacons had a good idea, they would handle it without any of this nonsense. How can I go and tell them that their damn silly short-sighted fatuous bloody ignorant criticism has just turned out right all the time?'

Yet, though he might feel more ashamed than Martin, though he would have no guard at all when he heard what Mounteney and the others had to say, he would recover sooner. Even in his wretchedness, his powers were beginning to reassert themselves. It was frustration to him to feel those powers deprived, to know that through his own fault he had not fulfilled them; until the pile was running, he would know self-reproach like a hunger of flesh and bone; but underneath the misery and self-accusation his resolve was taking shape.

'It was just on the edge of being right,' he said. 'Why in God's name didn't I get it quite right?

'What is stopping them (the neutrons)?

'Brother Rudd will have a nice sleep tonight. Well, I can't grudge him that.

'The heavy water is all right.

'The electronics are all right.

'The engineering is all right.

'I only hope the Germans are capable of making bloody fools of themselves like this. Or anyone else who gets as far. I tell you we've got as near as kiss your hand.

'*The engineering is all right.*

'*The heavy water is all right.*

'*The uranium is all right.*

'*The uranium is all right.*

'No, it blasted well can't be.

'*That must be it.* It must be the uranium – there's something left there stopping the neuts.'

Martin, who had been sitting so still that he might not have heard Luke's outburst, suddenly broke in. From the beginning they had known that the uranium had to be pure to a degree that made them need a new metallurgy. After all, that still might not be pure enough. Was there an impurity, present in minute quantities, which happened to have great stopping power? I heard names strange to me. One Luke kept repeating (it was gadolinium, though on the spot my ear did not pick it up). 'That's it,' he cried.

'There might be others,' said Martin.

'No,' said Luke. '*That's it.*'

'I'm not convinced,' said Martin.

But he was. Even that night, Luke's authority had surged up again.

Later, other scientists said there was nothing wonderful about Luke's diagnosis; anyone would have reached it, given a cool head and a little time. What some of them did praise (even those who only passed compliments on those securely dead) was his recuperative power.

They did not see him just a moment after his flare of certainty. He knew what was wrong, he could stiffen himself to months' more work: but there was something to do first.

He stopped his pacing, put a hand on the desk and spoke to Martin.

'Do you think they rumbled?'

(He meant the other scientists waiting by the pile.)

'I doubt it,' said Martin.

'I should have thought they must. They must be thinking that I've given them the laugh of a lifetime.'

'I don't think so,' said Martin.

'They've got to be told.'

Martin nodded. His own face pale, he was watching Luke's. Luke broke out:

'I can't do it.' His bounce had quitted him; his active nature had gone dead.

Martin pressed in his lips.

'I'll do it,' he said.

Then Luke took hold of the desk and shook himself, shook his heavy shoulders like a dog on the beach.

'No, I must do it,' he said. 'You've got more nerve than I have, but you'd be too diplomatic. It's a mistake to be diplomatic about a bloody fiasco.'

'You're right,' said Martin. For the first time since I came into that office, there was a comradely glance between them.

Luke went straight to the door.

'Here we go,' he said.

But, as they stood in the open hangar, with the crowd between them and the pile, Luke muttered:

'I'm going to try another reading, just on the off chance.'

Even now he was hoping for a miracle to save him. He walked, arms swinging, to the instrument bench, and once more studied the graph. He called out:

'Take her up to ·6.' Martin stood by his side. They had been gone less than twenty minutes. There was a stir in the spectators round me, but I did not hear any word of doubt. Mary Pearson's hair was close to the table as she read the indicator. With a slow sweep, like the movement of someone drugged, retarded but not jerky, her hand moved over the graph paper. The instant her pen point came to rest, Luke snatched the sheet from her. He glanced – showed it to Martin – threw it on to the bench – more quickly than a man could light a cigarette. He took a step forward, and in a loud, slow, inflexible voice said:

'It's a flop. That's all for tonight. We'll get it right, but it's going to take some time.'

A hush. An hysterical laugh. A gasp. Men talking at once. Pushing up her glasses, Mary Pearson began to sob, tears rolling down her face. I caught sight of young Sawbridge, his mouth open with pain like a Marathon runner's: for once I saw emotion on his face, he too was nearly crying.

Drawbell, Rudd, and Mounteney pushed towards the graph.

'What is all this?' Mounteney was asking irritably. 'What has the k got up to?'

Rudd said to Martin: 'Never mind, old chap. It might happen to anyone.'

'Not quite like this,' said Martin, looking straight into Rudd's eyes, in search of the gloating that he expected in all eyes just then.

In the hubbub, the high questions, the hot wash of feeling more alive that men get from any catastrophe not their own, Drawbell took command. Mounting on Mary Pearson's chair he shouted for attention; and as they huddled round him, as round an orator in Hyde Park, he stood quite still with an expression steady, friendly, undisturbed.

When they were looking up at him, he spoke, with the same steadiness:

'Now I'm going to send you home. We'll begin the inquest to-morrow, and I shall give you a statement all in good time. But I don't want you to go home tonight in the wrong frame of mind. It's true that the experiment hasn't worked according to plan, and Luke was right to tell us so. I'm not going to raise false hopes, so I shan't say any more about that. But I do tell you something else: that even if the worst comes to the worst, this experiment has taught us more about our job than any establishment in the world, except our friends across the Atlantic. We shall finish up better because we've had our setbacks. This isn't the end, this is the beginning.'

Without a flash of his own disappointments, free from the honours receding from him that night, without a tremor of *schadenfreude* at Luke's fall, Drawbell stood there, happier with a crowd than ever with a single person, engrossed in infecting them with his own curious courage, delighted (as the complex sometimes are) because he was behaving well. It was he who cleared the hangar, to allow Luke and Martin to get back to their office undisturbed. Outside on the floor round the pile, there was soon no one left, except Nora Luke; we looked at each other without a word, unable to go away.

'We'd better ask,' she said at last, as we stood helplessly there, 'whether we can be any use.'

In the office, Luke and Martin were both sitting down. As Nora saw her husband she said, awkwardly, wishing from the bottom of her heart that she could let herself go:

'Bad luck.'

It was Martin who replied, picking up Drawbell's speech with harsh irony:

'We shall finish up better because we've had our set-backs.'

To his wife, Luke said,

'Let's have some tea.'

That was the first pot of tea. Nora made five others before the night ended. Like other men of action, Luke talked more as he grew more tired. What to do? – decisions of his kind were not made in mono-syllables, they were made in repetitious soliloquies, often in speeches that got nowhere, that were more like singing than the ordinary give and take of talk. Yet out of that welter sprang, several times that night, a new resolve, one more point ticked off.

Meanwhile, Nora sat by, calculating for him how many (if his assumption were right) uranium slugs would have to be replaced, before the pile would run. It was a long calculation; she carried it out like the professional mathematician that she was; sometimes she glanced at Luke, distrusting herself, thinking that another woman might have given him rest. But she was wrong. His bad time was behind him, of us all he was the least broken.

As Luke talked more, Martin became more silent. He took in each new plan, he answered questions; but through the small hours he sat volunteering no words of his own, giving his opinion when Luke asked for it, like a sensible second-in-command – and yet each time I heard that controlled voice I knew that he was eating himself up with hopes in retrospect, with that singular kind of might-have-been that twists one's bowels because it still grips one like a hope.

As I looked at Martin, my disappointment for him, which had started anew, the instant I caught the glance between him and Luke over the graph, was growing so that it drained me of all other feelings, of patience, of sympathy, of affection. This might have been the night of his success. Now it came to the test, that was my only hunger. I had none to spare for the project; on the other hand, I did not give a thought for our forebodings with Mounteney by the river. I had none of the frustration that Luke felt and perhaps Martin also, because they were being kept at arm's length from a piece of scientific truth. For me, this ought to have been the night of Martin's success. I was bitter with him because it had gone wrong.

At last Luke said, his voice still resonant, that we had done enough for one night, and Martin and I walked together out of the hangar door. The sky was dark, without any stars, but in the east there was a pallor that seemed less comforting.

'First light,' said Martin.

I could not help myself. I broke out of control:

'Is this ever going to come off?'

'Is what ever going to come off?'

It was one of his stoical tricks, to pretend not to understand.

'You know what I mean.'

Martin paused.

'I should think your guess is about as good as mine,' he said.

I tried, but I could not keep quiet:

'Perhaps it's a pity that you burned your boats.'

'That's possible,' said Martin.

'Perhaps it wasn't sensible to invest all your future in one man.'

'I've thought of that,' said Martin.

'Luke's enemies have always said that he'd make one big mistake,' I said. I could hear in my own voice, and could not hold it down, the special cruelty that can break out of any 'unselfish' love, of a father's or a brother's, with anyone who is asking nothing for himself – except that the other person should fulfil one's dreams, often one's self-identificatory dreams. If you see yourself in another, you see all you would like to be: so you can be more self-sacrificing than in any other human relation, because it does not seem like sacrifice: for the same reason you can be more cruel.

'I've thought of that also.'

'Is this going to be his big mistake?' I asked.

For the first time, Martin turned against me; his voice was quieter but as bitter as mine.

'You're not making it any easier,' he said.

Ashamed, suddenly stricken by his misery, I said that I was sorry, and we walked in silence, making our way towards the Drawbells' house. We had quarrelled only once before, when I interfered over his marriage, and that had been just skin deep. Finding I could not put the words together to comfort him or tell him my regret for the past minutes, I muttered that I would see him home.

'Do,' said Martin.

Neither of us said much, as we walked along the footpath in the cold, slow dawn. What we had said could not be taken back; yet it seemed to have passed. Once Martin made a formal attempt to console me. He said:

'Don't worry too much: it may turn out all right.'

A little later, he said:

'If I had the choice about Luke to make all over again, I should do exactly the same as before.'

The hedges smelt wet, the blackthorn blossom was ectoplasmic on the morning dark. We came to the little road that led to Martin's. In front of us, stretching from the path to a cottage roof, was the dim shape of a ladder. As I went under, I could feel Martin hesitate and then take three quick steps round. He said, with a sarcastic smile: 'I need all the luck I can get.'

Making out his face in the twilight, I was wondering whether he, too, in that moment of superstition, had thought of our mother: who also had been superstitious: who, with her toes pointed out, would go round any ladder: who possessed just his kind of stoicism, invented to conceal an insatiable romantic hope: and who in his place, this morning after the fiasco, would be cherishing the first new pictures of wonderful triumphs to come.

It was strange to think that the same might be true of him.

PART THREE

A RESULT IN PUBLIC

CHAPTER 18

Request for an Official Opinion

As soon as I woke, the night's fiasco clinched itself out of the morning light. It was midday, not many hours since I left Martin outside his house.

Unable to keep myself away, hurrying to the laboratories to hear remarks that I did not want to hear, I found Luke and Martin already there. They might have been following old Bevill's first rule for any kind of politics: if there is a crisis, if anyone can do you harm *or* good, he used to say, looking simple, never mind your dignity, never mind your nerves, but *always be present in the flesh*.

Even that morning, Martin might have had the self-control to act on such advice: but it was more likely, in Luke's case certain, that they had come in order to argue a way through the criticisms and get to work the same day.

There were many criticisms. There was – to my ears, used to a different climate, less bracing and perhaps more hypocritical – astonishingly little sympathy. Most people had no thought to spare for Luke's or Martin's feelings; they were concerned with why the pile had not run last night, whether Luke's diagnosis was correct, how long the 'mods' (modifications) would take.

There were scientists' jokes. Was this, Mounteney asked, the most expensive negative result in scientific history? It was their own kind of jibing, abstract, not specially ill-natured. I would have preferred to go on listening, rather than return to London and make my report to Hector Rose.

Arriving in the office late that afternoon I found a message waiting for me: Sir Hector's compliments, and, when I could spare the time, would I make an opportunity to call on him?

I went at once to get the interview over. Rose's room, which was on the side of the building opposite to mine, looked over the trees of St James's Park, stirring that evening in the wind, bright in the cold sunshine. Rose was standing up, bowing from the waist, greeting me with his elaborate courtesy.

'It's very, very good of you to spare me a minute, my dear Eliot.' He put me in the armchair near his desk, from which I could smell the hyacinths on the little table by the window: even in wartime, he replaced his flowers each day. Then he offered me his cigarette case. It was like him to carry cigarettes for his visitors, though he did not smoke himself. Had my journey that afternoon been excessively uncomfortable, he asked, had I been able to get a reasonable luncheon?

Then he looked at me, his face still unnaturally youthful, expressionless, his eyes light.

'I gather that everything did not go precisely according to expectation?'

I said that I was afraid not.

'You will appreciate, my dear Eliot, that it is rather unfortunate. There has been slightly too much criticism of this project to be comfortable, all along.'

I was well aware of it.

'It may have been a mistake,' said Rose, 'not to take the course of least resistance, and pack them all off to America.'

'It may have been,' I said. 'If so, I helped to make it.'

'I'm afraid you did,' said Rose, with his usual cool justice. With the same justice, he added: 'So did I.'

'It may have been a mistake,' he went on smoothly, 'but it was Dr Luke and his comrades who led us up the garden path.'

Suddenly the smooth masterful official tone cracked: he had a blaze of ordinary human irritation.

'Good Lord,' he snapped, 'they talk too much and do too little!'

But Rose had the gift of being able to switch off his disappointment. Sometimes I thought it the most useful gift a man of affairs could possess, sometimes the most chilling.

'However,' said Rose, 'all that can wait. Now I should like to benefit by your advice, my dear Eliot. What do you suggest as the next step?'

I had been waiting for it.

I said, as honestly as I could, that there seemed to me two possible courses: one, to cut our losses, break up Barford, and distribute the scientists among the American projects (for Luke and Martin, that would be open failure): two, to reinvest in Luke.

'What is your personal opinion?'

'I'm not entirely impartial, you know,' I said.

'I'm perfectly sure that you can see the problem with your admirable detachment,' said Rose. The remark had the sarcastic flick of his tongue: but it was not meant as a sarcasm. For Rose it was easy to eliminate a personal consideration, and he would have despised me if I could not do the same.

I tried to. I said, as was true, that most people at Barford believed the pile would ultimately work; it might take months, it might (if Luke's diagnosis were wrong) take several years. There was a chance, how good I could not guess, that the pile would still work quickly; it meant giving Luke even more money, even more men.

'If you're not prepared for that,' I said, hearing my voice sound remote, 'I should be against any compromise. You've either got to show some faith now – or give the whole thing up in this country.'

'Double or quits,' said Rose, 'if I haven't misunderstood you, my dear chap?'

I nodded my head.

'And again, if I haven't misunderstood you, you'd have a shade of preference, but not a very decided shade, for doubling?'

I nodded my head once more.

Rose considered, assembling the threads of the problem, the scientific forecasts, the struggles on his committees, the Ministerial views.

'This is rather an awkward one,' he said. He stood up and gave his polite youthful bow.

'Well,' he said, 'I'm most indebted to you and I'm sorry to have taken so much of your valuable time. I must think this one out, but I'm extremely grateful for your suggestions.'

CHAPTER 19

A New Whisper

THOUGH Hector Rose had left me in suspense about his intention, I did not worry much. Despite our mutual dislike I trusted his mind, and for a strong mind there was only one way open.

Thus Luke, in the midst of disapproval, got all he asked for, and went back to playing his piano. There were months to get through before the pile was refitted. He and Martin had to set themselves for another wait.

It was during that wait that I had my first intimation of a different kind of secret. One of the security branches had begun asking questions. They had some evidence (so it seemed, through the muffled hints) that there might have been a leakage.

As men spoke of it, their voices took on that hushed staccato in which all of us, even on the right side of the law, seemed like conspirators. None of us knew what the evidence was, and the only hints we received were not dramatic, merely that a Barford paper had 'got loose'. We were not told where and the paper itself was unimportant. It was nothing but a 1943 estimate of the destructive power of the nuclear bomb. I looked it up in our secret files; it was signed by a refugee called Pavia, by Nora Luke and other mathematicians, and was called *Appreciation of the Effects of Fission Weapons*.

The typescript was faded, in the margin were some corrections in a high, thin, Italian hand. Much of the argument was in mathematical symbols, but, after twenty pages of calculation, some conclusions were set out in double spacing, in the military jargon of the day, with phrases like 'casualization', 'ground zero', 'severe destruction'.

These conclusions meant that, in one explosion over the centre of a town, about 300,000 people would be killed instantly, and a similar number would later die of injuries. This was the standard Barford calculation at that time, and it was the figure that we had in mind when Mounteney, Martin, and I talked by the river at Stratford.

Anyone who worked on the inside of scientific war saw such documents. And most men took it as part of the day-by-day routine, without emotion; it had to be done, if you were living in society, if you were one ant in the anthill. In fact most men did not need to justify themselves, but just performed their duty to society, made the calculations they were asked to make, and passed the paper on.

Once, alone in my office in the middle of the war, it occurred to me: there must exist *memoranda* about concentration camps: people must be writing their views on the effects of a reduction in rations, comparing the death rate this year with last.

I heard of the leakage, I re-read the appreciation, I heard the name of Captain Smith. He was high up, as I already knew, in one of the intelligence services. I also knew that he was a naval officer on the retired list, several times decorated in the first war, the son of a bishop. But when he came to visit me, I did not know what to expect.

He was a man in the fifties, with fairish hair and a lean, athletic figure. His face was stiff and strained, both in the cheeks and mouth. His eyes seemed to protrude, but more exactly had a fixed, light-irised stare. He was dressed with the elegance of an actor. His whole bearing was stiff, and soon after he came in, when a flying bomb grunted and vibrated outside, cut off, and then jarred the floor beneath us (it was by now the July of 1944), all the notice he took was a slight stiff inclination sideways, arms straight by his side.

That impression might have been both putting off and appropriate when one knew in advance his berserk record; but it did not last. It was destroyed, very oddly, by a smile which was so sudden, so artificial, that it might have been switched on. I had never seen a smile so false, and yet somehow it sweetened him.

He had come, he said, for a 'little confab' about some of our 'mutual friends' at Barford.

'I've been told,' I said, 'that you've been having a bit of trouble.'

'We don't want to blot our copy book,' said Captain Smith mysteriously, in a creaking and yet ingratiating voice.

'Nothing very serious has got out, has it?'

'I wish I knew: do you?' he said with his formidable stare, then switched on his smile.

'If one thing gets out, another can. That's why we get all hot and bothered,' he added.

Suddenly he asked:

'Know anything of a young man called Sawbridge?'

I had imagined that he might bring out other names. I felt relief because this one meant little to me. I explained that I had been present at Sawbridge's interview, and since then I had talked to him alone just once at Warwick, the night before the failure of the pile.

'I didn't get much out of him,' I said.

'I just thought you might have known him at home,' said Smith.

He had found out – it was one up to his method – that Sawbridge's family had lived close to mine. I said that, when I left the town for London in 1927, he could only have been eight or nine. My brother Martin was more likely to know him.

'I haven't forgotten M. F. Eliot,' said Smith, with his false, endearing smile.

I had spent enough time with security officers to leave the talking to him: but he was too shrewd to do what some did, and bank on the mystery of his job. He stared at me.

'I suspect you're wondering what all this is in aid of,' he said.

I said yes.

'There are one or two straws in the wind, and we've got an idea that the young man may not have been altogether wise.'

He gave me two facts, maybe in order to conceal others. Sawbridge had attended anti-war meetings, organized by the Communist Party, in 1940–1: at the University he had been a member of a pro-Communist group.

'He's certainly gone off the rails a bit,' said Smith.

At Barford they thought that Smith was a fool. They were quite wrong; he was highly intelligent, and very far, much further than many of the scientists, from being a commonplace man. The trouble was, he did not speak their language.

His axioms of behaviour were simple, though his character was not. Duty: obedience: if you were told to make a weapon you did so, and kept it secret. There was nothing more to it than that.

To him, the race in nuclear bombs was as natural as a race in building battleships. Your enemies were in it: so were you, so was Russia. You told no one anything, certainly not the Russians. Good fighters, yes, but almost a different species.

Intellectually, he knew something of communism; but he could no more imagine becoming a communist himself, or his friends or relations doing so, than I could imagine becoming a professional burglar.

He had not lived among scientists, their habits of feeling were foreign to him and his to them. As for his axioms of behaviour, most of the scientists, even those not far to the left, could not feel them so; what to him was instinct, to them meant a moral uneasiness at each single point.

Some days after Smith's call, I talked to Martin. It was our first serious talk since the fiasco; his tone sounded unwilling and hard, though that could have been the effect of long-drawn-out suspense. For the first time, his face was pallid and carried anxious lines. He was waiting for the last batch of the purified uranium, with unfillable time on his hands.

I asked him if Captain Smith had interviewed him.

Martin nodded.

'I think we ought to have a word,' I said.

He would have liked to put me off. Without showing his usual even temper, he went with me into the Park; at times we felt a neurosis of security, and only talked freely in an open space.

The Park was empty. It was a windy afternoon with black and ragged clouds; in the distance we heard, as we took two chairs on to the patch of grass nearest the Mall, the cranking of a flying bomb. I said:

'I suppose Smith told you about Sawbridge?'

'Yes.'

'How much is there in it?'

'If you mean,' said Martin, 'that Smith has cleverly found out that Sawbridge is left wing, that's not exactly news.' He went on: 'If Smith and his friends are going to eliminate all the left wing people working on fission here and in America, there won't be enough of us left to finish off the job.'

'Do you think Sawbridge has parted with any information?'

'I haven't the slightest idea.'

'Would you say it was impossible?'

Martin said: 'You know him nearly as well as I do.'

I said: 'Do you like him any better?'

Martin shook his head.

'He's a bit of a clod.'

That was my impression. Heavy: opaque: ungracious. I asked if Martin could imagine him fanatical enough to give secrets away.

Martin said: 'In some circumstances, I can imagine better men giving them away – can't you?'

Just for an instant he was speaking without constraint. At that time, his politics were like mine, liberal, considerably to the right of Mounteney, a little to the left of Luke. He had more patience than either with the practical running of the state machine, he was less likely to dismiss Smith out of hand.

Nevertheless, as he heard Smith's inquiries, he felt, almost as sharply as Mounteney, that his scientific code was being treated with contempt.

Martin was a secretive man; but keeping scientific secrets, which to Smith seemed so natural, was to him a piece of evil, even if a necessary evil. In war you had to do it, but you could not pretend to like it. Science was done in the open, that was a reason why it had conquered; if it dwindled away into little secret groups hoarding their results away from each other, it would become no better than a set of recipes, and within a generation would have lost all its ideals and half its efficacy.

Martin, who was out of comparison more realistic than Mounteney or even Luke, knew as well as I did that a good many scientists congratulated themselves on their professional ethic and acted otherwise: in the twenties and thirties, the great days of free science, there had been plenty of men jealous of priority, a few falsifying their results, some pinching their pupils'.

But it had been free science, without secrets, without much national feeling. Men like Mounteney hankered after it as in a murky northern winter one longs for the south of France. In the twenties and thirties, Mounteney had felt more at home with foreigners working in his own subject than he ever could with Captain Smith or Rose or Bevill.

Some of that spirit had come down to the younger men. Pure science was not national; the truth was the truth, and, in a sensible world, should not be withheld; science belonged to mankind. A good many scientists were as unselfconscious as Victorians in speaking of their ideals as though they were due to their own personal excellence. But the ideals existed. *That* used to be science; if you were ashamed of a sense of super-national dedication, men like Mounteney had no use for you; in the future, *that* must be science again.

Meanwhile, the war had forced their hands; but they often felt, even the most realistic of them, that they were mucking away in the dark. Though they saw no option but to continue, there were times, at this talk of secrets, leakages, espionage, when they turned their minds away.

It was startling to hear Martin break out, because of a violated ideal. In most respects, I thought of him as more earthbound than I was myself. But he would not take part in any more discussion about Sawbridge.

Soon he fell silent, the thoughts of pure science drained away, and he was brooding over the next test of the pile. His nerves had stayed steady throughout the fiasco, but now, within months or weeks of the second chance, they were fraying at last. In the windy August afternoon, the low black clouds drove on.

'If it doesn't go this time,' he said to me, more angrily than he had spoken after the failure, as though holding me to blame, 'you needn't reckon on my future any more.'

CHAPTER 20

The Taste of Triumph

NIGHT after night that September I stayed by my sitting-room window with the curtains open, watching the swathe of light glisten on the dusty bushes in the square. The flying bombs had ceased, and it should have been easy to sleep; often I was wondering when I should get a message from Barford, giving the date of the second attempt to start the pile.

I decided that this time I would not go – but was the date already fixed? From Martin's state I felt it could not be far off.

Sitting by the open window, tasting the autumn nights for the first time since 1939, I thought with regret of my own past troubles – with regret, not because I had undergone them, but because I was living through a quiet, lonely patch. Occasionally I thought of Martin: how many months in his adult life had been free from some ordeal approaching? Was this new one the biggest? Sometimes, from my quiet, I wished I were in his place.

One night at the end of the month, the telephone slowly woke me out of a deep sleep. Faintly it burred, in the hall, as though far away. When at last I understood the noise, I went towards it with dread.

The blue paint had not yet been taken from the hall bulb. In the crepuscular, livid light, I found the receiver: I heard Martin's voice, active, repeating 'Hallo, hallo, hallo.' Up to that moment I had not thought of him, just of the pounce of bad news, any bad news.

As I muttered his voice came:

'Is that you?'

'Yes.'

'*It's all right.*'

I was stupefied, half awake, half comprehending:

'What's all right?'

I heard:

'The pile began to run an hour ago. 3.5 a.m., the night of September 27–28 – just for purposes of reference.'

The words had been steady, but the flourish gave his joy away.

'Why didn't you tell me you were starting?' I answered with exultation, yet heard my temper rise.

'I thought it was better like this.'

Then I congratulated him.

'Yes, it's something. They can't take this from us.'

In his voice I could hear pure triumph, the words came out with the attack of triumph. At last he held success in his hands. If I had heard a friend speak so, even a most intimate friend, I should have known a splinter of rancour – the jag of the question: 'Why hasn't this happened to me?'

Listening to a brother in the pride of triumph, you could not feel even that splinter. It had been the same when I heard the news of his child. Just as in 'unselfish' love you can be crueller (as I was in Martin's failure, which we had neither of us forgotten), so for the same reason you can be less envious. The more unassailable they are in success, the more total your rejoicing: for it is your own.

He could not resist telling me some details, there and then, in the middle of the night. It had been his idea to hold a 'dress rehearsal'. During the summer, they had built a syphoning plant for the heavy water, so they had not required many hands: even of those present, few realized that this was the 'real thing'. They had begun just after midnight, and the filling was still going on. For ten minutes, at the half-way stage, the graph points seemed to be going wrong again. 'That was pretty hard to take,' said Martin. Then the points began to come out according to calculation. In fact, they were coming out slightly better than calculation. Martin for once forgot his listener, and broke into technical language: 'The k is 1.2 already, it's too hot to put in more than three-quarters of the heavy water.

'It's embarrassing that it's gone too well,' he added. 'Still, it's quite a tolerable way to be embarrassed.'

The following afternoon, when he met me at the station, he was just as happy. It was no longer self-discipline that kept his expression firm; one could see the happiness beneath the skin; he was not a man to lose appetite for triumph the moment he had it.

We shook hands, which we did not often do.

'The pile, I think,' said Martin, without asking me where we should go first. He said, as we walked along:

'When it looked as though we were due for another fiasco last night – that was getting near the bone.'

Contentedly browsing over past dramas, Martin led me into a hangar. It was empty, not a single human being in sight; it was noiseless, the pile standing silent in the airy space.

'There she goes,' said Martin. But he did not see the curious sinister emptiness of the place. He was thinking not of the silent, blank-faced pile but of the reaction going on within. He took me to the control room, a cubby hole full of shining valves with one kitchen chair placed, domestic and incongruous, in front of a panel of indicators. Sitting there was the only other man I had seen that afternoon.

'All well?' asked Martin.

'All well, Dr Eliot,' said the duty officer.

'I still can't quite believe it,' Martin said to me.

As we went out, there was a hallooing from close by, and Luke, who had just tramped in, called us into his office.

'Well, Lewis,' he said, 'this is a bit better.'

'To say the least of it,' I said.

'They ought to have known it was the neatest way to do it.'

'They' were Luke's collection of enemies and detractors, and without malice, or even much interest, he dismissed them. He was sitting on his desk, and suddenly his whole face and body became vigorous.

'There's only one thing that matters now, as I've been saying to

Martin this morning,' he said, 'and that is, how soon can we finish it off?'

Martin smiled. For himself, he would have been glad of a breathing space, to luxuriate in the success; to him, it was real success, the first he had had. But then Martin, less humble than Luke as a man, was far more so as a scientist. Luke knew his powers; he knew that this project had not stretched them; it had tested his character, but in terms of scientific imagination, it had needed little. He did not take much pride in the achievement; this was no place to rest; with all his energies, he wanted to push on.

'We've got to make the bloody bomb while we're about it,' said Luke. 'Until we've got the plutonium out, I shan't be able to put my In-tray on top of my Out-tray and go back to something worth doing.'

As I already knew, making the pile work was only the first stage, though the most important, in producing a bomb; second by second, the pile was now changing minute amounts of uranium into plutonium. In a hundred and fifty to two hundred days, they calculated, the transformation would have gone far enough: the slugs could then be taken out to cool: in another ninety days Luke and Martin could begin extracting the plutonium. Luke said they might cut a little off those periods, but not much.

'Perhaps we can begin extracting in March,' he said. 'Which leaves one question sticking out, when is the war going to end?'

This was late September 1944: we all agreed that there was no chance of an end that year. The intelligence teams in Germany were reporting that the Germans had got nowhere with their pile – but Luke and others at Barford found it hard to credit.

'What we can do, so can they,' said Luke. 'Which is one reason why I want to whip that plutonium out. It would be too damn silly if they lifted this one out of the bag before us.'

'What are the other reasons?'

Luke said quietly:

'To tell you the truth, Lewis, I'd rather we got it first – so that we should have some influence in case any maniac wants to use the damned thing.'

It was the first time I had heard Luke talk about anyone using the bomb.

'That is a point,' said Martin.

'But it isn't the real point,' said Luke, his face open and truculent once more. 'Let's come clean with you, Lewis. That's a very good reason, but it isn't the real reason, and you both know that as well as I do. The real reason is just that I can't bear not to come in first.'

They could not touch the rods before March 1st; what was the earliest possible date to possess the plutonium?

Martin said: 'The operative word is "possible".'

Luke said: 'I'll get that stuff out in six weeks from March 1st if it's the last thing I do.'

Martin said: 'It may be.'

'What is the matter?' I said.

Luke and Martin looked at each other.

'There are some hazards,' said Luke.

That was the term they used for physical danger. Luke went on being frank. The 'hazards' might be formidable. No one knew much about handling plutonium; it might well have obscure toxic properties. There would not be time to test each step for safety, they might expose themselves to illness: conceivably grave illness, or worse.

'Is that fair?' Luke said to Martin, when he had finished.

'Quite fair,' said Martin.

There was a silence, which Martin broke:

'I agree with you,' he said, speaking straight to Luke. 'There are good reasons for pushing ahead.'

'I'm glad you admit it at last, anyway,' said Luke.

'I also agree that we've got to take certain hazards,' said Martin. 'I'm not happy about it, but I'm prepared to take a few modest risks. I don't think, though, that I'm prepared to take the risks you are. I don't believe the reasons justify them.'

'They're ninety per cent conclusive,' said Luke.

'I don't think so,' said Martin.

'I haven't thought it out yet,' said Luke. 'I must get it clear with myself where I stand about the risks. But I think I shall take them.'

'You're not the only person involved,' said Martin.

'Look here,' Luke said, 'this is going to be like walking blindfold, and I am not beginning to answer for anyone but myself.'

Some of this repertee sounded as though they were repeating the morning's argument, but, for a few moments past, they had seemed surprised by each other. Martin's voice was sharp:

'What do you mean?'

'I mean that I can't ask any of our chaps to put their hands inside the blasted stew,' Luke replied. 'If anyone is going to dabble in chemistry with the lid off, it's me.'

'Just before Lewis arrived,' said Martin, on his side producing something new, 'someone was waiting to volunteer.'

'Who?'

'Sawbridge.'

'Good for him,' said Luke, 'but I can't let him.'

'Yes, I'm quite sure,' said Martin slowly, 'we can't ask any of the others, or even let them volunteer.'

Luke's face was flushed; his tone was quiet and sincere. 'I'm not even asking you,' he said.

Martin considered, rubbing the back of his forefinger across his lip. He was steady with the well-being of success; but he was also resentful, pinched with shame, as a prudent man is on being rushed by a leader much braver than himself.

'I wish I could let you risk it by yourself,' said Martin. 'If I thought it was quite justified, I think I might.'

'I'd rather do it myself,' said Luke.

'It may not be possible to let you.'

Suddenly Luke jumped down from the desk.

'Well,' he said, 'there's no need to make the decision yet awhile. It's something that we should be fools to settle until we can look at it in cold blood.'

'If you ask me,' said Martin, rubbing his forefinger across his lip again, 'I'm afraid the decision is already made.'

CHAPTER 21

Beam of Light over the Snow

THE decision was, in fact, already made. There were months in which to draw back, but no one suggested that Luke could or would. Even to those who disliked and envied him, he gave an impression of simple physical courage; it was the one virtue which, like any other group of men, the Barford scientists uncritically admired.

In those months, he received more respect than ever before.

'Perhaps we ought to be *doing* something for Luke,' I heard a rotund voice say in the Athenaeum. That meant, give him a decoration: he was passing into the ranks of solid respectable men.

Just about the same time, people at Barford noticed that Drawbell, whose Christian name no one had been known to utter, whose friends called him 'CF', had begun to sign himself with a large, plain, mesomorphic 'Cyril Drawbell'.

'A bad case of knight starvation,' said someone. It was the kind of joke the scientists did not get tired of.

It was true that Drawbell spent many days in London, calling on Rose and the new Minister; no longer non-committal, but instead proclaiming 'the success of our Barford policy'. With urgency he told Rose one day that the 'team' deserved some public credit. Rose, who had decided not to meet him half way, responded with even more than his usually civility.

Drawbell tried his set of personal arts against Rose's politeness, but could not get the response he was playing for. Yes, it was wonderfully exciting, yes, the Minister was well informed of the history of the project, Rose went on mellifluously, but gave no outright official praise to Drawbell, who, with the meeting inconclusive, returned with me to my room.

For once he looked dejected and tired, as though his vitality had sunk low. Suddenly he asked:

'Eliot, do you hate this life?'

He meant the life of officials.

'Sometimes I hate it,' said Drawbell.

He stared at me.

'If anyone asked my reason for existence, what should I tell them?'

I tried to cheer him up, but he interrupted me:

'I'm just a pedlar of *other men's* dreams.'

Like many tricky men, he was wishing his character were simpler. He wished he were not self-seeking. But he did not exude the pathos one often finds in tricky men; his nature was harder than most of theirs. He was angry with himself, still more angry with Rose, and he took it out of me as Rose's proxy.

At Barford he made one intervention, after trying to persuade Luke and Martin to go slow until the health risks were worked out. The only thing he had a right to insist on, he said, was this: they must not both expose themselves to danger at the same time. If one should happen to be laid out, the other must be left intact. It was reasonable and the two of them promised it.

All that winter they were experimenting with protective clothing, with various kinds of divers' suits in order to do chemistry-at-a-distance. Sawbridge, who was still asserting his claim to take part, had developed a set of instruments for manipulating the rods out of sight.

Martin spent many of his evenings reading case histories of radiation illness. It seemed probable, he decided, that they would find, as well as the radiation hazards, that plutonium was also a chemical poison.

Luke scoffed at what he called Martin's 'visits to the morgue'. To him, if you could do nothing about a danger, it was best to forget it. But Martin's attitude was the exact opposite; if he were going to face a danger, he wanted to live with it beforehand. If he could become familiar in advance with the radio-active pathologies, he could more easily bear the moment of test. His clinical researches, which seemed to the others morbid, stiffened his resolve. With nothing like Luke's or Sawbridge's bravery of the fibres, Martin was training himself to face the March experiments with resignation.

Meanwhile, he continued to enjoy his taste of success. He was getting rather more than the credit due to Luke's right-hand man; scientific elder statesmen, civil servants like Rose, found him comfortable to talk to, after Luke; he was cagey in speech, he showed some respect for etiquette, he had good manners; they were glad when he attended London committees instead of his chief, and on those visits he was taken to the Athenaeum more frequently than Luke had ever been.

He liked it. He seemed to view this official life with detachment, but really he saw it through a magnifying glass. I thought to myself that those like Martin, who were born worldy, were always half taken in by the world.

Even with March 1st coming on him, he still kept his satisfaction at having, in a modest sense, 'arrived'. In January, he and Irene, when they came to London for a week's leave, stood me a celebratory dinner. They had borrowed a flat in the first stretch of the Bayswater

Road, just opposite the Albion Gate; it was still a luxury to let light stream out across the pavements, striking blue that night from the unswept snow. As we looked out, the middle of the road was dark, for the street lamps had not yet been lit.

We were saying (it was the kind of commonplace that we did not want to escape, since we were so content) how time had slipped by unnoticed, how the street lamps had now been dark for five and a half years. It was six years since Irene and I first met in my old rooms in Cambridge.

'Too long for you, dear?' said Irene to me, mechanically asking for approval.

'You won't go back there, will you?' said Martin to me.

I shook my head: we were each talking at random, the past and future both seemed close.

'You'll have to make your plans, this can't last much longer,' said Martin. We all knew that the war must soon end; as he spoke, Irene started to reply, but stopped herself, her eyes restive.

Martin asked her to bring in the child to say goodnight. As she carried him in he stayed quiet, and Martin took him in his arms. Their glances met, the child's a model of the man's, fixed, hard, transparently bright; then, with a grave expression, the child turned in to his father's shoulder.

Martin's glance did not move from the child's head.

'We must make some plans for you too,' he said. 'I've told you, we've made one or two plans for you already.'

It was after dinner that Martin spoke with an openness that came out of the blue, that I had not heard more than twice in his life. He was smoking a cigar, emblem of the celebration that night, but he had drunk little and was cold sober. He had just been mentioning Hector Rose, for whom perversely he had taken a liking – and I teased him about his friends at court.

Martin smiled and without any preliminary said:

'It's nice to have a little confidence.'

He said it simply, naturally, and with gratification.

'I never had enough,' he said to me.

Perhaps it was true, I was thinking: in his struggle to be a scientist, to live in the same air as Mounteney or Luke, he had never believed in himself.

He was still speaking to me:

'I got a bad start.'

'We both did,' I said.

'Mine was worse.'

'How?'

He said:

'You always overshadowed me, you know.'

It was so unexpected that I could not have left it there, but he went on:

'This has done me good.'

I was just beginning to speak when Irene, who had been biting back a worry all the evening, could keep quiet no longer. She cried:

'Then why don't you sit tight when you've got it?'

'That's not so easy,' said Martin.

'Just when we're getting everything we wanted, you're ready to throw it away.'

He said to her:

'We've talked this out, haven't we?'

'I can't let you go on with this madness. Do you expect me just to sit quiet and wait for the end of the war to stop you? I suppose if the war does end you will have a glimmer of sense?'

'If the war ended there wouldn't be any necessity to go so fast,' he said, curiously stiff. His smile had an edge to it: 'I shouldn't be sorry if the necessity didn't arise.'

'You know you're frightened.'

'I am extremely frightened,' said Martin.

'Then why don't you think of yourself?'

'I've told you.'

What had he told her? Probably the coldest motive – that, if he did not follow Luke's lead, he would lose the ground he had won.

'Why don't you think of me?'

'I've told you that, too.'

Her face puckered, she said:

'All you've done is to think of Lewis (the baby). And I don't know whether you believe it's enough just to insure yourself for him. Do you believe it really matters whether he goes to the sort of school that you two didn't go to?'

For the first time, Martin's tone showed pain. He said:

'I wish I could do more for him.'

Suddenly she switched off – to begin with it was so jarring that one's flesh crept – into a wail for her life in London before her marriage. Though she was wailing for past love affairs, her manner was fervid, almost jaunty; she was talking of a taxi drive in the snow. I had a vivid picture of a girl going hot-faced on a night like this across the Park to a man's flat. I believed, though she was just delicate enough not to mention the name, that she was describing her first meeting with Hankins, and that she was using private words so that Martin should know it. Bitterly she was provoking his jealousy. To an extent she succeeded, for neither then nor later was he unmoved by the sound of Hankins' name.

As I listened, I thought I must do like other friends of his, and finish with her. Then I saw the look in her eyes – it was not lust, it was not malice, it was a plea. She had no self-control, she would always be strident – but this was the only way she knew to beg him to be as he used to be.

All of a sudden, I understood a little. I could hear her 'I am defeated' in my flat that night last year which, if it had led one to think that she was leaving Martin, was totally misleading. It was he before whom she felt defeat. I could hear the tone in which, ten minutes later, she had pressed him about the child. Their marriage was changing, in the sense that marriages which start with their disparities often do; the balance of power was altering; their marriage was changing, and she was beating about, lost, bewildered, frightened, trying to keep it in its old state, which to her was precious.

Perhaps it was that the birth of the child had, as Hanna Puchwein had foreseen, disturbed the bond between them. But if so, it had disturbed it in the diametrically opposite direction from that which Hanna had so shrewdly prophesied. It was Martin who was freer, not Irene.

It seemed possible that the birth of the child had removed or weakened one strand in his love for her. He still had love for her, but the protective part, so powerful in him, so much a part of his whole acceptance of her antics, had been diverted to another. Hearing him speak to his son that evening, or even hearing him speak to her about his son, I felt – and now I knew she felt it also – that all his protective love had gone in love for the child. He would be too anxious about his son, I thought, he would care too much, live too much in him – just as I had at times lived too much in Martin.

So, although he had much feeling left for Irene, he no longer felt driven to look after her. All that was gone; he wanted her to be happy; in his meticulous fashion he had made arrangements for her future in case, in the March experiments, he should be incapacitated, or killed; but when he thought of the danger, both of what he might lose and those who might miss him, his only fear that counted alongside his own animal fear was for the child.

While Irene, who when he loved her passionately and protectively had wanted to get away from the protective clutch, now wished it back. She wished him to think first of her, she was anxious about him with all the hungers of vanity, self-esteem, habit, anything that makes us want someone who has drawn into himself.

With another switch, she began asking, with a nagging insistence, about the programme for March.

'This is supposed to be a celebration,' said Martin.

She nagged on. As both she and I knew, the date for the first dissolving of the rods had been put back from March 1st to March 10th.

'That's all right,' she said, 'but which of you is going to make a fool of himself first?'

'Unless anyone insists, which won't be me, I suppose we might have to toss up for it.'

'Have you settled that?' she cried.

He shook his head. 'I haven't spoken to Walter Luke about it recently.'

It was the flat truth.

Wildly she turned to me. I was her last hope. Could not I make him behave decently?

I knew that it was no use. Both he and I were behaving with consideration for each other, but any authority I had had was worn away. For me to interfere in his life again would be too much of a risk. I knew it, and so did he. I had to accept that it was not only marriage relations which changed.

CHAPTER 22

Swearing in a Hospital Ward

ALTHOUGH none of us knew it at the time, Luke and Martin did not toss up. Even they themselves had not settled, until March was on them, which should 'go first': and how they settled it, they kept secret. It was long afterwards that I found out what had happened.

Martin had been as good as his word, no better, no worse. With his feeling for precision and formality, he had actually written Luke a note a week before the experiment, suggesting that they tossed up, defining what the toss should mean – heads Martin went first, tails Luke. Luke would not have it. Swearing at getting a letter from Martin whom he saw every day, he said that the extraction was his idea, his 'bit of nonsense', and the least he could do was have the 'first sniff'.

Luke got his way. Martin did not pretend to himself that he was sorry to be overruled.

The results of his being overruled came so fast that even at Barford, much more so in London, they were hard to follow. First Luke decided that he could not begin the experiment without another pair of hands; after his and Martin's arrangement with the Superintendent, which meant that Martin was excluded, they had to give Sawbridge his wish.

During the last waiting period, Luke had had a 'hot' laboratory built, rather like a giant caricature of a school laboratory, in which, instead of dissolving bits of iron in beakers under their noses, they had a stainless steel pot surrounded by walls of concrete into which they dropped rods of metal that they never dared to see. In each section of the hot laboratory were bell pushes, as though it were a bath arranged for a paralysed invalid who for safety was in need of a bell within inches of his head.

Luke and Sawbridge went alone into the hot laboratory on a morning in March. The next that Martin heard, just three hours later, was the sound of the bell. That same evening I received news that Luke and Sawbridge were both seriously ill, Luke much the worse. The doctors would have said not fatally, if they had known more of the pathology of radiation illness. So far, they looked like cases of severe sunstroke. It might be wise for their friends to be within reach.

Sawbridge had carried Luke away from the rods, and it was Sawbridge who had pushed the bell. The irony was, they had been knocked out by a sheer accident. They had got safely through the opening of the aluminium cans, in which the rods were taken from the pile; the cans had been stripped off under ten feet of water. Then something 'silly' happened, as Sawbridge said, which no one could have provided against. A container cracked. Luke went down, and Sawbridge a matter of minutes afterwards.

The next day's news was hopeful. Sawbridge seemed scarcely ill, and was a bad patient; Luke was able to talk about the changes they could make in the hot laboratory, before he or Martin had 'another go'.

They went on like this for several days, without anything the doctors could call a symptom. Several times Luke wanted them to let him out of bed. Eight days after the stroke, he broke out: '*What is the matter with me?*' Though he could not explain how, he felt physically uneasy; soon he was said to be low-spirited, a description which shocked anyone who knew him. He was restlessly tired, even as he lay in bed.

Within three more days he was ill, though no one had seen the disease before. His temperature went up; he was vomiting, he had diarrhoea, blood spots were forming under his skin; the count of his white blood cells had gone steeply down. In two more days, he was bleeding inside the mouth.

Sawbridge escaped some of the malaise, and the blood spots had not formed. Otherwise his condition seemed a milder variant of the same disease. I was ready to go to Barford at short notice to visit Luke, but during those days he was so depressed that he only wanted to be alone. Once a day he saw his wife; he sent for Martin but spoke very little when he came; he tried to give some instructions, but they were not intelligible. His chief comfort seemed to be in following the scientific observations of his illness. He and Sawbridge had been moved into a special ward at the establishment hospital; not only the Barford doctors, but others studying the clinical effects of radiation watched each measurement. There was a mutter from Luke's sickbed which spread round Barford: 'The only thing they (the doctors) still don't know is whether to label mine a lethal dose or only near lethal.'

Mounteney told me that much, one afternoon in my office. More physically imaginative than most men, Mounteney was enraged at the thought of Luke's illness. His eyes burnt more deeply in their sockets, his face looked more than ever Savonarola-like.

'It oughtn't to have been let happen, Eliot,' he said. 'It oughtn't to have happened to anyone, let alone a man we can't spare. Some of you people ought to have realized that *he's* one of the men we *can't* spare.'

Although his distress was genuine, it was like him to turn it into an attack. Somehow he implied that, instead of Luke being ill, Whitehall officials ought to be. But, as the afternoon went on, he became gentler though more harassed.

'I should like anyone who's ever talked about using the nuclear bomb to have a look at Luke now,' he said.

I was thinking of that night in Stratford, which now seemed far away and tranquil, when Martin fed the swans.

'It would teach them what it means. If ever a nuclear bomb went off, this is exactly what would happen to the people it didn't kill straight off.' He added:

'There are enough diseases in the world, Eliot. It's no business of science to produce a new one.'

That visit from Mounteney took place three weeks after Luke and Sawbridge were pulled out of the hot laboratory. In another few days – E + 29, as the scientists called it in the jargon of the day, meaning twenty-nine days after the exposure – Luke was said to be brighter, the bleeding had lessened. It might only be an intermission, but at least he was glad of people at his bedside.

Although I arrived in Barford the day I got that message, I was not allowed in the ward until the following morning. And, just as I was going inside, Mrs Drawbell, watching from the nurses' ante-room, intercepted me. Her husband detested Luke; when he was healthy she herself had never shown any interest in him; but now – now there was a chance to nurse. Triumphantly she had argued with Nora Luke. Nora had a piece of mathematical work to finish: anyone could do part-time nursing, only Nora could complete that paper. The wives who had no careers of their own criticized Nora, but it was Mrs Drawbell who became installed as nurse.

'You mustn't tire him, Mr Eliot,' she said accusingly. *She* (Nora Luke) was already in the ward, Mrs Drawbell said. She went on, stern and obscurely contented: 'They used to be such fine strong men!'

I had not heard her so articulate. She said: 'It's a case of the wheel of fortune.'

The first time I heard Luke's voice, it sounded husky but loud and defiant. I was only just inside the door; the ward was small, with a screen between the two beds, Sawbridge's in the shade and further from the window. The light spring sunshine fell across Nora sitting by the other bed, but I could not see Luke's face.

'I've got a bone to pick with you, Lewis,' he said.

It was the kind of greeting that I used to expect from him. He went on:

'We must have more bods.'

'Bods' meant bodies, people, any kind of staff: scientists were bods, so were floor cleaners, but as a rule Luke used the words in demanding more scientists.

I felt better, hearing him so truculent – until I noticed Nora's expression. At a first glance, she had looked, not cheerful, certainly, but settled; it was the set tender expression one sees in many wives by a husband's sick-bed, but that some would have been surprised to see in Nora. But, as Luke shouted at me, pretending to be his old rude, resilient self, that expression changed on the instant to nothing but pain.

As I moved out of the sunlight I saw Luke. For a moment I remembered him as I had first met him, in the combination room of our college, when he was being inspected as a fellowship candidate ten years before. Then he had been ruddy, well fleshed, muscular, brimming with a young man's vigour – and (it seemed strange to remember now) passionately self-effacing in his desire to get on. Now he was pale, not with an ordinary pallor but as though drained of blood; he was emaciated, so that his cheeks fell in and his neck was like an old man's; there were two ulcers by the left-hand corner of his mouth; bald patches shone through the hair on the top of his head, as in an attack of alopecia.

But these changes were nothing beside the others. I said, answering his attempt to talk business:

'We'll go into that any time you like. You'll get all the people you want.'

Luke stared at me, trying to concentrate.

'I can't think what we want,' he said.

He added, in a sad, exhausted tone:

'You'd better settle it all with Martin. I am a bit out of touch.'

He could not get used to the depression. Into his sanguine nature it seemed to grow, as though it was seeping his spirits away; he had never had to struggle against a mood before, much less to feel that he were losing the struggle.

Propped up by his pillows, his back had gone limp. His eyes did not focus on Nora or me nor on the trees in the hospital garden.

I said, hearing my voice over-hearty as though he were deaf:

'You'll soon get in touch again. It won't take you a week, when you get out of here.' Luke replied:

'I may not be good for much when I get out of here.'

'Nonsense,' I said.

'Are you thinking of *that* again?' said Nora.

'What is it?' I said.

'He's worried that he might be sterile,' said Nora.

Luke did not deny it.

'Are you having that old jag again?' said his wife.

'The dose must have been just about big enough,' he said blankly, as though he had nothing new to say.

'I've told you,' said Nora, 'as soon as the doctors say yes we'll make them have a look. I shall be very much surprised if anything is wrong.'

With the obstinacy of the miserable, Luke shook his head.

'I told you that if by any miracle there is anything wrong, which I don't credit for a minute, well, it doesn't matter very much,' said Nora. 'We've got our two. We never wanted any more.'

She sounded tough, robust, maternal.

Luke lay quiet, his face so drawn with illness that one could not read it.

I tried to change the subject, but Nora knew him better and had watched beside him longer.

She said suddenly:

'You're thinking something worse, aren't you?'

Very slightly, he inclined his head.

'Which one is it?'

Does it matter?'

'You'd better say,' she said.

'There must be a chance,' he said, 'that some of this stuff will settle in the bone.'

There was a silence. Nora said:

'I wish I could tell you there wasn't a chance. But no one knows one way or the other. No one can possibly know.'

Luke said:

'If I get through this bout, I shall have that hanging over me.'

He lay there, imagining the disease that might lie ahead of him. Nora sat beside him, settled and patient, without speaking. Sawbridge coughed, over by the wall, and then the room stayed so quiet that I could hear a match struck outside. We were still silent when Mrs Drawbell entered. Martin had come to visit Dr Luke; only two people were allowed in the ward at a time; when one of us left, Martin could take his place. Quickly Nora got up. She would be back tomorrow, whereas this was my only time with Luke. I thought that she was, like anyone watching another's irremovable sadness, glad to go.

With a glance towards Sawbridge, Martin walked across the floor towards Luke's bed. As he came, it struck me – it was strange to notice such a thing for the first time – that his feet turned out, more than one would expect in a good player of games. He looked young, erect, and well. With bright, hard eyes he scrutinized Luke, but his voice was gentle as he asked:

'How are you?'

'Not so good,' replied Luke from a long way off.

'You seem a bit better than when I saw you last.'

'I wish I believed it,' said Luke.

Martin went on to inquire about the symptoms – the hair falling out, the ulcers, the bleeding.

'That (the bleeding) may have dropped off a bit,' said Luke.

'That's very important,' Martin said. 'Don't you see how important it is?' He was easier with illness than I was, ready to scold as well as to be gentle. But after he had learned about the symptoms – he was so thorough that I longed for him to stop – he could not persuade Luke to talk any more than Nora or I could. Luke lay still and we could not reach the thoughts behind his eyes.

Martin gave me a glance, for once tentative and lost. He said quietly to Luke: 'We're tiring you a bit. We'll have a word with Sawbridge over there.'

Luke did not reply, as Martin, with me following, tiptoed over to the other bed.

'I'm not asleep,' said Sawbridge, in a scornful and unwelcoming tone. We stood by the bed and looked down on him; his skin in health had its thick nordic pallor, and the transformation was not as shocking as in Luke; but the bald patches of scalp shone through, his eyes were filmed over, half opaque. When Martin inquired about him, he said:

'I'm all right.'

Martin was reading the charts – white blood counts, red blood counts, temperature – over the bed head.

'Never mind that,' said Sawbridge, 'I tell you, I'm all right.'

'The figures look encouraging,' said Martin.

'I've never been as bad as he was – ' Sawbridge inclined a heavy eye towards Luke's bed.

'We've been worried about you, all the same.'

'There was no need.' Sawbridge said it with anger – and suddenly, under the shroud of illness, under the familiar loutishness, I felt his bitter pride. He did not want to admit that he was ill or afraid; he had heard the fears that Luke let fall, he could not help but share them; but neither to the doctors nor his relatives, certainly not to his fellow sufferer or to us, would he give a sign.

It was a kind of masculine pride that did not make him more endearing, I was thinking; in fact that it made him more raw and forbidding; it had no style. Until this accident I had heard little of him from Martin. No one had mentioned the security inquiries, which I assumed had come to nothing; the little that Martin said had not been friendly, and at the bedside he was still put off. But he managed to keep, what Sawbridge could not have borne, all pity out of his voice.

Of the three in the ward, the two invalids and Martin, Luke and Sawbridge were beyond comparison the braver men. Like many brave men, they did not bear a grudge against the timid. But, like

many ill men, they resented the well. Sawbridge was angry with
Martin, and with me also, for being able to walk upright in the sun.

Martin could feel it, but he would not let silence fall. Both he and
Sawbridge cultivated an amateur interest in botany, and he mentioned
flowers that he had seen on his way to the hospital.

'There's a saxifrage in the bottom hedge,' he said.

'Is there?'

'It seems early, but there's one spire out on the flowering chestnut.'

Then Sawbridge broke out, slowly, methodically, not hysterically
but with a curious impersonal anger, swearing at the flowering chestnut. The swear words of the midland streets ground into the room,
each word followed by the innocent tree, '— the flowering chestnut.'
The swearing went on and on. Strangely, it did not sound as though
Sawbridge were losing his head. It did not even sound as though
he were trying to keep his courage up. Somehow it came, certainly
to me, as the voice of a man cursing his fate, dislikeable, but quite
undefeated.

It must have come to Luke so, for during a break in Sawbridge's
machine-like swearing, there sounded a husky whisper from the other
bed.

'Bugger the flowering chestnut,' whispered Luke. Somehow the
younger man's brand of courage had tightened his.

We all listened to him, and soon Sawbridge's voice stopped, while
Martin stood between the beds. Luke's face had changed from blank-
ness to pain, but there was sight in his eyes. He spoke fast and ration-
ally, lying there supine, calling on his fibres for an effort they could
scarcely make, calling on the will behind his fibres.

'How fast are you getting on with the new bay?' he croaked to
Martin.

After a moment's stupefaction, Martin replied as coolly as though
they were in the hangar.

'How long are you going to take about it?' said Luke. 'Good
Christ, how long?'

'The new hot laboratory,' said Martin, 'should be ready by June.'

'It's too long.'

There was a voice from Sawbridge's bed. 'It's absolutely essential
not to let the others get years ahead.'

Luke strained himself to the effort. He and Martin, with one or two interruptions from Sawbridge, talked sharp and quick, words coming out like 'hazard points', 'extracts', 'cupferron'.

'By the end of June at the outside, we must start again,' said Luke. Hoarsely he went on:

'I expect it will have to be you this time.'

'Yes,' said Martin. He had been studying Luke and Sawbridge with a clinical curiosity that unnerved me, because he wanted to know what might happen to himself. But, as Luke made his effort, as he called on an ultimate reserve of hope when his body had none, for an end which to them all seemed at that moment as simple as getting first to the top of a mountain, Martin lost the last peg of his detachment.

It was not that he felt fonder of Luke or overwhelmed with sorrow for him; just then none of these three men was interested in another; there was something to do, that was all; in this they were one.

Luke was tired out, but as we stood over the bed, he still kept up a harsh whisper.

'We must have more bods. Tell them we must have more bods.'

CHAPTER 23

'Events Too Big for Men'

I WAS in suspense during the last days of the German war. The scientific teams in Germany had reported, months before, that the Germans had got nowhere with their pile; but now, when one could count days to the surrender, I kept thinking – could there have been one hidden? In terms of reason, I told myself, it was impossible, it was superstitious nonsense – but during those last few days I became nervous when I heard an aircraft.

It was not until the formal end that I could go to my flat and sleep twelve hours in anti-climax and relief. It was because the anti-climax stayed with me, because I did not want to share the sadness of the first weeks of peace, that I saw nothing of my Barford friends that May. Later I wished that I had heard them talk, immediately the German war finished. All I heard in fact was that the new laboratories were being built ready for the second attempt in June; that

Sawbridge was a good deal better, and that Luke was now definitely expected to live.

Then came the morning of Pearson's news.

The rain had just stopped; through the windows of Rose's room drifted the smell of wet leaves from the Park. It was right at the end of May, and the kind of dark warm morning which brought back days of childhood, waiting at the county ground for the umpires to come out again. Instead, Rose was meeting his five senior colleagues on a problem of reconstruction – 'an untidy one', he said. We were getting towards the end of the morning, when his personal assistant brought in a note for Rose. He read it, and passed it to me. It said:

Dr Pearson has just arrived back from Los Alamos, and says he wants to see the Perm. Sec. at once. He says it can't wait.

Rose glanced at me under his lids. Himself the most ceremonious of men in dealing with others' dignity, he never stood on his own. He said:

'I really am most apologetic, but this is something I probably ought to attend to, and perhaps we've got nearly as far as we can go today. I do apologize.' He asked me to stay, and, when the others had left, Rose and I sat looking out over the rainwashed trees. Just once Rose, who did not spare time for useless speculation, remarked:

'I wonder if there really is anything in the wind, or whether this man has just dropped in to pass the time of day.'

As soon as the girl brought Pearson in, Rose was on his feet, bowing, showing Pearson the armchair opposite mine, hoping that he had had a pleasant journey.

'As pleasant as flying the Atlantic in bumpy weather can be,' said Pearson.

'When did you actually arrive?'

'I wanted to get rid of this commission' ('commission' was one of their formal words, and simply meant that he had been asked to give news by word of mouth) 'so I came straight here.'

'That was very, very good of you, Dr Pearson, and I can't tell you how extremely grateful I am. I do hope you're not too tired?'

'As tired as I want to be, thanks. I shan't be sorry to sleep in my own bed tonight.'

Rose, unwearying in politeness, said:

'We are grateful to you for many other reasons, of course, Dr Pearson. We have heard the most glowing accounts of you from the American authorities. They told us that you've been of inestimable value, and it's very nice to have you and some of our other friends putting up our stock over there. I do congratulate you and thank you.'

It was all true. Pearson had been a great success in America, working on the actual fixing mechanism of the bomb.

'Oh, I don't know about that,' he said, with a diffidence that was awkward and genuine, but lay on top of his lazy invulnerable confidence.

'*You* may not know, but *we* do,' said Hector Rose. Then lightly: 'You said you had a little business for us, did you?'

Pearson did not reply at once but glanced edgewise through his spectacles at me. He said to Rose:

'I've got a piece of information that I am to give you.'

'Yes, Dr Pearson,' said Rose.

'I've no authority to give it to anyone else,' said Pearson.

Rose was considering.

'I take it,' he said, 'this information is to go to the committee?'

'The sooner the better,' said Pearson.

'Then I can authorize you to speak in front of Eliot, with many thanks for your precautions. Because you see, Dr Pearson, Eliot is part of the secretariat of the committee, and in any case I should have to pass him this information at once.'

Pearson tilted back his head. He did not care for me, but that was not moving him; he was a rigid, literal, security-minded man. On the other hand, he was a practical one.

'If Eliot's got to channel it through the committee, he might as well know now as after lunch, I suppose,' he said.

'That would be my view,' said Hector Rose.

'As long as it's understood that this is a time when there mustn't be one word out of school. I'm not authorized to speak to anyone at Barford, and neither are you. This is for the committee and no one else in this country.'

'We take that point, Dr Pearson.' Rose inclined his head.

'Oh, well then,' said Pearson, in a flat casual tone, 'we've got a bomb.'

He announced it as though it were an off-hand matter of fact, as though he were informing two people, neither of whom he thought much of, that he had bought a new house.

Rose's first reply was just as flat.

'Have you indeed?' he said. Then he recovered himself:

'I really must congratulate you and our American colleagues. Most warmly.'

'We're just putting the final touches to the hardware,' said Pearson. 'It's nearly ready for delivery.'

Rose looked from Pearson's face, pale from travel but relaxed, out to the soft, dank, muggy morning. Under the low sky the grass shone with a brilliant, an almost artificial sheen.

'It really is a remarkable thought,' said Rose.

'I always expected we should get it,' said Pearson.

I broke in: 'What happens now?'

'Oh, before we make many more, there are lots of loose ends to tie up,' said Pearson.

I said:

'I didn't mean that. What happens to the bombs that do exist?'

Pearson pushed up his spectacles.

'They're going to explode one in the desert soon,' he said, 'just to see if it goes off all right.'

'And the others?'

'I didn't have much to do with the military,' he said, in the same offended tone, 'but there's some talk they'll try one on the Japs.'

I said:

'How do the scientists over there take that?'

'Some of them are getting a bit restive.' He might not have heard the feeling in my question, but he was not a fool, he knew what lay behind it. 'Some of the people at Barford will get restive, too,' he said. 'That's why they mustn't hear until there's proper authority for them to do so.'

It was no use arguing just then. Instead, I asked about friends of mine working on the American projects, O—, S—, Kurt Puchwein.

'Puchwein moved from Chicago to Los Alamos,' said Pearson. 'He was said to have done a good job.'

He yawned, stretched his legs, and announced,

'Oh, well, I think that's all, I may as well be going.'

'Thank you very, very much for coming here so promptly this

morning,' said Rose. 'I'm immensely grateful to you, many, many, many thanks.'

When Pearson had shut the door, we heard his slow steps lolloping down the corridor. Rose was sitting with his arms folded on his desk, his glance meeting mine; we were each thinking out consequences, and some of our thoughts were the same.

'I must say I'm sorry we didn't get in first,' he said.

'Yes.'

'It's clear to me that the Pearson man is right. This information is restricted to us and the committee, and that there's nothing that we can usefully do at this juncture.'

'When can we do anything?'

'I think I know what's on your mind,' he said.

'What do you mean?'

Rose said:

'Now that the American party has produced this bomb, you're thinking it's obviously unreasonable for our people to break their necks trying to save a couple of months. I need hardly say that I agree with you. I propose to take it upon myself to prevent it happening.' He added in a polite, harsh, uneasy tone: 'Please don't think I'm taking care of this arrangement for the sake of your brother. We simply want to avoid unnecessary waste, that's all.'

I thanked him, uneasy in my turn. Even that morning, we could not be natural to each other. Curiously, although Rose had picked out and settled what was most likely to be worrying me, at that moment it happened to be taking second place.

'It's important,' I broke out, 'that the Barford people should know what we've just heard.'

'Why is it important, Eliot?' asked Rose in his coolest voice.

Watching me as I remained silent, he went on, sounding as competent as ever:

'I think I can go some of the way with you. If there is any temptation to make a practical demonstration of this weapon – on the whole I shall believe that when I see it – then the scientists are likely to have their own views. In fact, they might have more influence with the soldiers and politicians than any of us would have. In that case, I suggest to you that two points arise: first, the scientists concerned won't be listened to if they get the information through a security leakage; second, that there is every conceivable advantage in the scientists acting entirely by themselves. I put it to you that, even if you and I were free agents, which we're very far from being, the balance of sense would be in favour of leaving it strictly to the scientists.'

I was looking at him, without being ready to say yes or no.

'Mind you,' said Rose, 'I can appreciate the argument that it's totally unreasonable for scientists to make a fuss at this stage. A good many people hold the perfectly tenable view that all weapons are scientific nowadays and you can't draw a division between those we've already used and this new one. It's arguable that any scientific hullabaloo on this affair would be a classical case of straining at the gnat and swallowing the camel.'

'I can't see it as quite so simple,' I said.

I was thinking, this was what official people might come to. Rose was always one jump ahead of official opinion; that was why they called him a man of judgement. His judgement was never too far-sighted for solid men, it led them by a little but not too much, it never differed in kind from theirs.

Yet, as we sat together beside his desk, he gave me a heavy glance. 'There are times, it seems to me,' he said, 'when events get too big for men.'

He said it awkwardly, almost stuttering, in nothing like his usual brisk tone; if I had taken the cue, we might have spoken off guard for once. Almost immediately he went on:

'That may conceivably be the trouble with us all. If so, the only course that I can see is to play one's particular game according to the rules.'

It was one of his rare moments of self-doubt, the sharpest I had seen in him. Neither then nor later did I know whether that morning he had any sense of the future.

He got up from his chair and looked out at the sky, so dark and even that one could not see the rim of any cloud.

'At any rate,' he said, 'our first job is to call the committee at once. Perhaps you will be good enough to look after that?'

I said that I would do it first thing in the afternoon.

'Many, many thanks.' He put on his neat raincoat, his black trilby hat.

'I suppose I can't have the pleasure of giving you luncheon at the Athenaeum?'

It was not just his formal cordiality; the news had been a shock, and he wanted a companion – while I, after the same shock, wanted first of all to be alone.

CHAPTER 24

'What is Important?'

THE news rippled out. More scientists followed Pearson across. By the end of June, not only the Whitehall Committee, but the top men at Barford all knew that completed bombs were in existence: that the trial was fixed for the end of July: that there was a proposal, if the trial went according to plan, to use a bomb on a Japanese town. Of my acquaintances, perhaps thirty were in possession of those facts.

Among those I was closest to, the first responses were variegated. Several men of good will felt above all excitement and wonder. In the committees there was a whiff almost of intoxication; the other conquests of nature were small beside this one; we were within listening distance of the biggest material thing that human beings had done. Among people who had been flying throughout the war between America and England, who had been giving a hand on both sides and who had, like so many scientists, little national feeling, there was a flash of – later I did not wish to over-state it, but I thought the emotion was awe; a not unpleasurable, a self-congratulatory awe.

In the first days of the news reaching London, I did not catch much political prevision. But I did hear someone say: 'This will crack Russia wide open.'

At Barford, the response was, from the moment the news arrived, more complex. For Luke and Martin, it was a time of desolating disappointment, so that they had hours of that dull weight of rancour, of mindless, frustrating loss, that Scott and his party felt as, only a few miles away, they saw the ski marks of Amundsen's party and then the black dot of the tent at the South Pole.

To Luke it seemed that he had wasted years of his life, and perhaps his health for good, just to have all snatched away within sight of the end. On the other hand, Martin found considerable comfort for himself. There were great consolations, he remarked, in reverting to being as timid as he chose. Beside that relief, the disappointment had an agreeable look, and he began to count his blessings.

But Martin, like others at Barford, showed one radical difference from those I met round committee tables, waiting for the news from America. They all heard the bomb might 'conceivably' or 'according to military requirements' be used on Japan. It was mentioned only as a possibility, and most people reacted much like Hector Rose; they did not believe it, or alternatively felt there was nothing they could do. '*War is war*', someone said.

The Barford scientists were nothing like so resigned. Rumour of the bomb coming into action reached them late in June, and there was some sort of confirmation on July 3rd. From that day they took it seriously; like their elders on the committees, some believed that it could not happen, that the report was misjudged: but none of them was for sitting still. Some of the engineers, such as Pearson and Rudd, held off, but the leading scientists were unanimous. Drawbell tried to cajole them – it was not their business, he cried, it would do Barford harm – but they threw him over.

On July 4th they held a meeting in Luke's hospital ward. How long had they got? The trial would not take place before July 20th, and American scientists had sent messages about a joint deputation. Was there a better way to stop it? How could they make themselves heard?

No one in London knew what they intended – and only those they trusted, such as Francis Getliffe and I, knew that they intended anything. All through that July, my information lagged days behind the events.

On July 5th I received a telephone call from my office: it was Emma Mounteney, whom I had known at Cambridge, but had scarcely had a word with since: she wanted to see me urgently, and had a confidential note for me. I was surprised that they should use her as a messenger, but asked her to come round at once. She entered, wearing her youthful, worn, cheeky smile, dressed in a summer frock and a pre-war picture hat. She slid a letter on to my blotting pad, and said:

'Billet-doux for you.'

I was cross with her. I was even more cross when I saw that the envelope was addressed in Irene's handwriting. As soon as I opened it, I saw that it had no connexion with the scientists' plans – it just said (so I gathered at the first glance) that she could not worry Martin when he was worried enough, that Hankins was still at her to pick up where they left off, would I explain as much to him as I safely could?

Unless I had seen Irene, that evening of our celebration in the Albion Gate flat, I should have wondered why she was brandishing bad behaviour to prove that she could be temporarily decent. There was no need for it; she could have turned Hankins down by letter (even if her story were true); she could have avoided this rackety fuss. The answer was that, once she felt part of Martin's love had slipped away, she was losing her confidence: once you lost your confidence in a love relation, you made by instinct, not the right move, but the one furthest from being right.

She was trying to prove to Martin, through me, that she was thinking of his well-being. She was trying, in case the day came when she was going to be judged, to accumulate a little evidence to speak for her.

A few days later, as a result of Irene's letter, I was giving dinner to Edgar Hankins. It was years since we had met, and at once he was exuding his own brand of interest, his bubbling malicious fun. He was getting fat now (he was five years older than I was), his fair hair had gone pepper-and-salt; as in the past, so that night, as soon as he came to my table in the restaurant, we enjoyed each other's company. It was only when we parted that neither of us felt like meeting again.

Hearing him flatter me, recognizing that more than most men he raised the temperature of life, I had to remind myself that his literary personality contained little but seedy, dispirited, homesick despair. He was a literary journalist of the kind not uncommon in those years, who earned a professional income not so much by writing as through broadcasting, giving official lectures, advising publishers, being, as it were, high up in the civil service of literature.

We had a good many friends in common, and, sitting in a corner at the White Tower, we began to exchange gossip. Very soon we were talking intimately; I realized, finally, that part of Irene's stories was true. There was no doubt about it; he could not get her out of his imagination, he was, despite his hesitations and comings-and-goings, in love with her.

'It was only after she married that I realized her husband was your brother,' he said.

'That doesn't make it easier to say what I've got to say,' I said.

'I don't think that should make it any harder,' said Hankins. He was apprehensive, but stayed considerate.

'I'd rather you told me,' he said. Then, with the defiance of a man who is keeping his courage up:

'But don't if it's embarrassing. If you don't, I shall have to make her see me.'

I looked at him.

'That is the trouble,' I said.

'Isn't she going to see me?'

'I've got to tell you that she can't see you: that she asks you not to write: that she wants to stop communication between you, but can't tell you why.'

'Can *you* tell me why?'

For a moment he had the excitement, the excitement that is almost pleasure, of someone in touch with the person he loves, even if he is going to hear bad news. I thought how the phenomena of love did not lose their edge as one got older. Here was this middle-aged, experienced man feeling as he had felt at twenty. Perhaps it got harder to bear, that was all.

'I can tell you the reason she gave me,' I said. 'My brother is in the middle of a piece of scientific politics. She says she's not prepared to do anything that might put him off his stroke.'

Hankins' face went heavy.

'That's not the real reason,' he said. After a moment, he said: 'There aren't many reasons for not seeing someone you want to. What does it sound like to you?'

I shook my head.

He was too subtle a man to bluff.

'All I can say is that she is speaking the truth –'

'What on?'

'There is a scientific struggle going on, and my brother is mixed up in it. I can't tell you anything about it, except to say that she isn't exaggerating.'

'How do you know?' He was the most inquisitive of men; even at that moment he could not resist the smell of a secret. I put him off, and he asked:

'Is it important?'

'Yes.'

Hankins' interest faded, his head sank down, the flesh bulged under his chin.

'It was futile, asking you whether it was important. What is important? If you were lying ill, and expected to die, what use is it if one of your scientific friends comes bounding up and says, "Old chap, I've got wonderful news! I've found a way – which won't come into effect for a few years as a matter of fact – of prolonging the life of the human race".'

A smile, malicious, fanciful, twisted his lips.

'What is important? Is your brother's piece of politics important? Is it important to know whether Irene is shouting goodbye or whether she's just expecting me to press her?' He continued to smile at me. 'Would you consider that an important question, Lewis, or is it the most trivial one you've ever heard?'

CHAPTER 25

Standard Roses in the Sunshine

FOR a fortnight after my dinner with Hankins there was no firm news from America. One rumour was, that the decision about using the bomb had been postponed. Among the people that I met, no one knew the truth, not ministers nor Hector Rose nor any of the scientists.

Late in July – from a record I could later place it as the morning of July 27th – Francis Getliffe entered my office.

He was a thin-faced, fine-looking man, with whom I had been friendly since we were both young. He was a good scientist, who had come into his own during the war. As he entered he gave a creased smile, but his face, as a young man's high-strung and quixotic, had grown more closed. Now we usually did not speak to each other out of our immediate experience. In recent years, he had carried much responsibility, and I some; in public and in private we had each had to hide a good deal; we were becoming middle-aged.

Before he said anything to the point, he walked with his plunging stride across my room, from door to window, back again, back to the window. He made some small talk, staring down Whitehall, so that I could see his knave of diamonds profile. Then he turned full on me.

'Look, Lewis,' he said, 'it might be useful if you came down to Barford with me. Can you make it?'

'When?'

'At once.'

I looked at my In-tray, then shook myself out of the neurosis of routine; Francis was not the man to invite one for a jaunt.

I nodded. 'Yes, that's all right.'

'Good work,' said Francis.

I asked: 'Is anything new happening?'

'Slightly,' said Francis. He added:

'We've just had a signal from New Mexico.'

That meant the trial.

'It went off?'

'Oh yes, it went off.'

Neither of us spoke, then I said:

'What happens now?'

'I wish I knew.'

He had telephoned the Barford scientists (who heard this kind of official news later than we did in the London offices) and they asked him to go down. As we were driven out of London, in Francis' departmental car, along the Bayswater Road, I asked:

'Why do they want me too?'

'I don't know that they do,' Francis said. 'But I thought you might help.'

'Why?'

'In case they try to do something silly. I don't mind them doing something silly if it achieves the object – but I'm afraid they might do it just because there's nothing else to do.'

The shabby streets, the peeling house fronts, shrank under the steady sun. In that wet and windy summer, it was one of the few halcyon days – out in the country the hedges were still as though they were painted, over the river meadows the air quivered like a water mark.

Suddenly, after neither of us had spoken for some miles, Francis said:

'They *can't* be such fools.'

For an instant, I imagined he was still thinking of the Barford scientists, but he went on:

'You can't expect decency from any collection of people with power in their hands, but surely you can expect a modicum of sense.'

'Have we seen much of that?' I asked.

'They can't drop the bomb.'

The car drove on, past the unshaded fields. Francis went on to say that, even if we left moral judgements out, even then it was unthinkable for a sensible man to drop the bomb. Non-scientists never understood, he said, for how short a time you could keep a technical lead. Within five years any major country could make these bombs for itself. If we dropped them first –

At the establishment, which lay well ordered in the sunlight, by this time as neat, as hard, as a factory in a garden suburb, Francis left me in the room where we were to meet. It was a room in a red-brick range, a single storey high; between the ranges were lawns, lush after the weeks of rain, with standard roses each few yards looking like presentation bouquets wired by an unimaginative florist. I remained alone in the room, which was trim, hygienic, as the rest of the establishment had become, with a blackboard on the wall in a pitch pine frame. From the windows one saw the roses, the lawns, the next red-brick range, the roof of the new hot laboratory, all domesticated, all resting in the sun.

Martin was the first to join me; but before we had done more than greet each other, Hanna Puchwein followed him in. She came so quickly after him that she might have been keeping watch – and almost at once there was another constraint in the room.

'Where have you been these days?' she said to Martin. 'You knew I wanted to see you.'

As she spoke, she realized that I was also there. She gave a smile, curiously tomboyish for anyone so careful of herself. I found Martin guiding the conversation, leading me so as not to mention her husband's name. I could not tell whether he just guessed that she and Puchwein had finally parted.

Then I found him guiding the conversation in another sense.

'What brings *you* down here, Lewis?' she asked in a light tone.

Quickly, but as though indifferently, Martin replied for me:

'Oh, just an ordinary visit from headquarters.'

'I didn't know we had much to visit, till you and Walter had got going again,' she said. She said it with a toss of her head that made her seem both bad-tempered and young. In fact, she was standing the years better than any of us, with her small strong bones, her graceful Hamitic head.

'I don't think there is much to visit,' said Martin, telling her it was no good going on.

'Why are you wasting your time?' she turned on me. But, as I was replying, she flashed out at Martin: 'Do you really believe that no one has any idea what's in the wind?'

'No, I don't believe that,' he said, and in the same breath began to talk of what we should do the following day.

Hanna's eyes filled with what seemed like tears of anger. Just for a second, as Mounteney and others entered the room and she left us, Martin glanced at me. He was frowning. Even when he had been snubbing her, he had sounded as though they had once been in each other's confidence, to an extent which came as a surprise.

The room was noisy, as the scientists sat themselves at the desks, one or two banging the lids, like a rowdy class at school. Most of them wore open-necked shirts, one or two were in shorts.

It struck me that all the top scientists at Barford were present, but none of the engineers. As an outsider, it had taken me years to understand this rift in technical society. To begin with, I had expected scientists and engineers to share the same response to life. In fact, the difference in the response between the physicists and engineers often seemed sharper than the difference between the engineers and such men as Hector Rose.

The engineers, the Rudds and Pearsons, the people who make the hardware, who used existing knowledge to make something go, were, in nine cases out of ten, conservatives in politics, acceptant of any régime in which they found themselves, interested in making their machine work, indifferent to long-term social guesses.

Whereas the physicists, whose whole intellectual life was spent in seeking new truths, found it uncongenial to stop seeking when they had a look at society. They were rebellious, questioning, protestant, curious for the future and unable to resist shaping it. The engineers buckled to their jobs and gave no trouble, in America, in Russia, in Germany; it was not from them, but from the scientists, that came heretics, forerunners, martyrs, traitors.

Luke was the last to arrive, a stick supporting him on one side and his wife on the other. If one had seen him near his worst, one no longer thought of him as ill, though the improvement made him look grotesque, for his hair had begun to grow again in tufts, shades fairer than the wings over his ears. With an attempt at jauntiness, he raised his stick before he sat down, while men asked him if he had heard details of the New Mexico explosion.

Luke shook his head.

'All I know is that the bloody balloon went up all right.'

Someone said, with more personal sympathy than the rest:

'It's a pity it wasn't yours.'

'Ours ought to go a bit higher when it does go,' replied Luke.

Francis Getliffe sat on a desk, looked down the small room, began to talk about reports from America – the argument was still going on, the scientists there were pressing the case against using the bomb, the military for; and all the statements for and against most of us knew by heart.

Then there was an interruption.

Mounteney leaned back, protruded his lean prow of a chin, and said, with unexpected formality:

'Before we go on, I should like to know who invited L. S. Eliot to this meeting.'

'I did,' said Francis Getliffe. 'I take it no one objects.'

'I do,' said Mounteney.

For a second, I thought it was a scientist's joke, but Mounteney was continuing: 'I understood that this was a meeting of scientists to find ways of stopping a misuse of science. We've got to stop the people who don't understand science from making nonsense of every-thing we've said, and performing the greatest perversion of science that we've ever been threatened with. It's the general class of people like Eliot who are trying to use the subject for a purpose none of us can tolerate, and I don't see the point in having one of them join in this discussion. Not that I mean anything against L. S. Eliot, of course. I don't suppose he personally would actually authorize using the fission bomb.'

It was only later that I remembered that he liked me, and that this was a triumph of impersonality.

Getliffe raised his voice. 'We all know that Eliot thinks as we do. He also knows a great deal more than any of us about the government machines. That's why he can be useful this afternoon.'

'I don't want anyone who knows anything about government machines,' said Mounteney. 'People who know about government machines all end up by doing what the machine wants, and that is the trouble we have got ourselves in today.'

Luke and Martin were exchanging glances, and Luke spoke.

'We want Lewis Eliot in on this,' he said.

'Why?' asked Mounteney.

'Because you're a wild man, Arthur, and he's a cunning old dog.'

'If you really do want him,' said Mounteney, 'I suppose I'm prepared to stay.'

'I should think you are.'

'But I still object in principle.'

Later, a good many scientists, not so wild as Mounteney, would have considered that in principle he was right.

Getliffe returned to the arguments in America. For weeks everyone in that room had thrashed them out.

Some of them gave an absolute no to the use of the bomb for reasons which were too instinctive to express. For any cause on earth, they could not bear to destroy hundreds of thousands of people at a go.

Many of them gave something near to an absolute no for reasons which, at root, were much the same; the fission bomb was the final product of scientific civilization; if it were used at once to destroy, neither science nor the civilization of which science was bone and fibre, would be free from guilt again.

Many, probably the majority, gave a conditional no with much the same feeling behind it: but if there were *no other way* of saving the war against Hitler, they would be prepared to drop the bomb. I believed that that was the position of Francis Getliffe; it was certainly Luke's.

None of those attitudes were stated at this meeting. They had been agreed on long before, and they gave us much common ground. But those who answered with a conditional no could not dismiss the military counter argument out of hand. In America, so Getliffe said, those in favour of the bomb were saying: Our troops have got to invade Japan, this bomb will save our men's lives; a soldier must do anything, however atrocious, if by doing so he could save one single life under his command.

As Getliffe said, that was a case which one had to respect. And it was the only case one could respect. Using the bomb to forestall the Russians or for any kind of diplomatic motive – that was beneath the human level.

Yet, if the dropping of a bomb could make the Japanese surrender, the knowledge that we possessed it might do the same?

'Several of us,' said Francis Getliffe, 'had made a scheme, in case we had it before the end of the German war. Step one. Inform the enemy that the bomb was made, and give them enough proof. Step two. Drop one bomb where it will not kill people. Step three. If the enemy government will not budge, then' – Getliffe had faced his own thoughts – 'drop the next on a town.'

By this time, the meeting was in a state of deep emotion. 'If there is any sense or feeling left,' said Francis Getliffe (it was only afterwards that I recalled that 'sense and feeling' was the one emotional phrase in his speech), 'don't begin by using this bomb on human beings.'

That was the case which scientists were putting up in Washington.

'How are they taking it?' asked a refugee.

'Some are listening,' said Francis.

'Is that going to be good enough?' said someone.

'No one knows yet,' said Francis. He added:

'We've had one optimistic message.'

'Who from?'

Getliffe gave the name.

Luke shook his head.

'He'd believe anything that a blooming general told him. I must say, it doesn't sound safe enough to leave.'

'I agree,' said Francis Getliffe.

'What more can we do?' came a voice.

'There's plenty we can do,' said Luke.

'There's plenty we can do,' said Mounteney, speaking into space, 'but there's only one way we can make it impossible for them.'

'What's that?' said Francis.

'Issue a statement saying what has happened about the bomb and what is proposed. That will settle it in one.'

'Who is to issue the statement?' said Nora Luke.

'We are.'

'Breaking the law?' said Francis.

'I know that,' said Mounteney.

'Breaking our oaths?' said Francis.

Mounteney hesitated for some moments.

'I don't like that. But there's no other way.'

'We're still at war,' said Luke. 'We shall never get the statement out.'

'I think we should,' said Mounteney.

'It'd all be hushed up. A few of us would be in jug, and the whole bloody game would be discredited.'

'We might be unlucky,' said Mounteney. 'In that case a few scientists would be discredited. If we do nothing, then all scientists will be discredited. I can understand some of you fighting shy of signing the statement. I shan't mind putting it out by myself.'

That was a false note. He was a daring man, but so were others there. He was a man of absolute integrity, but most of them did not trust his judgement. Just at that turning point, they were undecided.

Francis Getliffe had expected some such suggestion all along; for himself, he was too disciplined to act on it. So was Luke. But it was Martin who spoke.

'No, Arthur,' he said, smiling to Mounteney. 'That's not fair. What's more important, it isn't realistic, you know. We couldn't let you do it unless (a) it was certain to work, (b) there was no alternative. It just wouldn't work. The only result would be that a Nobel prize-winner would be locked up for trying to break the Official Secrets Act, and the rest of us wouldn't be able to open our mouths. Don't you see that, if you try something illegal and it doesn't come off – then *we've completely shot our bolt*? Whatever governments decided to do with the bombs, we should have lost any influence we might have had.'

There was a murmur in the room. If you were used to meetings, then you knew that they were on Martin's side. I was astonished at the authority he carried with them.

It happened to be one of those occasions when it was easier to make a prudent case than a wild one. Nearly everyone there was uneasy about breaking an oath – uneasy both out of fear and out of conscience. They were not men to whom gesture-making came lightly: they could not believe, that sunny afternoon, that it was demanded of them. So they took Martin as their spokesman.

But also, I thought, he was speaking with an inner authority of his own; his bit of success had been good for him; he carried the weight of one who is, for the first time, all of a piece.

'I don't see any other way,' said Mounteney.

'We do,' said Martin.

Mounteney, as well as being cantankerous, was the most obstinate of men. We were ready for him to argue for hours. Yet without explanation he gave way. I did not even wonder how mysterious his surrender was; we were too much in the middle of events to care.

Immediately, Martin brought out his proposal: that two or three English scientists should be flown over to America to say again what they had said that afternoon. It was known that a number of the scientists working on the American project had signed a protest: the English emissaries would take over a corresponding list of names. Those names were already known – of the scientists at Barford, every-one was willing to sign except Drawbell himself, and two obscure chemists. There would also be some signatures, but a much smaller proportion, from the engineers and technicians.

Everyone in the room agreed; they were active men, and they were soothed by action for its own sake. Getliffe could arrange for an official aircraft within twenty-four hours. Who should go? There was a proposal, backed by Mounteney, that it should be Luke and Martin, the people who had done the work.

Luke was willing to agree, but Martin would not have it. Neither of them was known in America, said Martin: it was no use sending local reputations. Whereas Mounteney had his Nobel prize and Francis Getliffe a great name in Washington for his war work: they were the two who might count.

It was agreed. They would be in America by July 29th. Francis

Getliffe said that they would hope to send us news before the middle of August.

CHAPTER 26

Need for a Brother

ON those first days of August, I had little to do in the office except wait for news. The 'leave season' had set in, as it had not done for six years; rooms round me were empty; the files ended 'cd we discuss on my return?'

When I arrived in the morning, I looked for a despatch from America: but none came. I got through my work in an hour. Then I rang up Martin at Barford, hoping that Getliffe might have signalled to them and not to London: no news. There was nothing to do. Often, in the afternoons, I went off by myself to Lord's.

It was the week before Bank Holiday. The days were like the other days: a sharp cool wind was blowing, more like April than full summer, the clouds streamed across the sky, at the cricket ground one watched for the blue fringe behind them.

On the Friday, I had still had no word from America; when I telephoned Martin (it was becoming a routine), nor had he. 'We're bound to hear before long,' he said.

Saturday was the same. On the Sunday I stayed in my flat all day, half expecting that Martin was right, that a message was on the way.

Next morning I was restless; once more I went off (half thinking as when one waits for a letter in a love affair, that if I were out of the way, a message was more likely to arrive) to St John's Wood, and sat there watching the game.

The ground was shabby that summer. The pavilion was unpainted; like the high Victorian afternoon of which it might have been the symbol, it had sunk into decay. Yet the smell of the grass was a comfort; it helped me to tell myself that though I had cares on my mind, they were not the deepest. Like the scientists, more often than not I felt this trouble about the bomb could be resolved. And in myself I was lonely rather than unhappy; at forty I had not reshaped my life. Perhaps that was why I took to heart this trouble at one remove. So

I sat, watching those hours of cricket in the flashing rainsharp sunshine, taken over by well being, thoughtless, and secure.

It must have been about a quarter to six when I left Lord's. I walked in a meaningless reverie down to Baker Street and then along the Marylebone Road; the light was brilliant after rain, and in it the faces of passers-by stood out sharp-edged. At last I went at random into a pub in Portland Place. I heard my name. There, standing at the bar beside a man in a polo sweater, was Hankins.

I began by saying something banal, about not meeting for years and then twice in a month, but he cried loudly:

'This is my producer. I've just been giving a talk on *Current Shakespeareana*.'

He said that he had had only one drink, but his bright, heavy face was glistening, he was talking as if he were half drunk.

'And all the time I was thinking of my words going out to the villages and the country towns and clever young women saying "That was a good point!" or "I should like to take that up with him". And then I came out of the studio and met the man who had been reading the six o'clock news just before I went on.'

'Is there any news?' I asked.

'There is,' said Hankins.

I knew.

'So they've dropped it, have they?' I asked dully. I felt blank, tired out.

'Were you expecting something then?' said Hankins. But his inquisitiveness for once was swamped: yes, the six o'clock news had contained the announcement about the bomb and he, in innocence, had broadcast just after.

'I wonder how many people listened to my immortal prose!' cried Hankins. '*Current Shakespeareana*. I wish it had been something slightly more obscure. The *influence of the Duino Elegies on the later work of C. P. Cavafy* – that's how I should like to have added the only comment literary culture was entitled to make on this promising new age.'

He was upset and hilarious, he wanted an audience, human bodies round him, drink.

'The chief virtue of this promising new age, and perhaps the only one so far as I can tell, is that from here on we needn't pretend to be any better than anyone else. For hundreds of years we've told ourselves in the west, with that particular brand of severity which ends up in paying yourself a handsome compliment, that of course we cannot live up to our moral pretensions, that of course we've established ethical standards which are too high for men. We've always assumed, all the people of whom you,' he grinned at the producer and me, 'and I are the ragtag and bobtail, all the camp followers of western civilization, we have taken it for granted that, even if we did not live up to those exalted ethical standards, we did a great deal better than anyone else. Well, anyone who says that today isn't a fool, because no one could be so foolish. He isn't a liar, because no one could tell such lies. He's just a singer of comic songs.'

The producer said that next day he had a programme on the care of backward children. 'One can't help thinking,' he said, 'whether there'll be any children left to care for.'

Hankins suddenly clapped a hand to his head.

'I suppose this wasn't the piece of scientific policy we were interested in, you and I, Lewis, last time we met?'

'It was.'

'You said it was important,' he said, as though in reproof. I nodded.

'Well, perhaps I could concede it a degree of importance. What is important, after all?' He had a writer's memory for the words we had each spoken. 'Did Irene know about this?' he flashed out.

'No.'

'Did your brother and the rest of them?'

'None of them knew that this bomb was going to be dropped.'

'But they'd been working heroically on it, I suppose,' said Hankins. 'And now they're getting the reward for their labours. It must be strange to be in their shoes tonight.'

It was also strange to hear him speak with such kindness, with his own curious inquisitive imagination.

We went on drinking, as Hankins talked.

'The party's nearly over,' he said. 'The party for our kind of people, for dear old western man – it's been a good party, but the host's getting impatient and it's nearly time to go. And there are lots of people waiting for our blood in the square outside. Particularly as we've kept up the maddening habit of making improving speeches from the window. It may be a long time before anyone has such a good party again.'

If I had stayed I should have got drunk, but I wanted to escape. I went out into the streets, on which the anonymous crowds were jostling in the summer evening. For a while I lost myself among them, without a name, among many who had no name, a unit among the numbers, listening but hearing no comment on the news. In the crowd I walked down Oxford Street, was carried by the stream along Charing Cross Road: lights shone in the theatre foyers, the plays had all begun, in the wind relics of newsprint scuffled among our feet.

Near Leicester Square I drifted out of the crowd, into another pub. There some had heard the news, and as they talked I could pick out the common denominator of fear, sheer simple fear, which, whatever else we thought, was present in us all, Hankins and his producer, the seedy travellers, agents, homosexuals in the Leicester Square bar. Hankins' rhetoric that night: Francis Getliffe's bare words on the way down to Barford: they were different men, but just for once their feelings coincided, they meant the same things.

But in the pub there were also some indifferent. They had heard, and thrown it off already.

One, an elderly man with a fine ascetic face, sat with strained eyes focused on the doors. From a passing remark, I gathered that he was waiting for a young man, who had been due at six.

I walked across Piccadilly Circus, up Vigo Street and then west of Bond Street, through the deserted fringes of Mayfair, towards my club. As soon as I entered, acquaintances spoke to me with interest, with resignation, with the same damped-down fear. Had I known? Was there a chance that we could make ourselves safe again? What would happen to this country in another war? To this town? There was one interruption, as I stood in a party of four or five, standing round the empty grate. A young member, elected that year, asked if he could have a word with me. He had been invalided out of the Navy, his face was sallow, he had a high-strung, delicate, humorous look. But he spoke with urgency:

'Is this bomb all they say?'

I answered yes, so far as I knew.

'Do you think it will finish the Japanese? Do you think the war's going to stop?'

'I should have thought so,' I replied.

'I don't believe it. Bombs don't end wars.'

I was puzzled, but the explanation was straight-forward. He was arguing against his own hopes. He had an elder brother, who was booked to fight in the invasion of Malaya. He could not let himself believe that the war would end in time.

When I left the club, I began to walk across London, trying to tire myself. But soon the energy of distress left me, almost between one step and another: although it was not yet eleven I found myself tired out. I took a taxi back to Pimlico, where from the houses in the square the lights were shining, as serene as on any other night of peace, as enticing to a lonely man outside.

I went straight off to sleep, woke before four, and did not get to sleep again. It was not a bad test of how public and private worries compare in depth, I thought, when I remembered the nights I had lain awake because of private trouble. Public trouble – how many such nights of insomnia had *that* given me? The answer was, just one. On the night after Munich, I had lain sleepless – and perhaps, as I went through the early hours of August 7th, I could fairly count another half.

As I lay there, I wished that I were able to speak to someone I was close to. The thoughts, the calculations of the future, pressed on me out of the morning dusk; it might have taken the edge off them if I could have admitted them to Martin. Soon after breakfast, I rang him up.

'So this is it,' I said.

'Yes, this is it,' came his voice, without any stress.

For some instants neither of us spoke, and I went on:

'I think I should like to come down. Can you put up with me?'

A pause.

'It might be better if I came to London,' he replied. 'Will that do?'

'I can come down straight away,' I said.

'The other might be better. Is it all right for you?'

I said it was, but I was restless all morning, wondering why he had put me off. It was just after one when he came into my room.

As soon as I saw him, I felt, as often when we met, the familiar momentary wiping away of fret. I had felt the same, over five years before, when he visited me in that office, and we talked of the bomb, and I induced him to work on it.

'Well, it's happened,' I said.

'I'm afraid so,' said Martin.

It was a curious phrase, inadequate and polite.

'I don't find it easy to take,' I said.

'It's not pretty,' said Martin.

I looked at him. His eyes were hard, bright, and steady, the corners of his mouth tucked in. I felt a jolt of disappointment; I was repelled by his stoicism. I had turned to him for support, and we had nothing to say to each other.

Without pretending to be lighthearted, Martin kept up the same level, disciplined manner. He made some comments about his journey; then he asked where we should eat.

'Where you like,' I said.

His eyes searched mine.

'Would you rather wait a bit?'

'I don't care,' I said.

'I mean,' said Martin, his eyes harder, 'would you rather wait and talk? Because if so it may take some time.'

'It depends what we talk about –'

'What do you think I'm going to talk about?'

His voice was not raised – but suddenly I realized it was unsteady with anger.

'I thought you felt it wasn't any use –'

'It may be a *great deal* of use,' said Martin. His voice was still quiet, his temper utterly let go.

'What do you mean?'

'You don't expect me to sit by and hear about this performance, and not say that I should like my dissent recorded in the minutes?'

'I've felt the same,' I said.

'I know you have,' said Martin. 'But the question is: what is a man to do?'

'I doubt if you can do anything,' I said.

Martin said: 'I think I can.'

'It's happened now,' I said. 'There's nothing to do.'

'I disagree.'

At that moment, each of us, staring into the other's eyes, shared the other's feeling, and knew that our wills must cross.

PART FOUR

A RESULT IN PRIVATE

CHAPTER 27

An Uneffaceable Afternoon

BIG BEN had just struck, it must have been the half hour, when Martin said:

'I disagree.'

He continued to look at me.

'I oughtn't to have stopped Arthur Mounteney sending his letter,' said Martin. Just then, that was the focus of his remorse.

'It wouldn't have done any good,' I said.

'It would have done the trick,' said Martin.

I shook my head. He said:

'So now I shall have to send a letter myself.'

He added, in a tone that was casual, cold, almost hostile:

'Perhaps you'd better have a look at it.'

He opened his wallet, and with his neat deliberate fingers unfolded a sheet of office paper. He leant across and put it on my blotter. The words were written in his own handwriting. There were no corrections, and the letter looked like a fair copy. It read:

To the Editor of *The Times* (which failing, *Daily Telegraph*, *Manchester Guardian*). Sir, As a scientist who has been employed for four years on the fission bomb, I find it necessary to make two comments on the use of such a bomb on Hiroshima. First, it appears not to have been relevant to the war: informed persons are aware that, for some weeks past, the Japanese have been attempting to put forward proposals for surrender. Second, if this had not been so, or if the proposals came to nothing, a minimum respect for humanity required that a demonstration of the weapon should be given, e.g. by delivering a bomb on unpopulated territory, before one was used on an assembly of men, women, and children. The actual use of the bomb in cold blood on Hiroshima is the most horrible single act so far performed. States like Hitler's Germany have done much wickedness over many years, but no State has ever before had both the power and the will to destroy so many lives in a few seconds. In this respect, our scientists and our government have been so closely interwoven with those of the U.S.A. that we have formed part of that power and that will . . .

'You've not sent this?' I said, before I had finished reading.

'Not yet.'

'How many people know you've written it?'

'Only Irene.'

That was the reason, I thought, that he had not wished me to go to Barford.

If this letter were published, it meant the end of his career. I had to get him out of it. From the moment he said that he was proposing to act, I had known that I must prevent him.

Even though I agreed with almost all he said.

As I began to make the first opposing moves, which he was already expecting, I was thinking, his was a letter which an able man only writes when he is near breaking point. Only his mask was stoical, as he sat there, his fingers spread like a starfish on the arms of his chair. In his letter – whatever he had written I should be trying to suppress it – he had not made the best of his case.* Yet I agreed with him in all that mattered. Looking back years later, I still agreed with him.

I felt it so, that afternoon, when I set myself to make Martin keep quiet. I shut away the sense of outrage, my own sense of outrage as well as his, and brought out the worldly wise, official's argument, such as we had displayed at Barford in July, such as he had used himself. It was not worth while making gestures for no result. One such gesture was all you were allowed; you ought to choose a time when it could do good. We had found ourselves in responsible positions; we could not give them up overnight; for everyone's sake we had to get through the next few years without a war; then one could make gestures.

There was something in what I said, but they were not the reasons, they were nowhere near the reasons, why I was calling on each ounce of nature that I possessed to force him to conform. It was, in fact,

---

*The passage about diplomatic overtures, for example, only complicated the argument.

incomparably more simple. For a brother as for a son, one's concern is, in the long run, prosaic and crude. One is anxious about their making a living; one longs for their success, but one wants it to be success as the world knows it, reputation among solid men. For myself, my own 'respectable' ambitions had damped down by now, I should perhaps have been able, if the choice was sharp enough, to throw them away and face a scandal. For myself; but not for him.

I had seen friends throw away what most men clung to, respectability, money, fame. Roy Calvert: Charles March: even old Martineau. I understood why they had done it, I should have been the last to dissuade them. But they were friends, and Martin was a brother. The last thing you want with a brother is that he should fulfil a poetic destiny.

Martin met my argument point by point; we were getting nowhere. All of a sudden he began looking down beside his chair, under the desk, by the hatstand.

'Did I bring in a briefcase?' he said.

I said that I had not noticed, and he went on searching.

'Does it matter?' I was put out.

He said that it contained notes of the new method for extracting plutonium: it was top secret. He must trace it. He thought he remembered leaving it in his car: would I mind walking to the garage with him? Irritated at the interruption, I followed beside him, down Whitehall, across Victoria Street: Martin, his forehead lined with anxiety was walking faster than usual, and we were both silent. The offices, the red-brick houses of Great Smith Street, glowed shabby in the sunshine. Just as on the night before, I felt a tenderness for the dirty, unfriendly, ugly streets such as I had never felt before. I even felt something like remorse, because what had happened to another town might happen here.

The briefcase was not in the car. Martin said nothing, except that he must ring up Barford from my office. Back there, he sat leaning forward, as though by concentrating he could make the call come through. It was minutes before the telephone whirred. Martin was talking to his secretary, his words fast but even then polite. 'Would you mind looking . . .?' He waited, then cried out:

'Thank God for that!' With elaborate thanks he put the receiver down, and gave me a sharp, deprecating grin.

'I never moved it. It's sitting there in its proper place.'

'It seemed a curious thing to worry about,' I said.

For an instant he looked blank. Then his face broke into a laugh, the kind of noiseless laugh with which as children we used to receive family jokes. But soon his expression hardened. He asked, had I anything more to say before he sent the letter?

'A good deal more,' I said.

'I wish you'd say it.'

His tone was so inflexible that I became more brutal.

'How are you going to live?' I said.

'A decent scientist can make some sort of a living,' he said.

'Whatever trouble you get into?'

'It wouldn't be a good living, but I can make do.'

'What does your wife think of that?'

There came a surprise. Martin smiled, not affectionately, but as though he held a trump which I had miscounted. He said:

'As a matter of fact, she wants me to do it.'

He spoke with absolute confidence. I had made a stupid mistake. I should have remembered the way she welcomed his first risk. I tried another tack.

'Have you thought of your son?'

'Yes, I've thought of him,' said Martin. He added:

'I've also thought of you. I'm sorry if it harms you, and I know that it must.' He said it formally.

I cast round again. He and I took too much responsibility on ourselves, I said. That was true in our human relations.

He stared at me, and for an instant I was silent.

I went on with the argument. We should be better men if we took less upon our shoulders. And scientists as a class had the same presumption. They thought too much of their responsibility. Martin that day had no more guilt to carry than any other man.

'Again I disagree,' said Martin. After a silence, he went on:

'In any case, I can make a more effective noise.'

'Yes,' I said, feeling another spot to probe – he and Luke and the others would be listened to. But if he were patient, some day he would be listened to in a way that did effective good. Not now. It would be a nine days' wonder, he would be ruined and powerless. But wait. In the next few years, if he and Luke brought their process to success, they would have more influence than most people. That was the only way in which Martin could gain authority: and *then*, if a protest had to be made, if a martyr were needed, *then* he could speak out without it being just a pathetic piece of defiance, a lonely voice in Hyde Park.

A girl brought us cups of tea. The argument went on, flashes crossed the wall from bus roofs reflected in the sun. Neither then nor afterwards did I detect the instant at which the hinge turned. Perhaps there was no such instant. Perhaps it was more like a turn of the tide. Towards the end of the afternoon, Martin knew, and I knew, that I had made him give up.

I did not, even then, believe that any reasons of mine had convinced him. Some had been sound: some were fabricated: some contradicted others. So far as reasons went, his were as good as mine. The only advantage I had was that, in resolving to stop him acting, I had nothing to dilute my purpose. Whereas he intended to act, but deep down he had his doubts. Some of these doubts I had brought into the open: the doubt that fed on responsibility, on caution, on self-interest, on a mixture of fears, including the fear of being disloyal.

As the afternoon sun made blazing shields of the windows across the street, Martin said:

'Very well, I shall just do nothing.'

He spoke sadly, admitting what, for some time past, we had each known.

I asked him to have dinner with me, and stay in my flat. For a second his face had the look of refusal, but then his politeness came back. We were both constrained as we walked across the parks to Hyde Park Corner. In Green Park we stood for a while watching some boys of eight or nine play, in a clearing by the bandstand, a primitive game of cricket. The trees' shadows stretched across the lumpy grass, and we saw something that had the convincing improbability of a dream; at three successive balls the batsman made a scooping shot, and gave a catch which went in a gentle curve, very softly, to point; the first catch was seriously and solemnly missed. So was the second. So was the third.

'We shall never see that again,' I said to Martin.

Usually he would have been amused, but now he only gave a token smile.

We walked along the path.

'By the way,' said Martin, in a tone dry and without feeling, 'I heard one story about tactics that might interest you.'

He had heard it from someone present after the bomb was made.

'There was a good deal of discussion,' he said, 'about how to drop it with maximum results. One ingenious idea was to start a really spectacularly pretty flare a few seconds before the bomb went off.'

'Why?'

'To make sure that everyone in the town was looking up.'

'Why?'

'To make sure they were all blinded.'

I cried out.

'That's where we've got to in the end,' he said. He added: 'But I agree with you, now I've got to let it go.'

We walked on, set apart and sad.

CHAPTER 28

'What do you Expect from him Now?'

TWO days later, as we drove down to Barford in the afternoon, Martin and I talked civilly of cricket and acquaintances, with no sign on the surface of our clash of wills.

In Banbury I bought an evening paper. I saw that another bomb had been dropped. Without speaking I passed the paper to Martin, sitting at the wheel, the car drawn up in the market place beside the kerb. He read the paragraph under the headline.

'This is getting monotonous,' he said.

His expression had not changed. We both took it for granted that the argument was not to be reopened. He was too stable a character to go back on his word. Instead, he commented, as we drove into Warwickshire, that this Nagasaki bomb must have been a plutonium one.

'The only point of dropping the second,' said Martin, his tone neutral, the last edge of feeling dried right out, 'must have been for purposes of comparison.'

As soon as we went inside the canteen at Barford he made a

similar remark, and was immediately denounced by Luke as a cold fish. Martin caught my eye; just for an instant, his irony returned.

Inside that room, four floors up in the administration building, so that one looked out over the red-brick ranges towards the dipping sun and then back to the tea cups and the white linoleum on the tables, the voices were loud and harsh.

There were a dozen people there, Mary Pearson, Nora Luke, Luke himself, erect and stiff-backed as he had not been for a year; I had never seen them so angry.

The news of Hiroshima had sickened them; that afternoon had left them without consolation. Luke said: 'If anyone had tried to defend the first bomb, then I might just have listened to him. But if anyone dares try to defend the second, then I'll see him in hell before I listen to a single word.'

They all assumed, as Martin had done, that the plutonium bomb was dropped as an experiment, to measure its 'effectiveness' against the other.

'It had to be dropped in a hurry,' said someone, 'because the war will be over and there won't be another chance.'

'Not just yet,' said Luke.

I had known them rancorous before, morally indignant, bitter: but it was something new to hear them cynical – to hear that last remark of Luke's, the least cynical of men.

Eric Pearson came in, smiled at his wife, nodded to others, threw back his quiff of hair. He sat down at the table, where most of us were standing. Suddenly I thought I should like to question him. Of them all, he was the only one who had worked directly on the actual bombs, that is, he had had a small part, a fractional part, in what they would call 'the hardware', the concrete objects that had been dropped on those towns. Even if it was only a thousandth part, I was thinking, that meant a good many lives.

'How do you feel about it?' I asked.

'Nothing special,' said Pearson.

As usual he irritated me with his off-hand manner, his diffidence, his superlative inner confidence.

'I should have thought,' I said, 'you might wish it hadn't happened?'

'Oh,' he said, 'I haven't lost any sleep about it.'

Suddenly his wife broke out, her face flaming, tears starting from her eyes:

'Then you damned well ought to have!'

'I'm sorry.' His manner changed, he was no longer jaunty. 'I only meant that it wasn't my business.'

She brushed away the tears with the back of her hand, stared at him – and then went out of the room. Soon Pearson followed her. The others dismissed him as soon as he had gone, while I wondered how long that breach would last. Pitilessly they forgot him, and Luke was shouting to me:

'Lewis, you may have to get me out of clink.'

He stood between the tables.

'It's no use belly-aching any more,' he cried. 'We've got to get something done.'

'What is to be done?' said a voice.

'It stands out a mile what is to be done,' said Luke. 'We've got to make a few of these damned things ourselves, we've got to finish the job. Then if there's going to be any more talking, we might have our share.'

In the midst of their indignation, the proposal did not startle them. Luke was a man of action, so were many of them. Political protests, associations of scientists – in their state of moral giddiness, they were looking for anything to clutch on to. For some, Luke was giving them another hold. He had always been the most nationalistic of them. Just as old Bevill kept the narrow patriotism of the officer élite, so Luke never quite forgot that he had been brought up in a naval dockyard, and kept the similar patriotism of the petty officer.

That afternoon the scientists responded to it.

'Why is it going to lead you in clink?' I cut across the argument.

'Because if we don't get the money to go ahead, I don't mean next month, I don't mean tomorrow, I mean *now*, I'm going to stump the country telling them just what they're in for. Unless you old men' – he was speaking to me – 'get it into your heads that this is a new phase, and that if we don't get in on the ground floor there are just two things that can happen to this country – the best is that we can fade out and become a slightly superior Spain, the worst is that we get wiped out like a mob of Zulus.'

Nora said:

'When you see what the world is like, would that matter so much?'

'It would matter to me,' said Luke. Suddenly he gave up being a roughneck. 'I know it seems as though any chance of a little decency in the world has been wiped out for good. All I can say is that, if we're going to get any decency back, then first this country must have a bit of power.'

Someone asked how much time he needed.

'It depends on the obstacles they put in our way,' said Luke. He said to Martin: 'What do you say, how long do we need?'

Since we entered the canteen Martin had been standing by the window, just outside the group, and as I turned my eyes with Luke's question, I saw him, face half averted, as though he were watching the western sky, the blocks of buildings beneath, rectangular, parallel, like the divisions in a battle map. It was many minutes since he had spoken.

He gazed at Luke with a blank face. Then, businesslike, as in a routine discussion, he replied:

'Given the personnel we've got now?'

'Double it,' said Luke.

'Two years, at the best,' said Martin. (By this time, even Luke admitted that his early estimates had not been realistic.) 'About three, allowing for an average instalment of bad luck.'

All he had promised me was to keep quiet. Now he was going further. He was taking the line I had most urged him to take. They began arguing about the programmes: and I left them to it.

As I walked along the path to Martin's flat, where Irene had been told to expect me, the evening was serene; it should have been the end of a calm and nameless day. The sky was so clear that, as the first stars came out, I could distinguish one that did not twinkle, and I was wondering which planet it was, as I made my way upstairs to Irene.

When I got inside their sitting-room, I found that she had just begun to wash her hair.

She asked, without leaving the bathroom, whether I would not go into the village and have a meal alone. No, I said, I was tired; any kind of snack, and I would rather stay. Still through the open door, she told me where to find bread and butter and tinned meat. Then she ignored me.

Sitting on the drawing-room sofa, I could see her across the passage, her hair, straight and fine, hanging down over the basin. Later, hooded in a towel, she was regarding herself in the looking-glass. Her face had thinned down and aged, the flesh had fallen away below the cheek-bones, while on her body she had put on weight; some men would find excitement in the contrast, always latent in her, but now in her mid-thirties established, between the body, heavy, fleshly and strong, and the nervous, over-exhausted face.

In towel and dressing-gown she surveyed herself sternly, as though, after trying to improve her looks for years, she was still dissatisfied.

She had finished washing, there was no reason to prevent her chatting with me, but still she sat there, evaluating her features, not paying any attention that I had come. I had no doubt that it was deliberate; she must have decided on this toilet as soon as she heard that I was on the way. It was quite unlike her, whose first instinct was to be ready to get a smile out of me or any other man.

I could not resist calling out:

'Aren't you going to talk to me tonight?'

Her reply took me aback. Her profile still towards me, and gazing at her reflection, she said:

'It could only make things worse.'

'What is all this?' I said roughly, as though she were sulky and needed shaking. But she answered without the least glint of sex:

'It will be better if we don't talk until Martin comes back.'

It sounded like melodrama, of which she had her share: but also, like much melodrama, it was meant. I went into the bathroom and she turned to confront me, the towel making her face open and bald. She looked nervous, frowning – and contemptuous.

'This isn't going to clear up without speaking,' I said.

She said:

'You've done him harm, haven't you?'

I was lost. For a second, I even thought she was speaking of Hankins, not Martin. She added:

'He's going to toe the line, isn't he? And that can only be your doing.'

Then, in the scent of powder and bath salts, a remark swung back from the previous afternoon and I said:

'You'd rather he ruined himself, would you?'

'If that's what you call it,' said Irene.

Like the scientists in the canteen I was morally giddy that day.

'He makes up his own mind,' I said.

'Except for you,' she cried. She burst out, her eyes bright with resentment, with an obscure triumph:

'Oh, I haven't fooled myself – and I should think you must have a glimmering by now – I'm perfectly well aware I haven't any influence on him that's worth a row of beans. Of course, he's easy going, he's always good natured when it doesn't cost him anything. If I want to go out for a drink, he never grumbles, he just puts down whatever he's doing: but do you think on anything that he cares about, I could ever make him budge an inch?'

It was no use contradicting.

'You can,' she cried. 'You've done it.'

She added:

'I hope you'll be satisfied with what happens to him.'

I said:

'We'd better wait till we've got over this shock –'

'Oh, never mind *that*,' she said. 'I wash my hands of that. It's him I'm thinking of.'

She looked at me with eyes narrowed.

'Do you know,' she said, 'I'm beginning to wonder whether you understand him at all?'

She broke off. 'Don't you like *extravagant* people?' she asked.

'Yes,' I said.

'Unless it comes too near home.' She went on: 'He's one at heart, have you never seen that?'

She stared at her reflection again.

'That's why he gets on with me,' she said, as though touching wood.

'That might be true,' I said.

'He's capable of being really extravagant,' she broke out. 'Why did you stop him this time? He's capable of throwing the chains right off.'

She stared at me and said:

'I suppose you were capable of it, once.'

It was said cruelly, and was intended to be cruel. For the first time in our relation she held the initiative. Through her envy of my intimacy with Martin, through her desire to be thought well of, through the attraction that smoulders often between in-laws, she could nevertheless feel that she was thinking only of him.

When I replied, I meant to tell her my real motive for influencing him, but I was inhibited.

Instead, I told her that he was not alone, he was not living in a vacuum, nor was I. What he did affected many others. Neither he nor I could live as though we were alone.

She said:

'He could have done.'

I said:

'Not this time.'

'It would have been a glorious thing to do,' she cried.

She rounded on me:

'I've got one last word for you,' she said. 'You've stopped him doing what he wanted to. I won't answer for the consequences. I should like to know what you expect from him now.'

CHAPTER 29

Hushed Voices under the Beams

ONE night soon after, coming out of the theatre at Stratford, I was forced to remember how – the evening the news of Hiroshima came through – I had walked through the West End streets in something like wretchedness. Now I was leaving the play, the sense of outrage had left me alone for days, I was one among a crowd, lively and content in the riverside lights. Around me was a knot of elderly women whom I had noticed in the theatre, who looked like school-teachers and to whom, by some standards, life had not given much; yet their faces were kind, shining with a girlish, earnest happiness, they were making haste to their boarding house to look up the text.

It was there by the river, which was why I was forced to remember, why I became uncomfortable at being content under the lamplit trees, that Martin and Mounteney and I, on the dark wartime night, so tunnel-like by the side of this, agreed that there was no serious chance that the bomb could be used.

Yet I was lighthearted under the belts of stars.

How long can you sustain grief, guilt, remorse, for a horror far away?

If it were otherwise, if we could feel public miseries as we do private ones, our existences in those years would have been hard to endure. For anyone outside the circle of misery, it is a blessing that one's public memory is so short; it is not such a blessing for those within.

Should we be left with only one reminder, that for thoughtful men there would stay, almost like a taste on the tongue, the grit of fear?

In the following days at Stratford, where I was taking my first leave that year, all I heard from the establishment was that Luke was driving his team as though in his full vigour, and that Martin was back in place as second in command. Martin had not spoken to me alone.

For most of that August there was no other news from Barford except that Mounteney had made his last appearance in the place, taken down the nameplate from his door, emptied his In-tray on top of his Out-tray, as he and Luke had once promised, and gone straight back to his university chair.

A few days later, without any warning, Drawbell came into Stratford to see me with a rumour so ominous that he spoke in whispers in the empty street. The rumour was that there had been at least one 'leakage', perhaps more: that is, data about the American experiments, and probably the Barford ones also, had been got through to Russia.

Within a few hours of that rumour – it was the end of August, and my last week in Stratford – I received a telephone call at my hotel. It was from Luke: Martin and he had a point to raise with me. I said I could come over at any time, but Luke stopped me. 'I don't like the cloak and dagger stuff,' he said, 'but it might be better just this once if we happen to run across you.'

They drove into Stratford that evening, and we met at the play. In the intervals, there were people round us; even outside on the terrace in the cool night, we could not begin to talk. Afterwards, with the wind blowing like winter, we went to the hotel sitting-room, but there for a long time, while Luke breathed hard with impatience, a couple of families were eating sandwiches after the theatre. The wind moaned outside, we drank beer, the beams of the low room pressed down on us as we waited; it was a night on which one was oppressed by a sense of the past.

At last we had the room to ourselves. Luke gave an irritable sigh, but when he spoke his voice, usually brazen, was as quiet as Martin's.

'This is Martin's show,' he said.

'I don't think so,' said Martin.

'Damn it,' said Luke, and it was curious to hear him angry in an undertone, as we sat with heads bent forward over the gate-legged table, 'we can't pass the buck as though we were blooming well persuading each other to sing.'

'No,' said Martin, 'I'd speak first if I had the responsibility.'

Luke glowered at him. Martin looked blank-faced.

'The problem,' said Luke brusquely, 'is security. Or at least you' – he thrust his lip towards Martin – 'are making it a problem.'

'I'm not making it,' said Martin. 'The world's doing that.'

'Blast the world,' said Luke. Luke was frowning: he uttered 'security' like a swear word, but he could not shrug it off: in the fortnight since the dropping of the bombs, it had fallen upon them more pervasively than ever in the war. Now they knew, as I did, that the rumour of the leakages was more than a rumour. So far as one could trust the intelligence sources, it was true.

Already that day, Luke had been forced to concede one of Martin's points. Kurt Puchwein, who had been working at Berkeley, had recently arrived back in England, and wanted to return to Barford as Luke's chief chemist. Luke had admitted that it was too dangerous to take him. None of us believed that Puchwein had been spying, but he was a platform figure of the Left; if the leakages became public, Martin had made Luke agree, they could not stand the criticism of having re-engaged him at Barford. So Puchwein had arrived home, found that Hanna was finally leaving him and that he had no job. As for the latter, Luke said that he was 'taking care' of that; there were a couple of universities who would be glad to find a research readership for Puchwein; it would happen without commotion, one of those English tricks that Puchwein, for all his intellect and father-in-Israel shrewdness, could never completely understand.

That point was settled, but there was another.

'Martin is suggesting,' said Luke, 'that I ought to victimize someone.'

Our heads were close together, over the table; but Martin looked at neither of us, he seemed to be set within his carapace, guarded, official, decided.

'I think that's fair comment,' he said.

'You want to dismiss someone?' I asked.

'Yes,' said Martin.

'On suspicion,' said Luke.

'It may save trouble,' said Martin.

They were speaking of Sawbridge. I had heard nothing of Captain Smith's investigations for over a year. I had no idea whether Sawbridge was still suspected.

'Do you know anything I don't?' I said to Martin.

For once he replied directly to me, his eyes hard and with no give in them at all.

'Nothing,' he said.

All they knew was that, in the last few months, since his recovery, Sawbridge had spoken like a milk-and-water member of the Labour Party.

'What does it prove?' said Martin.

'All right, what does it prove?' said Luke. 'He might have gone underground. How do you know that I haven't, as far as that goes? How do I know that *you* haven't been for years – both of you? I expect we were all tempted, ten years ago.'

'This isn't getting us very far,' said Martin.

'Do you think you're getting us very far? You want me to get rid of my best radio-chemist – ' Luke said it with anger (his professional feeling had risen up, he was thinking of the project, of the delay that losing Sawbridge might mean), and then lowered his voice again. 'I don't pretend that as a chap he's much my cup of tea, but he's been in this thing with us, he's entitled to his rights.'

Luke was not a sentimental man. He did not mention that Sawbridge had taken his share of the risks, and had suffered for it.

'We've got to balance his rights against the danger,' said Martin without expression.

'You've not given one single piece of evidence that he's got anything to do with the leakage,' said Luke.

'I don't intend to. That's not the point.'

'What *is* the point?'

'I've made it clear enough before. I'm not prepared to say whether he is or is not connected with the leakage, or whether there's any danger that he ever will be. I'm saying something quite different and much simpler. For the purpose of anyone running Barford, the world has divided itself into two halves. Sawbridge belongs to the other. If we keep him at Barford, it is likely to do the place finite harm. And it may not be nice for you and me.'

'I've told you before, and I will tell you again,' said Luke, 'you're asking me to throw Sawbridge out because a lot of old women may see bogies. Well, I'm not prepared to do it, unless someone can give me a better reason than that. There's only one reason that I should be ready to listen to. That is, is he going to give anything away?'

We all knew that Martin was right in his analysis. The world had split in two, and men like us, who kept any loyalty to their past or their hopes, did not like it. Years before, people such as Luke or Francis Getliffe or I had sometimes faced the alternative – if you had to choose between a Hitler world or a communist world, which was it to be? We had had no doubt of the answer. It had seemed to us that the communists had done ill that good might come. We could not change all the shadows of those thoughts in an afternoon.

It had been different, of course, with men like Thomas Bevill and his friends, or many of my old colleagues at Cambridge and the Bar. Most of them, in their hearts, would have given the opposite answer: communism was the enemy absolute: incidentally, it said something for the patriotism of their class that, full of doubts about the German war, knowing what it meant for them, win or lose, they nevertheless fought it.

Now it was men like Luke and Francis Getliffe and me who felt the doubts, the scientists most of all. Often they were sick at heart, although despair was unnatural to them and they believed that the split in the world – the split which seemed to them the anti-hope – would not last for ever.

Martin said:

'I've explained to you, that doesn't begin to be the point.'

'For me,' Luke's voice became loud, 'it's the beginning and the end. Here's someone who, as far as you know, will never be any closer to a leakage than you or me. And you're saying we ought to find a bogus reason for putting him in the street – just because some old women might natter. I'm simply not playing that game. Nor would Lewis. If we have to start insuring ourselves like that, we might as well pack up.'

As he knew, my sympathies were on his side. It was he, not Martin, who had insisted on seeing me that night – because he wanted my support. But also he had asked for my advice as an official, and I had to give it. No prudent man could ignore Martin's case. True, the responsibility for security rested with Captain Smith and his service: true, also, that Martin's proposal to get rid of the man out of hand was indefensible. But the risks were as great as Martin said.

As I was advising Luke (I wanted him at the least to talk to the new Chairman), I watched them both and thought – yes, Martin's case was clear, he was showing his usual foresight, and yet there was another motive behind it. Luke was frowning, his head bent over the table; Martin was sitting slightly back, his forehead unlined, more controlled, more like an official, than the other two of us that night. He seemed remote from any sign or memory of the conflict in my office, only three weeks before. But, though he was remote, I believed I could see his motive.

As the hushed voices, his and Luke's and mine, whispered and hissed under the beams, I saw him for a moment with the insight of kinship: I thought I knew what he was aiming at. If I were right, I did not like it.

We had talked for a long time, when Luke pushed the table away. He had just repeated that he would not budge unless someone gave him new evidence; this was the finish.

'I'm damned if I get rid of Sawbridge,' he said, and his force was formidable.

Martin replied, unmoved:

'In that case I shall send you my views on paper.'

'Damn it, man,' for the third time Luke forgot to be quiet, 'we've talked it out, I don't want any bumf.'

Martin said:

'I'm sorry, but I want to have it on the record.'

CHAPTER 30

A Joyous Moment in the Fog

THAT autumn it was strange to hear the scientists alone, trying to examine their consciences, and then round a committee table.

Outsiders thought them complacent, opaque: of those that I knew best, it was not true.

'There aren't any easy solutions,' said Luke. 'Otherwise we should all take them.'

He was speaking first of scientists, but also of all others in a time of violence; for the only root-and-branch 'solutions' which could give a man an absolute reason for not working at Barford on the bomb, were not open to many. Unqualified pacificism or Communism – if you believed either, your course was clear. But no other faith touched the problem. Among the new recruits to Barford, there were a number who were religious, but none of the churches gave them a direction.

Either/or, said Luke. Either you retired and helped to leave your country defenceless. Or you made a weapon which might burn men, women, and children in tens of thousands. What was a man to do?

'I don't think we've got any option,' said Francis Getliffe to me in the club, one night after his return from America. 'Luke's right, the Barford boys are right, we've got to make the infernal thing.'

After these conversations, I saw the same men in their places on the committees, experienced in business after six years of war, many of them, including Getliffe himself and Martin, having become skilful at the committee arts, disposing of great budgets, all caught up, without so much as a stumble of reservation, on getting the plutonium made at Barford. No body of men could have sounded less introspective; as their new Chairman said, with the jubilation of a housemaster who sees the second eleven at the nets, they were the *keenest* committee he had ever had.

The new Chairman was – to the irritation of his own friends and the Government backbenchers – old Thomas Bevill. In those first months of office, the Government had a habit of resurrecting figures from early in the war. Bevill was an ex-Minister, a Tory, but atomic energy had started under him; now it was in the limelight, he might soften criticism; so he was brought out of retirement like an old man of the tribe. On his side, he havered about taking a job under a Labour administration, but he was by this time seventy-six, they would be in for five years, he might never get another job and he just could not resist it.

At his first committee he slipped unobtrusively, happily into the chair, as though in literal truth, not in his own inexorable cliché, he was 'glad to be back in the saddle'. He gazed round the table and greeted each man by name. No one was less effusive by nature, but he always felt that effusiveness was called for on such occasions, and so he called out 'Dr Getliffe! old friend!' and so on clockwise round the table. 'Mr Drawbell! old friend!' 'Dr Luke! old friend!' and finally round to me, at his right hand: 'Our secretary, Mr Eliot! old friend!'

Mounteney, sitting near me, was disgusted. One might have asked why he was there at all, after his disappearance from Barford, never to return. Actually, Mounteney's self-exile from atomic energy had lasted exactly two months. He remained in his professorship, but accepted a seat on the committee. He was so austere that no one dared to ask why. Duty? Yes. The desire that real scientists should have a voice? No doubt. But for myself, I believed that his chief motive was the same as Bevill's, whom he so much despised – that he could not bear to be out of things.

So, in the autumn of 1945, Bevill was listening to the scientists, hearing Mounteney's minority opinion, trotting round the corner to the Treasury with Rose. It was on one of his committee afternoons, the technical sub-committee which I did not attend, that Irene came up with Martin for the day. On this committee Martin had a place as well as Luke, and as I took Irene out through the Park, in the foggy afternoon, to tea, I pointed up to a window whose lights streamed out into the whirling white.

'There they are,' I said.

'Busy as beavers,' said Irene.

She was smiling with a tenderness unusual in her. Perhaps she felt the safety we all snuggle in, when someone about whom we worry is for a couple of hours securely locked away. Certainly she was gratified that he was up there, in the lighted room, among the power-ful. Had her prediction – 'I should like to know what you expect from him now' – been nothing more than hitting out at random? She had not seen him that night at Stratford; she showed no concern for what he might be planning.

Although she had been behind him in his outburst, had quarrelled with me so bitterly that we had not been reconciled till that afternoon, she nevertheless, with a superb inconsistency, had blotted all that out and now simmered with content because he was 'getting on'.

But her smile, tender, coming from within, held more than that.

'I love the fog, don't you?' she said. She said a little more: and I realized that this scene of subfusc grandeur, the back of Whitehall with window lights tumbling out in the fog of St James's Park, at first lay heavy on her mind, as though there were a name she had forgotten and yet was lurking near her tongue, and then suddenly lifted, to let rise a memory not so grand but full of mellowing joy: another foggy afternoon years before, a street in Bayswater, the high shabby genteel houses, the joy of a childhood autumn.

Under a lamp in the Mall, I looked at her, and thought I had never seen her face so happy. Her youth was going, she still had her dash, she still looked a strapping, reckless woman – and on her mouth was a tender, expectant, astonished smile. I wonder if she had smiled so before she began her adventures. I wondered if she had come to the end of them, if she were what she called 'settled down'?

How would she take it, when that end came? I had not yet seen a woman, or a man either, who had lived a life of sexual adventure, give it up without a bitter pang that the last door had clanged to. Nevertheless, I had a suspicion that she might struggle less than most. I did not believe that she was, in the elemental sense, passionate. There were many reasons which sent people off on their sexual travels, and sheer passion was one of the less common. If you were searching for a woman moved by passion, you would be more likely to find her in someone like Mary Pearson, who had not been to bed with a man except her husband. Of these two, it was not Mary Pearson, it was Irene, who had racketed so long, it was she who would in the long run, and not unwillingly, give way to age and put her feet up with a sigh.

If that day came, I wondered – walking through the fog, taking her to tea as a sign that there was peace between us – whether she and I would at last cease to grate on each other? Was that walk through the Park a foretaste? I had not noticed her restlessness, she spoke as though she trusted me, remembering in the sight of the lighted window a spate of joy which seemed, as such joys of memory seem to us all, like the intimation of a better life from which we have been inexplicably cut off.

CHAPTER 31

Situation Designed for a Clear Head

On New Year's Eve, just as the Whitehall lamps were coming out, Bevill sent for me. The room which had been found for him as chairman was at the end of the passage, and even more unpretentious than his room as Minister; Bevill did not grumble, he had never in his life grumbled at a minor slight, he settled there and called it his 'hutch'. But that afternoon, as soon as I entered, I saw his face heavily flushed, with an angry blood pressure flush that one did not often see in so spare a man, the relics of grey hair twisted over his head so that he looked like a ferocious cockatoo.

Rose was sitting with him, arms folded, unaffected except that the pouches under his eyes seemed darker.

'This is a nasty one,' Rose was saying. 'Yes, it is a distinctly nasty one.'

'The swine,' said Thomas Bevill.

'Well, sir,' said Rose, 'it means some publicity that we could do without, but we can cope with that.'

'It knocks the feet from under you, that's what it does,' said Bevill.

In the war, whatever the news was like, he had been eupeptic, sturdily hopeful – not once rattled as he was that afternoon.

He turned to me, his eyes fierce, bewildered.

'Captain Hook's just been in,' he said.

'Captain Hook' was his name – partly one of his nursery jokes, partly for secrecy's sake – for Smith, the retired naval captain, the chief of the security branch. 'One of your scientists has been giving us away to the Russians. A chap who's just come back from Canada. They're going to put him inside soon, but it's locking the stable door after the horse is lost.'

I asked who it was.

'I didn't get the name. *One of your Cambridge men*.' Bevill said it accusingly, as though I were responsible for them all.

Rose told me that it was a man who had at no time been employed at Barford.

'That isn't the half of it,' said Bevill. 'There's another of them at

least who they're waiting for. *They oughtn't to have to wait,*' he burst
out. 'We're too soft, any other country in the world would have
risked a bit of injustice! Sometimes I think we shall go under just
because we put too high a price on justice. I tell you that, Rose,
though I don't want it to go outside this room.' He said to me: 'This
chap's still knocking about at Barford now. He's a young chap called
Sawbridge. Do you know him?'

'A little,' I said.

'Is he English?' said Bevill.

'As English as I am,' I said.

The blood was still heavy in Bevill's temples, as he shook his
head.

'I can't understand it.'

He shook his head again. 'I don't want to set up as better than anyone else, and I can understand most things at a pinch. I expect we've
all thought of murder, haven't we?' said the old man, who as a rule
looked so mild. He went on, forgetting his nursery prattle, and
speaking like a Hanoverian. 'As for rape and' – he listed the vices of
the flesh – 'anyone could do them.'

Hector Rose said, surprisingly: 'We're none of us spotless.'

'But as for giving away your country, I can't understand it,' said
Bevill. 'I could have done the other things, but I couldn't have done
that.

'I don't want to put the clock back,' he said. 'But if it were in my
hands, I should hang them. I should hang them in Trafalgar Square.'

At Barford next day, Bevill himself sat in with Captain Smith as
he broke the news to the leading scientists one by one. He interviewed
them, not in Drawbell's office, but his secretary's, sitting on typing
stools among the hooded typewriters and dictaphones; sometimes I
was called in to hear the same half-explanations, the same half-
questions.

It was only Drawbell, sitting alone with me during the morning,
who let out a spontaneous cry. This was the first day of 1946, which
in Drawbell's private calendar marked the last stage of the plutonium
process, with luck the last year of plain Mr Drawbell. He had to com-
plain to somebody, and he cried out:

'This isn't the kind of New Year's gift I bargained for!'

And then again:

'This isn't the time to drop bricks. They couldn't have picked a worse time to drop bricks!'

When I heard Smith talking to scientist after scientist, the monotony, the strain, seemed to resonate with each other, so that the light in the little room became dazzling on the eyes.

To the seniors, Smith had to tell more than he liked. In his creaking, faded, vicarage voice, he said that his 'people' knew that Sawbridge had passed information on.

'How do you know?' said one of them.

'Steady on, old son,' said Captain Smith. He would not explain, but said that beyond doubt they knew.

They also knew which information had 'gone over'.

Another of the scientists speculated on how much time that data would save the Russians. Not long, he thought; a few months at the most.

Bevill could not contain himself. He burst out:

'If our people are killed by their bomb, it will be this man's doing.'

The scientist contradicted him, astonished that laymen should not realize how little scientific secrets were worth. He and Bevill could not understand each other.

Bevill did not have to put on his indignation; it was not just the kind of politician's horror which sounded as though it had been learnt by heart. He was speaking as he had done yesterday, and as I was to hear others speak, not only among the old ruling classes, but among the humble and obscure for years to come. Bevill had not been shocked by the dropping of the bomb; but this was a blow to the viscera.

Whereas, as they heard the first news of the spies, the scientists were unhappy, but unhappy in a different tone from Bevill's. They had been appalled by Hiroshima, still more by Nagasaki, and, sitting in that typist's office, I thought that some at least had got beyond being appalled any more. They were shocked; confused; angry that this news would put them all back in the dark. They felt trapped.

To two of them, Smith, for reasons I did not know, said that one arrest, of the man who had been working in Canada, would happen within days. There had been at least three scientific spies, whom most of the men Smith interviewed that day had known as friendly acquaintances.

For once even Luke was at a loss. Smith seemed to be wasting his time. He had come for two purposes, first to satisfy himself about some of the scientists whom we knew least, and second, to get help in proving his case against Sawbridge. But all he discovered were men shocked, bewildered, sullen.

There was one man, however, who was not shocked nor bewildered nor sullen. It was Martin. His mind was cool, he heard the news as though he had foreseen it and made his calculations. I did not need to look at him, as Smith brought out his elaborate piece of partial explanation. I had expected Martin to see it as his time to act.

Smith asked to have a 'confab' with him and Luke together, since Sawbridge was working directly under them. As they sat on the secretary's desk, he told them, speaking frankly but as though giving an impersonation of frankness, that Sawbridge's was the most thorough piece of spying so far. The difficulty was, to bring it out against him. Smith's conclusive evidence could not be produced. The only way was to break him down.

'You've tried?' said Luke.

'We should be remiss if we haven't,' said Smith, with his false smile.

'Without any result?'

'He's a tough one,' said Smith.

'What does he say?'

'He just denies it flat and laughs at us,' said Smith.

Bevill's voice and Luke's sounded soggy with exasperation, but not Martin's, as he asked:

'How long can he keep that up?'

His eyes met Smith's, but Luke disturbed them.

'Anyway,' Luke was saying, 'the first thing is to get this chap out of the laboratory before we shut up shop tonight.'

'I don't think that's right,' said Martin.

'What are you getting at, Eliot?' asked Bevill.

'I suggest that the sensible thing, sir,' said Martin, speaking both modestly and certainly, 'is to leave him exactly where he is.'

'With great respect,' Smith said to Luke, after a pause, 'I wonder if that isn't the wisest course?'

'I won't have him in my lab a day longer,' said Luke.

'He might get away with your latest stuff,' cried old Bevill.

Martin answered him quietly:

'That can be taken care of, sir.'

'If we move him,' Smith appeared to be thinking aloud, 'we've got to make some excuse, and if he isn't rattled he might require a very good excuse.'

'How in God's name can you expect us to work,' Luke shouted, 'with a man we can't talk in front of?'

'If we leave him where he is,' said Martin, without a sign of excitement, 'he would be under my eyes.'

He added:

'I should very much prefer it so.'

In the middle of the argument, the telephone rang on the far table. It was from Drawbell's personal assistant, the only person who could get through to us; she was asking to speak to me urgently. In a whisper, only four feet from old Bevill, I took the call.

'I'm sorry, Mr Eliot,' she said, 'but Hanna Puchwein is pressing me, she says that she must speak to you and your brother this afternoon. I said that I mightn't be able to find you.'

'That's right,' I said.

'I suppose you can't speak to her?'

'No,' I said with routine prudence.

'She said, if I couldn't get you, that I was to leave a message. She's most anxious. She told me to say it was urgent for her – for you and Dr Eliot (Martin) to see her before dinner tonight.'

I went back to my place, wrote down the message, put it in an envelope (it was curious how the fug of secrecy caught hold of one, how easy it was to feel like a criminal) and had it passed across the room to Martin. I watched him staring at the note, with his pen raised. Without his face changing, he wrote: 'No, not until we have discussed it with Smith M.'

Uncertain of himself as I had not seen him, Luke soon gave way. Sawbridge was to stay under observation, and we left Smith alone with Luke and Martin, making arrangements about how Sawbridge must be watched.

Although Martin and I had not once talked without reserve since the August afternoon, I was staying, as usual, in his house. So I waited for him in his laboratory, while he finished the interview with Captain Smith.

As I waited there alone, I could not help trying to catch a glimpse of Sawbridge. His state of jeopardy, of being in danger of hearing a captor's summons (next week? next month?), drew me with a degrading fascination of which I was ashamed.

It was the same with others, even with Smith, who should have been used to it. The sullen, pale face had only to come within sight – and it was hard to force one's glance away. It might have been a school through which there moved, catching eyes afraid, ashamed, desiring, a boy of superlative attraction. On the plane of reason, I detested our secret; yet I found myself scratching at it, coming back to it.

Waiting for Martin, I manufactured an excuse to pass through Sawbridge's laboratory, so that I could study him.

He knew his danger. Just like us who were watching him, he was apprehending when the time – the precise instant of time – would come. It seemed that at moments he was holding his breath, and he found himself taking care of ordinary involuntary physical acts. Instead of walking about the laboratory with his heavy, confident clatter, he went lightly and jaggedly, sometimes on tiptoe, like a man in trepidation by a sick bed. He had grown a moustache, fair against the large-pored skin. He was working on, taking his measurements, writing results in his stationery office notebook. He knew that we were watching. He knew all we knew. He was a brave man, and his opaque, sky-blue eyes looked back with contempt.

Martin, sooner than I counted on, found me there. He called Sawbridge: 'How is it coming out?'

'Eighty per cent reliable.'

'Pretty,' said Martin.

They looked at each other, and as Martin took me out he called goodnight.

CHAPTER 32

Distress out of Proportion

As soon as we reached Martin's laboratory, he switched on the light behind an opalescent screen. He apologized for keeping me, said that he wanted to have a look at a spectroscopic plate; he stood there, fixing the negative on to the bright screen, peering down at the regiments of lines.

I believed his work was an excuse. He did not intend to talk about his action that day. I was out of proportion distressed.

Though nothing had been admitted, we both took it for granted that there was a break between us; but it was not that in itself which weighed on me. Reserve, separation, the withdrawal of intimacy – the relation of brothers, which is at the same time tough and not over-blown, can stand them all. And yet that night, as we did not speak, as he stood over the luminous screen, I was heavy-hearted. The reason did not seem sufficient; I disliked what he planned to do about Sawbridge; but I could not have explained why I minded so much.

I had had no doubt what he intended, from that night at Stratford, when he put forward his case in front of Luke. He had foreseen the danger about Sawbridge: he had also foreseen how to turn it to his own use. It was clear to him, as in his place it might have been clear to me, that he could gain much from joining in the hunt.

It was cynical, but I could not lay that against him. It might be the cynicism of the rebound, for which I was at least in part responsible. His suggestion at Stratford had been unscrupulous, but it would have saved trouble now. And I could not lay it against him that now he wanted to put Sawbridge away. We had never talked of it, but we both had the patriotism, slightly shamefaced, more inhibited than Bevill's, of our kind and age.

We took it out in tart, tough-sounding sentiments, that as we had to live in this country, we might as well make it as safe as could be. In fact, when we heard of the spies, we were more shaken than we showed.

Concealing our sense of outrage, men like Martin and Francis Get-liffe and I said to each other, in the dry, analytic language of the day – none of us liked the situation in which we found ourselves, but in that situation all societies had their secrets – any society which permitted its secrets to be stolen was obsolescent – we could not let it happen.

But accepting that necessity was one thing, making a career of it another.

Yet was that enough to make me, watching him, so wretched?

Was it even enough that he was throwing other scruples away, of the kind that my friends and I valued more? Among ourselves, we tried to be kind and loyal. Whereas I had no doubt that Martin was planning to climb at Luke's expense, making the most out of the contrast between Luke's mistake of judgement over Sawbridge and Martin's own foresight. That day he had taken advantage of Luke's confusion, in front of Bevill. And Martin had a card or two still to play.

Was that enough reason for my distress?

Carefully Martin packed the photographic plate in the box, made a note on the outside, and turned to me. He apologized again for keeping me waiting; he was expecting a result from another laboratory in ten minutes, and then he would be ready to go.

We made some conversation with our thoughts elsewhere. Then, without a preliminary and also without awkwardness, he said:

'I'm sorry we had to brush Hanna off.'

I said yes.

'I'm sure it was wise,' said Martin.

'Is there any end to this business?'

'Not yet.'

He went on: 'Hanna will understand. She's a match for most of us.'

I glanced at him, his face lit from below by the shining screen. He was wearing a reflective, sarcastic smile. He said:

'Why don't you and I marry women like that?'

I caught his tone. My own marriage had been even more untranquil than his.

'Because we wanted a quiet life,' I said. It was the kind of irony that we could still share.

'Exactly,' said Martin.

We seemed close enough to speak. It was for me to take the first step if we were to be reconciled. I said:

'We look like being in an unpleasant situation soon.'

Martin said:

'Which one?'

I said:

'About Sawbridge.'

'Maybe,' said Martin.

I said:

'It would be a help to me if I knew what you were thinking.'

'How, quite?'

'These are times when one needs some help. So far as I'm concerned I need it very much.'

After a pause, Martin said:

'The trouble is, we're not likely to agree.'

Without roughness, he turned the appeal away. He began asking questions about the new flat into which I was just arranging to move.

CHAPTER 33

Wife and Husband

THE spring came, and Sawbridge remained at liberty. But the scientist about whom the warning came through on New Year's Eve had been arrested, had come up at the Old Bailey, pleaded guilty and been given ten years. His name, which Bevill had forgotten that day, made headlines in the newspapers.

Later, I realized that most of us on the inside hid from ourselves how loud the public clamour was. We knew that people were talking nonsense, were exaggerating out of all meaning the practical results; and so, just like other officials in the middle of a scandal, we shut our ears off from any remark we heard about it, in the train, at the club bar, in the theatre-foyer, as though we were deaf men who had conveniently switched off our hearing aid.

Myself, I went into court for the trial. Little was said there; for many people it was enough, as it had been for Bevill, to add to the gritty taste of fear.

Always quick off the mark, Hankins, in his profession the most businesslike of men, got in with the first article, which he called The Final Treason. It was a moving and eloquent piece, the voice of those who felt left over from their liberal youth, to whom the sweetness of life had ceased with the twenties, and now seemed to themselves to be existing in No Man's Land. For me, it had a feature of special interest. That was a single line in which he wrote, like many writers before him, a private message. He was signalling to Irene reminding her that she had not always lived among 'the new foreigners' – that is, the English scientists. For Hankins had come to think of them as a different race.

Soon after came news, drifting up from Barford to the committees, that Luke was ill. 'Poorly' was the first description I heard. No one seemed to know what the matter was – though some guessed it might be an after effect of his 'dose'. It did not sound serious; it did not immediately strike me that this put Martin in effective charge.

I thought so little of it that I did not write to inquire, until towards the end of March I was told by Francis Getliffe that Luke was on the 'certain' list for that year's elections to the Royal Society. I asked if I could congratulate him. Yes, said Francis, if it were kept between us. Luke himself already knew. So I sent a note, but for some days received no reply. At last a letter came, but it was written by Nora Luke. She said that Walter was not well, and not up to writing his thanks himself; if I could spare the time to come down some day, he would like to talk to me. If I did this, wrote Nora in a strong inflexible handwriting, she asked me to be sure to see her first. Then she could give me 'all the information'.

I went to Barford next morning, and found Nora in her laboratory office. On the door was a card on which the Indian ink gleamed jet bright: N. Luke, and underneath P.S.O., for Nora had, not long before, been promoted and was at that time the only woman at Barford of her rank.

As soon as I saw her, I said:

'This is serious, isn't it?'

'It may be,' said Nora Luke.

She added:

'He asked me to tell you. He knows what the doctors think.'

'What do they think?'

Sitting at her desk, with her hair in a bun, wearing rimless spectacles, her fawn sweater, her notebook in front of her, she looked as she must have done when she was a student, and she and Luke first met. Steadily she answered:

'The worst possibility is cancer of the bone.'

It was what he had feared, in his first attack.

'That may not happen,' Nora went on in a reasonable tone. 'It seems to depend on whether this flare up is caused by the gamma rays or whether it's races of plutonium that have stayed inside him and gone for the bone.'

'When will you know?'

'No one can give him any idea. They haven't any experience to go on. If this bout passes off, he won't have any guarantee that it's not going to return.'

I muttered something: then I inquired how many people knew.

'Most people here, I suppose,' said Nora. Suddenly she was curious: 'Why do you ask that?'

In my middle twenties, I also had been threatened with grave illness. I had tried to conceal it, because it might do me professional harm. Instead of telling Nora that, I just said how often I had seen people hide even the mention of cancer.

'He wouldn't have any patience with that,' said Nora. 'Nor should I. Even if the worst came to the worst' – she stared straight at me – 'the sooner everyone here knows the dangers the more they can save themselves.'

How open she was, just as Luke was himself! Sometimes their openness made the ruses, the secretiveness, of such as I seem shabby. Yet even so, learning from Nora about her husband's illness, I felt that she was too open, I was more embarrassed than if she could not get a word out, and so I was less use to her.

I asked where Luke was, and who was nursing him. In the establishment hospital as before, said Nora; Mrs Drawbell, also as before.

'She's better at it than I am,' said Nora.

She added, her light eyes right in the middle of her lenses, her glance not leaving mine:

'If he's knocked out for years, I suppose I shall have some practice.'

She went on: 'As a matter of fact, if I've got him lying on his back for keeps, I shall be grateful, as long as I've got him at all.'

She said it without a tear. She said it without varying her flat, sensible, methodical voice. Nevertheless, it made me realize how, even five minutes before, and always in the past, I had grossly misunderstood her. The last time Luke was ill, and she had left the ward, I had thought to myself that she was glad to escape, that like me she could not stand the sight of suffering. Nonsense: it was a carelessness I should not have committed about a wilder woman such as Irene; at forty I had fallen into the adolescent error of being deceived by the prosaic.

Actually Nora would have stayed chained to her husband's bedside, had it kept the breath of life in him a second longer. She had the total devotion – which did not need to be passionate, or even emotional – of one who began with no confidence in her charms, who scarcely dared think of her charms at all. Her self-esteem she invested in her mind which in fact she thought, quite mistakenly, was in her husband's class. But, in her heart, she was always incredulous that she had found a man for life. Rather than have him taken away she would accept any terms.

Illness, decay, breakdown – if only he suffered them in her care, then she was spared the intolerable deprivation of losing him. It was those total devotions which sprang from total diffidence that were the most possessive of all. Between having him as an abject invalid, and having him in his full manhood but apart from her, there would not have been the most infinitesimal flicker of a choice for Nora.

When I entered Luke's ward, the room was dark, rain was seeping down outside, he seemed asleep. As I crossed the floor, there was a rustle in the bed; he switched on the reading lamp and looked at me with a flushed, tousled face. The last patch of alopecia had gone, his hair was as thick as it used to be, the flush mimicked his old colour, but had a dead pallor behind it.

'I've heard the doctors' opinions,' I said, searching for some way of bringing out regret. To my amazement, Luke said:

'They don't know much. If only there hadn't been more interesting things to do, Lewis, I'd have liked to have a shot at medicine. I might have put some science into it.'

I could not tell whether he was braving it out – even when he went on:

'I shall be surprised if they're going to finish me off this time. I don't put the carcinoma theory higher than a twenty per cent chance.'

If that was his spirit, I could only play up. So I congratulated him again on the Royal Society election.

'Now that's the only bloody thing that really frightens me,' said Luke, with a grim, jaunty laugh. 'When the old men give you your ticket a year or two early, it makes you wonder whether they're hurrying to get in before the funeral.'

'I haven't heard any whispers of that,' I said.

'Are you lying?'

'No.' He had been elected on his second time up, while not yet thirty-five.

'That's a relief,' said Luke. 'I tell you, I shall believe that I'm done for when I see it.'

I thought, how easy he was to reassure.

'One thing about people trying to dispose of you like this,' said Luke, 'it gives you time to think.'

Half heartedly (I did not feel much like an argument) I asked what he had been thinking about.

'Oh, the way I've spent my life so far,' said Luke. 'And what I ought to do with the rest of it.'

He was not speaking with his old truculence.

'I couldn't help being a scientist, could I? It was what I was made for. If I had my time over again, I should do the same. But none of us are really going to be easy about that blasted bomb. It's the penalty for being born when we were – but whenever we have to look into the bloody mirror to shave, we shan't be a hundred per cent pleased with what we see there.'

He added:

'But what else could we do? You know the whole story, what else could chaps like me do?'

I mentioned that I had once heard Hector Rose say – Hector Rose, who stood for so much that Luke detested – that 'events may get too big for men'.

'Did he? Perhaps he's not such a stuffed shirt after all. Of course we've all thought events may be too big for us.'

He fell silent. Then he said:

'It may be so. *But we've got to act as though they're not.*'

He knew that I agreed.

'Curiously enough,' said Luke, 'it isn't so easy to lose hope for the world – if there's a chance that you're going to die pretty soon. The moment you feel these things aren't going to be your concern much longer, then you think how you could have made a difference.'

He said:

'When I get over this, I shall make a difference. And if I don't, I don't know who can.'

He was so natural that I teased him. I inserted the name of the younger Pitt, but Luke knew no history.

He went on:

'I've been lowering my sights, Lewis. I want to get us through the next twenty years without any of us dropping the bomb on each other. I think if we struggle on, day by day, centimetre by centimetre, we can just about do that. I've got to get the bomb produced, I've got to make the military understand what they can and cannot do with it, I shall have some fights on my hands, inside this place as well as outside, but I believe I can get away with it. Twenty years of peace would give us all a chance.'

He sat up against his pillows with a grin.

'It won't be good for my soul, will it?'

'Why not?'

It was nerve racking that he thought so much of the future.

'I like power too much, I'm just discovering that. I shall like it more, when I've got my way for the next few years.'

He broke off:

'No, it won't be good for my soul, but if I do something useful, if I can win us a breathing space, what the hell does it matter about my soul?'

He had not once inquired about Martin or referred to him, except perhaps (I was not sure) when he spoke of internal enemies.

He made an attempt to ask about my affairs, but, with the compulsion of illness, came back to himself. He said, in a quiet, curiously wistful voice:

'I once told you I had never had time for much fun. I wonder when I shall.'

A memory, not sharp, came back to me. Luke, younger than now, in the jauntiness of his health, grumbling outside a Barford window.

From his bed he frowned at me.

'When these people told me I might die,' he said, 'I cursed because I was thinking of all the things I hadn't done. If they happen to be right, which I don't believe, I tell you, I shall go out thinking of all the fun I've wasted. That's the one thought I can't bear.'

Just for an instant his courage left him. Once again, just as outside Drawbell's gate (the memory was sharper now) he was thinking of women, of how he was still longing to possess them, of how he felt cheated because his marriage had hemmed him in. His marriage had been a good one, he loved his children, he was getting near middle age; yet now he was craving for a woman, as though he were a virgin dying with the intolerable thought that he had missed the

182

supreme joy, the joy greater in imagination than any realized love could ever be, as though he were Keats cursing fate because he had not had Fanny Brawne.

In those that I had seen die, the bitterest thought was what they had left undone.

And, as a matter of truth, though it was not always an easy truth to take, I had observed what others had observed before – I could not recall of those who had known more than their share of the erotic life, one who, when the end came, did not think that his time had been tolerably well spent.

CHAPTER 34

Warm to the Touch

MARTIN was the last man to over-play his hand. The summer came, Sawbridge was still working in the plutonium laboratory, there was nothing new from Captain Smith. From Luke's ward there came ambiguous, and sometimes contradictory reports; some doctors thought that it was a false alarm. Whoever was right, Martin could count on months in control. The press kept up articles on traitors, and espionage, but Barford was having a respite out of the news.

In July, Martin let us know that the first laboratory extraction of plutonium metal was ready for test. Drawbell issued invitations to the committee, as though he were trying to imitate each detail of the fiasco with the pile. The day was fixed for the 16th July, and Bevill was looking forward to it like a child.

'I believe tomorrow is going to be what I should call a Red Letter Day,' he said earnestly, as soon as he met the scientists at Barford, as though he had invented the phrase. At dinner that night, where there came Drawbell, Martin, Francis Getliffe, Mounteney, Hector Rose, Nora Luke, ten more Barford scientists and committee members, he made a long speech retracing the history of the project from what he called the 'good old days', a speech sentimental, nostalgic, full of nursery images, in which with the utmost sincerity he paid tribute to everyone's good intentions, including those people whom he regarded as twisters and blackguards.

As we were standing about after dinner, Martin touched my arm. He took me to the edge of the crowd and whispered:

'There's no need to worry about tomorrow.'

Looking at him, I saw his mouth correct, his eyes secretive and merry. I did not need an explanation. In estrangement, it was still possible to read each other's feelings; he had just considered mine with a kind of formal courtesy, as he would not have needed to consider a friend's.

I was not staying with him that night, but he asked me to escape from the party for a quarter of an hour. We went inside the establishment wire, and walked quickly along the sludgy paths.

In an empty room of the hot laboratory, he found me a set of rubber clothes, cloak, cowl, gloves, and goloshes, and put on his own. He took me down a passage marked DANGER. 'Never mind that,' said Martin. He unlocked a steel door which gave into a slit of a room, empty except for what looked like a meat-safe. Martin twiddled the combination, opened the panel, and took out a floppy bag made of some yellowish substance, rather smaller than a woman's shopping basket. As he held the bag, one corner was weighed down, as though by a small heavy object, it might have been a lead pellet.

'That's plutonium,' said Martin.

'How much?'

'Not much. I suppose it's worth a few hundred thousand pounds.'

He looked at the bag with a possessive, and almost sensual glance. I had seen collectors look like that.

'Touch it,' he said.

I put two fingers on the bag – and astonishingly was taken into an irrelevant bliss.

Under the bag's surface, the metal was hot to the touch – and, yes, pushing under memories, I had it, I knew why I was happy. It brought back the moment, the grass and earth hot under my hand, when Martin and Irene told me she was going to have a child; so, like Irene in the Park under the fog-wrapped lights, I had been made a present of a Proustian moment, and the touch of the metal, whose heat might otherwise have seemed sinister, levitated me to the forgotten happiness of a joyous summer night.

For once, Martin was taken unawares. He was disconcerted to see me, with my fingers on the bag, lost in an absent-minded content.

'Are you all right?' he asked.

'Quite,' I said.

Next day, the demonstration was conducted as though Martin and his staff did not know whether it would work.

At the end, however, Martin would not accept the congratulations, insisting that they were due to Luke, and he took Bevill and the others to Luke's bedside.

Hector Rose and I followed behind.

'Are you going with them, Eliot?' said Rose.

I was surprised by the constraint in his voice.

'I think we'd better,' I said.

'As a matter of fact, I think I'll just take a stroll round the place,' he said.

It was so impolite, so unlike him that I did not begin to understand. Although I accompanied him, I could get no hint of the reason. Later I picked it up, and it turned out to be simple, though to me unexpected. Hector Rose happened to feel a morbid horror of cancer; he tried to avoid so much as hearing the name of the disease.

By ourselves, in Drawbell's office, he was for him relaxed, having extricated himself from an ordeal; he let fall what Bevill would have called one or two straws in the wind, about the future management at Barford. He and Bevill wanted to get it on a business footing: Drawbell was dead out of favour. If they made a change of superintendent, and if Luke were well, it would be difficult to sidetrack him – but none of the officials, and few of the elderly scientists, relished the idea. He had made mistakes: he talked too loud and too much: he was not their man.

Already they trusted Martin more. He was younger, he was not in the Royal Society, to give him the full job was not practical politics; but, if Luke's health stayed uncertain, was there any device by which they could give Martin an acting command of Barford?

The luck was playing into Martin's hand. I knew that he was ready, just as he had been ready since that night in the Stratford pub, to make the most of it. Even when he paid his tribute to Luke he had a double motive, he had one eye on his own future.

It was true that he was fair-minded, more so than most men. He would not receive more credit than he had earned. Better than anyone, he could estimate Luke's share in the project, and he wanted it made clear.

But although what he said of Luke was truthful, he also knew that men required it. Men liked fairness: it was part of the amenities, if in Bevill's and Rose's world you wanted your own way.

Now Martin was coming to his last move but one.

To Drawbell's room, Bevill and he and Drawbell himself returned from the sickbed. Mounteney and Getliffe accompanied them. Martin wanted those two on his side as well as the officials. If the opportunity did not arrive without forcing it, he was ready to wait. In fact, it came when Bevill asked about Luke's health.

'Is that poor chap,' said Bevill, 'going to get back into harness?'

'I hope so,' said Martin. 'The doctors seem to think so.'

'We just don't know,' said Drawbell.

'He may never come back, you mean?' said Bevill.

'I believe he will,' said Martin, once more speaking out deliberately on Luke's behalf.

'Well,' said Bevill to Drawbell, 'I suppose Eliot will carry on?'

'He's been doing it for months,' said Drawbell. 'I always tell my team no one is indispensable. If any of you go there's always a better man behind you!'

'I suppose you *can* carry on, Eliot, my lad?' said Bevill to Martin in a jollying tone.

At last Martin saw his opening.

Instead of giving a junior's yes, he stared down at his hand, and then, after a pause, suddenly looked straight at Bevill with sharp, frowning eyes.

'There is a difficulty,' he said. 'I don't know whether this is the time to raise it.'

Drawbell bobbed and smiled. Now that the young man had grown up, he was having to struggle for his say.

'I don't see the difficulty,' said Bevill. 'You've been doing splendidly, why, you've been delivering the goods.'

'It would ease my mind,' said Martin, 'if I could explain a little what I mean.'

Bevill said, 'That's what we're here for.'

Martin said: 'Well, sir, anyone who is asked to take responsibliity for this project is taking responsibility for a good deal more. I think it may be unreasonable to ask him, if he can't persuade his colleagues that we're shutting our eyes to trouble.'

Bevill said: 'The water is getting a bit deep for me.'

Martin asked a question:

'Does anyone believe we can leave the Sawbridge question where it is?'

'I see,' said Bevill.

In fact, the old man had seen minutes before. He was playing stupid to help Martin on.

'I am sorry to press this,' said Martin, 'but I couldn't let myself be responsible for another Sawbridge.'

'God forbid,' said Bevill.

'Is there any evidence of another?' said Getliffe.

'None that I know of,' said Martin. He was speaking as though determined not to over-state his case. 'But if we can't touch this man, it seems to me not impossible that we should have someone follow suit before we're through.'

'It's not impossible.' Francis Getliffe had to give him the point.

'It's not exactly our fault that we haven't touched your present colleague,' said Rose.

'I have a view on that,' said Martin quietly.

'We want to hear,' said Bevill, still keeping the court for Martin.

'Everything I say here is privileged?'

'Within these four walls,' the old man replied.

'I think there's a chance that Sawbridge can be broken down,' said Martin.

'Captain Hook has tried long enough.'

'That's true,' said Martin, 'but I think there's a chance.'

'How do you see it happening?'

'It could only be done by someone who knows him.'

'Who?'

'I'm ready to try,' said Martin.

Martin, in the same tone, went on to state his terms. If Sawbridge stayed at large in the project, it was not reasonable to ask Martin, feeling as he did, to take the responsibility. If he were to take it, he needed sanction to join Captain Smith and try to settle 'the Sawbridge question' for good and all.

Bevill was enthusiastically in favour; Rose thought it a fair proposal.

'We want two things,' said Rose. 'The first is safety, and the second is as little publicity as we can humanly manage. We should be eternally grateful, my dear Eliot,' (he was speaking to Martin) 'if only you could keep us out of the papers.'

'That won't be possible,' said Martin.

'You mean, there'll be another trial?' said Getliffe.

'It's necessary,' said Martin.

Martin had counted on support from Bevill and Rose; he had also set himself to get acquiescence from the scientists. Suddenly he got more than acquiescence, he got wholehearted support where one would have looked for it last. It came from Mounteney. It happened that Mounteney possessed, as well as his scientific ideals, a passionate sense of a man's pledged word. He forgot about national secrecy (which he loathed) and communism (which in principle he approved of) in his horror that a man like Sawbridge could sign the undertaking of secrecy and then break it. In his pure unpadded integrity Mounteney saw nothing but the monstrosity of breaking one's oath, and, like Thomas Bevill whom he resembled in no other conceivable fashion, he cried out: 'I should shoot them! The sooner we shoot them the better!'

In that instant I understood at last the mystery of Mounteney's surrender before the bomb was dropped, the reason his protest fizzled out.

It was Francis Getliffe who took longest to come round.

'I should have thought it was enough,' he said, 'for you to give Smith all the information you can. I don't see why you should get involved further than that.'

'I'm afraid that I must,' said Martin patiently.

'There are a great many disadvantages, and no advantages to put against them, in scientists becoming mixed up in police work, even now.'

'From a long-term view, I think that's right,' said Martin.

'Good work,' said Francis Getliffe.

'But,' said Martin, 'there are times when one can't think of the long-term, and I suggest this is one.'

'Why?'

'Because otherwise no one will make this man confess.'

'It isn't proved that you can make the difference.'

'No,' Martin replied. 'I may fail. But I suggest that is not a reason for stopping me.'

At last Francis shook his head, unwittingly assenting, and said:

'We've gone so far, someone was bound to go the whole distance.'

He, who carried so much authority, sounded for once indecisive: as though the things he and others had been forced to do had prepared the way for younger, harder men.

Then Martin put in his last word that afternoon:

'I think, before we settle it, that I ought to mention Luke and I have not been in complete agreement on this problem.'

'That's appreciated,' said Hector Rose.

Martin spoke as fairly, as firmly, as when he had been giving the credit to Luke.

'I proposed easing Sawbridge out last summer,' he remarked. 'I felt sufficiently strongly about it to put it on the file.'

'I take it,' asked Rose, 'that Luke resisted?'

'It's no use crying over spilt milk,' said Bevill. 'Now you put us straight.'

CHAPTER 35

The Brilliance of Suspicion

THE day after Martin's piece of persuasion I did what, at any previous time, I should not have thought twice about. Now I did it deliberately. It was a little thing: I invited Kurt Puchwein to dinner.

As a result, I was snubbed. I received by return a letter in Puchwein's flowing Teutonic script:

'My friend, that is what I should have called you when Roy Calvert brought us together ten years ago. I realize that in volunteering to be seen with me again you were taking a risk: I am unwilling to be the source of risk to anyone while there is a shred of friendship left. In the life that you and your colleagues are now leading, it is too dangerous to have friends.'

The letter ended:

'You can do one last thing for me which I hope is neither dangerous for yourself, nor, like your invitation, misplaced charity. Please, if you should see Hanna, put in a word for me. The divorce is going through, but there is still time for her to come back.'

Within a few hours Hanna herself rang up, as though by a complete coincidence, for so far as I knew she had not been near her husband for months. It was the same message as at Barford on New Year's Day – could she speak to me urgently? I hesitated; caution, suspiciousness, nagged at me – and resentment of my brother. I had to tell myself that, if I could not afford to behave openly, few men could.

In my new flat Hanna sat on the sofa, the sun, on the summer evening still high over Hyde Park, falling across her but leaving her from the shoulders up in shadow. Dazzled, I could still see her eyes snapping, as angrily she asked me:

'Won't you stop Martin doing this beastly job?'

I would not begin on those terms.

'It's shabby! It's rotten!' Her face was crumbled with rage.

'Look, Hanna,' I said, 'you'd better tell me how it affects you.'

'You ought to stop him out of decency.'

Without replying, I asked about a rumour which I had picked up at Barford: for years Hanna's name had been linked with that of Rudd, Martin's first chief. Martin, who knew him well, was sure that she had picked wrong. She was looking for someone to master her; she thought she had found it in Rudd, who to his subordinates was a bully; yet with a woman he would be dependent. I asked, did she intend to marry him?

'Yes,' said Hanna.

'I was afraid so,' I said.

'You have never liked him.'

'That isn't true.'

'Martin has never forgiven him.'

'I wouldn't mind about that,' I said, 'if he were right for you.'

'Why isn't he right for me?'

'You still think you'd like some support?'

'Oh, God, yes!'

'You had to bolster up Kurt for years, and now you're going to do the same again.'

'Somehow I can make it work,' she said, with an obstinate toss of her head.

She was set on it: it was useless, and unkind, to say more.

'That is,' she said, 'if Martin will let me marry him without doing him harm.'

'What do you mean?'

'I mean that it may be fatal to anyone at Barford to have a wife with my particular record.'

She seemed to be trying to say: 'I want this man. It's my last chance. Let me have him.' But she was extraordinarily inhibited about speaking from the heart. Both she and Irene, whom the wives at Barford envied for their sophistication, could have taken lessons from a good many of those wives in the direct emotional appeal. Anger, Hanna could express without self-consciousness, but not much else.

I asked if Rudd knew of her political past. Yes, she said. I told her (it was the only reassurance I could give her) that I had not heard her name in any discussion at Barford.

'Whose names have you heard?'

I told her no more than she already knew.

'Why don't you drag Martin out of the whole wretched business?'

I did not reply.

'I suppose he has decided that persecution is a paying line.'

Again I did not reply.

'If you will forgive a Jew for saying so,' she said with a bitter grin, 'it seems rather like St Paul going in the opposite direction.'

She went on:

'Does Martin know that he has been converted the wrong way round?'

Just then the rays of the sun, which had declined to the tops of the trees, began streaming into her eyes, and I drew the curtains across the furthest window. As I glanced at her, her face was open and bleached, as many faces are in anger, grief, pain.

She cried:

'Is there no way of shifting him?'

Then she said:

'Do you know, Lewis, I could have had him once.'

It might be true, I was thinking. When he had been at his unhappiest over Irene, in the first year at Barford – then perhaps Hanna could have taken him away. She threw back her neat small head, with a look that seemed most of all *surprised*. She said something more; she had considered him for herself, but turned him down because she had not thought him strong enough. Intelligent but lacking insight, with a strong will that had so long searched for a stronger, she had never been able to help under-rating the men she met, especially those of whom she got fond. It came to her with consternation, almost with shame, that, now her will had come up in earnest against Martin's, she, who in the past had thought him pliable, did not stand a chance. She was outraged by his behaviour, and yet in her anger and surprise she wished that when they first met she had seen him with these fresh eyes.

She made another attack on me.

'He cannot like what he is doing,' she said. 'It cannot be good for him.'

She turned full on me, when I was sitting near the window with my back to the sunlight.

'I always thought you were more heavyweight than he was – but that he was the finer man.'

Making her last attempt, she was using that oblique form of flattery, which delights a father by telling him how stupid he is compared to his son. But for once it had no effect. I had no room for any thoughts but two.

The first was, the time would have to come when Martin and I faced each other.

The second – it was so sharp that it dulled even the prospect of a final quarrel – was nothing but suspicion, the sharp-edged, pieces-fitting-together, unreal suspicion of one plumped in the room where a crime had taken place. How did Hanna know so much of Martin's actions? What was she after? How close was she really to Puchwein nowadays? Was their separation a blind?

In that brilliance of suspicion, one lost one's judgement altogether. Everything seemed as probable, as improbable, as anything else. It seemed conceivable, that afternoon, that Hanna had lived years of her life in a moment by moment masquerade, more complete than any I had heard of. If one had to live close to official secrets (or, what sounded different but produced the same effect, to a crime of violence) one knew what it must be like to be a paranoiac. The beautiful detective-story spider-web of suspicion, the facts of everyday clearer-edged than they have ever been, no glue of sense to stick them in their place.

That evening, each action of Puchwein's and Hanna's for years past, stood out with a double interpretation – on one hand, the plunging about of wilful human beings, on the other, the master cover of spies. The residue of sense pulled me down to earth, and yet, the suspicions rearranged themselves – silly, ingenious, unrealistic, exciting, feelingless.

CHAPTER 36

A Cartoon-like Resemblance

THE same evening that Hanna visited me, Martin was talking to Captain Smith. Sawbridge was called by telephone some hours later, and 'invited to a conference', which was Smith's expression, on the following day. Smith rang me up also; he wanted me there for the first morning (he assumed that the interrogation would go on for days) in order to retrace once more the facts of how Sawbridge first entered Barford.

In past interrogations Smith had questioned Sawbridge time and again about his movements, for those days and hours when Smith was certain (though he could not prove it in a court) that Sawbridge had walked down a street in Birmingham, watched for a man carrying two evening papers, exchanged a word, given over his information; and this, or something close to it, had happened not once but three times, and possibly four.

In the morning we waited for him. Smith had borrowed a room in an annexe outside New Scotland Yard, behind Whitehall on the side opposite my offices. The room smelt of paint, and contained a table, half a dozen shiny pitch-pine chairs, a small desk where a shorthand writer could sit; the walls were bare, except for a band of hat pegs and a map of Italy. I did not know why, but it brought back the vestry of the church where my mother used to go, holding her own through the bankruptcy, still attending parish meetings and committees for sales-of-work.

Smith walked about the room, with his actor's stride; he was wearing a new elegant suit. Most of the conversation, as we waited, was made by an old acquaintance of mine, a man called Maxwell, whom I had known when I practised at the Common Law Bar. He had just become a detective inspector in the Special Branch. He was both fat and muscular, beautifully poised on small, strong, high-arched feet. His eyes, which were hot and inquisitive, looked from Martin to me. We were both quiet, and apart from a good-morning had not spoken to each other.

To Smith, Martin talked in a matter-of-fact tone, as though this were just another morning. His face was composed, but I thought I noted, running up from eyebrow to temple, a line which had not fixed itself before.

Sawbridge was brought in. He had expected to see Smith but not the rest of us; he stared at Martin; he did not show any fear, but a touch of perplexity, as though this was a social occasion, and he did not know the etiquette.

The smell of paint seemed stronger. I felt the nerves plucking in my elbows.

'Hallo, old son,' said Smith in his creaking voice.

'Are you all right?' Sawbridge responded. It was the greeting that Martin and I used to hear on midland cricket grounds.

'Let's get round the table, shall we?' said Smith.

We sat down, Smith between Sawbridge and Martin. He shot from one to the other his switched-on, transfiguring smile.

'You two knew each other before ever you went to Cambridge, didn't you?'

Sharply Martin said:

'Oh yes, we peed up against the same wall.'

It might have been another man speaking. I had not heard him false-hearty before; and, as a rule, no one knew better how to wait. Just then, I knew for certain the effort he was making.

In fact, the phrase was intended to recall our old headmaster, who used it as his ultimate statement of social equality. Sawbridge took it at its face value, and grinned.

'I thought,' said Captain Smith, 'that it mightn't be a bad idea to have another yarn.'

'What's the point of it?'

'Perhaps we shall see the point of it, shan't we?'

Sawbridge shrugged his shoulders, but Martin held his eye, and began:

'You knew about how the Canadian stuff was given away?'

'No more than you do.'

'We're interested in one or two details.'

'I've got nothing to say about that.'

'You knew — ' (the man convicted that spring), 'didn't you?'

'No more than you did.'

'Your ring was independent of that one, was it?'

I could hear that Martin's opening had been worked out. He was master of himself again, at the same time acute and ready to sit talking for days. To my surprise Sawbridge was willing, though he made his flat denials, to go on answering back. If I had been advising him (I thought, as though I were a professional lawyer again), I should have said: At all costs, keep your mouth shut. But Sawbridge did not mind telling his story.

On the other side there was no pretence that anyone thought him innocent. As in most investigations, Smith kept on assuming that Sawbridge had done it, that it was only necessary for him to admit the facts that Smith produced.

Smith talked to him like an old friend going over anecdotes familiar to them both and well liked. 'That was the time you took the drawings . . .' '. . . but you had met — before, hadn't you?' . . . Smith, trying to understand his opponent, had come to have a liking for him – the only one of us to do so.

Even that morning, Smith was fascinated by the discovery he kept making afresh – that, at the identical time when (as Smith repeated, without getting tired of it) Sawbridge was carrying secrets of the Barford project to a contact man, he was nevertheless deeply concerned for its success. He had worked night and day for it; few scientists had been more devoted and whole-hearted in their science; such scientific ability as he had, he had put into the common task.

I remembered the night of Luke's fiasco; it did not matter personally to Sawbridge, and he was not a man who displayed much emotion; but it was he who had been crying.

Smith shook his head, half gratified, as when one sees a friend repeat an inexplicable oddity; but to Martin it did not seem an oddity at all. Science had its own imperatives; if you were working on a problem, you could not help but crave for it to 'come out'. If you could be of use yourself, it was unnatural not to. It was not Sawbridge alone, but most of the scientific spies who had their own share, sometimes a modestly distinguished share, in producing results which soon after (like Sawbridge, walking to a commonplace street corner, looking for a man with a daily paper) they, as spies, stole away.

All this Martin understood much better than I did. Watching him and Sawbridge facing each other across the table, I could hear them speaking the same language. The two young men stared at each other without expression, with the faces of men who had learned, more deeply than their seniors, to give nothing away. They did not even show dislike. At that moment, there was a cartoon-like resemblance between them, both fair, both blue-eyed: but Sawbridge's face was heavier than Martin's and his eyes glaucous instead of bright. Of the two, though at twenty-nine he was three years younger, he looked – although for the first time his expression was bitten into with anxiety – the more unalterable.

Martin's eyes did not leave him. He could understand much that to me was alien; to do so, one had to be both a scientist and young. Even a man like Francis Getliffe was set back by the hopes of his youth – whereas Martin by an effort seemed able to throw those hopes away, and accept secrets, spying, the persistence of the scientific drive, the closed mind, the two world-sides, persecution, as facts of life. How long had it been since he made such an effort? I thought, watching him without sympathy, though once or twice with a pulse of kinship. Was it his hardest?

CHAPTER 37

The Lonely Men

I LEFT the room at midday, and saw no more of him for several days, although I knew that he was going on with the interrogation. Irene did not know even that, nor why he was staying so long in London. One afternoon, while Martin was sitting with Captain Smith and Sawbridge in the paint-smelling room, she had tea with me and asked about him, but casually, without anxiety.

In fact, she showed both enjoyment at his rise to fame, and also that sparkle of ridicule and incredulity which lurks in some high-spirited wives when their men come off. It was much the same incredulity as when she told me that 'E.H.' (Hankins) was at last on the edge of getting married.

'Caught!' she said. 'Of course the old boy can still slip out of it. But he's getting on, perhaps he's giving up the unequal struggle.'

Her unrest was past and buried, she was saying – but even so she was not as amused as she sounded. I was thinking that she, to whom marriage had sometimes not seemed so much of a confining bond, regarded it in her old lover with the same finality as her mother might have done. Like most of us, she was more voracious than she admitted to herself; even if he had been a trivial capture, the news of his marriage would have cost her a wrench. As for Hankins – though I listened to the squeal of glee with which she laughed at him, within weeks of being domesticated at last – I felt that she was half thinking – 'If I wanted, I should still have time to break it up!'

Although she did not know it, I read that night, as on each night for a week past, what her husband was doing. Evening by evening Captain Smith walked along from the room to my office with the verbatim report of what he called 'the day's proceedings'. Those reports had the curious sodden flatness which I had come to recognize years ago at the Bar in conversation taken down word by word. Most of the speeches were repetitive, bumbling, broken-backed. The edge was taken off Martin's tongue, and the others sounded maundering. There was also, as in all investigations I had been anywhere near, very little in the way of intellectual interchange. Martin and Sawbridge were men trained in abstract thought, and Martin could use the dialectic as well as Sawbridge; but in practice neither of them found this the time to do so.

Over ninety per cent of all those words, day by day for more than a week already, were matter-of-fact. Captain Smith's organization was certain, from the sources they could not reveal, that Sawbridge had walked down a named street on a named day, and passed over papers. Ninety per cent, probably ninety-five per cent, of the records consisted of questions and answers upon actions as prosaic as that.

Out of the first day's transcript I read nothing but details. 'You were in Birmingham, at the corner of Corporation Street and High Street, on October 17th, '43?' (that was only a few months after Sawbridge arrived at Barford). Flat negatives – but one or two were broken down by ordinary police facts. Who could remember the events of an afternoon three years ago, anyway? Why not be vague?

Sawbridge denied being in Birmingham on any day that month: then he fumbled: Maxwell produced a carbon copy of a receipt (dated not October 17th but October 22nd) given him by a Birmingham bookshop.

The next impression, of the later days of the first week, was that Martin was taking more and more of the examination. It looked as though Smith and the Special Branch between them had run out of facts, certainly of producible facts. Was Sawbridge experienced enough to guess it? Or did he expect there was evidence to come?

From the first, Martin's questions were more intimate than the others. He took it for granted that, as soon as Sawbridge knew that Barford was trying to make the fission bomb, he did not feel much doubt about how to act.

E. (Martin). Did you in fact know what Barford was set up for before you arrived?

SA. (in the record, this symbol was used throughout to distinguish Sawbridge from Smith). No.

E. Hadn't you thought about it? (i.e. the bomb).

SA. I read the papers, but I thought it was too far off.

E. When did you change your mind?

SA. As soon as I was appointed there and heard about the background.

E. Then you believed it would happen?

SA. Of course I did, just like you all did.

E. That is, you believed this country or America would have the bomb within 3–4 years?

SA. We all did.

E. And you thought of the effect on politics?

SA. I'm not sure what you mean by politics.

E. You thought of the possibility that the West would have the bomb, and the Soviet Union wouldn't?

(Despite Sawbridge's last remark, Martin was using 'politics' in a communist sense, just as he steadily referred to the Soviet Union, as though out of politeness to the other man.)

SA. I thought if we'd seen that the thing might work then the Soviet physicists must have done the same.

E. But you didn't know?

SA. What do you take them for? Do you think you're all that better than they are?

E. No, but there are more of us. Anyway, you'd have felt safer if they knew what we were doing?

SA. I thought it was wrong to keep secrets from allies, if that's what you mean.

E. The Soviet Union wouldn't be safe until someone told them?

SA. I didn't say that.

E. But you thought it might be your duty to make certain?

SA. I thought it was the Government's duty.

E. You knew that wouldn't happen. You knew that the Soviet Union might be more at a disadvantage than they've been since the civil war?

SA. I didn't think they'd be far behind.

E. But they would be behind. They had to be kept up to date – even if none of them was able to extend to us a similar courtesy?

(That was the only sarcasm of Martin's that came through the record.)

SA. They weren't in the same position.

E. You were thinking all this within a month of getting to Barford, weren't you? Or it didn't take as long as a month?

SA. There wasn't much difficulty about the analysis.

E. You talked to a contact straight away, then?

SA. No.

All through that exchange, Martin assumed that in origin Sawbridge's choice had been simple. To introduce national terms, or words like treachery, was making things difficult for yourself, not for Sawbridge. He did not think of the Soviet Union as a nation, opposed to other nations; his duty to it over-rode all others, or rather included all others. It was by doing his duty to the Soviet Union that he would, in the long run, be doing his duty to the people round him. There was no conflict there; and those who, preoccupied with their own conflicts, transposed them to Sawbridge, could not make sense of the labyrinths they themselves invented in him. It was Martin's strength that he invented none: from the start, he treated Sawbridge as a man simple and tough, someone quite unlike a figure out of Amiel or Kierkegaard, much more like Thomas Bevill in reverse.

In fact, Martin assumed Sawbridge did not think twice about his duty until he acted on it. Then he felt, not doubt, but the strain of any man alone with his danger – walking the streets of Birmingham under the autumn sun, the red brick gleaming, the Victorian gothic, the shop fronts – so similar to the streets of the town twenty miles away, where both he and Martin had waited at other street corners. The cosy, commonplace, ugly street – the faces indifferent, the busy footsteps – no one isolated or in any danger, except one man alone, looking out for an evening paper, the homely evening paper which, not many years ago, he would have bought for the football results. That was the loneliness of action, the extreme loneliness of a man who was cutting himself off from his kind.

From Martin's questions, he understood that too, as pitilessly he kept on, waiting for an admission.

What had sent Sawbridge on those walks, cut off from the others safe on the busy street? I could not find a satisfactory answer. Nearly everyone found him dislikeable, but in a dull, unspecific fashion. His virtues were the more unglamorous ones – reliability, abstinence, honesty in private relations. In some respects he resembled my *bête noire*, Pearson, and like Pearson he was a man of unusual courage. He possessed also a capacity for faith and at the same instant for rancour.

No doubt it was the rancour which made him a dynamist. Compare him, for example, with Puchwein, whose communism sprang from a magnanimous root – who was vain, impatient, wanted to be benevolent in a hurry. And, just as with many Romans who turned to Christianity in the fourth century, Puchwein wanted to be on the side of history. He had no question intellectually that, in the long run, the communists must win. But those motives were not so compelling as to drive him into danger; to go into action as Sawbridge did, benevolence was not enough.

Then what was? The hidden wound, people said: the wound from which he never took the bandages and which gave him his sullen temper, his rancour. None of us knew him well enough to reach it.

Did Martin see the wound clearer than I did? Did he feel any resemblance to himself?

If so, he shut it away. Behaviour matters, not motive – doing what he was doing, he could have no other thought.

The visits to Birmingham, the autumn transaction (giving the news that the pile was being built), the three visits in the spring, one just before Sawbridge had accompanied Luke into the hot laboratory: on each visit, what data had he given over?

Denial, denial again.

Martin increased the strain.

He knew, via Captain Smith, the information that had passed. He knew, which no one else but Luke could, that one piece of that information was false; while waiting for the rods to cool, they had decided on which solvent to use for the plutonium – and then, a good deal later, had changed their minds. It was the first method which had been told to the agent; only Luke, Sawbridge, and Martin could know the exact circumstances in which it had been decided on, and also given up.

Martin asked Sawbridge about those decisions. For the first and only time in the investigation, Martin gained an advantage through being on the inside. So far as I could judge, he used his technical familiarity with his usual deliberate nerve; but that was not the major weight with which he was wearing Sawbridge down.

The major weight came from his use of Sawbridge's loneliness, and his sense of how it was growing as the days dripped by. Against it Martin brought down, not only his bits of technical knowledge, not only the facts of the meetings at the Corporation Street corner – but also all the opinions of Barford, every sign that men working there were willing to dismiss Sawbridge from their minds, so that he should feel separate even from those among whom he had been most at home.

No one knew better than Martin how even the hardest suffer the agoraphobia of being finally alone.

On the seventh day, the record ran:

E. I suppose you have got your notebooks about the work at Barford?
SA. Yes.
E. We shall want them.
SA. I shall want them if I go back.
E. Do you think you will go back?
SA. I hope you realize what it will mean to Barford if I do not.
E. You might have thought of that before.
SA. I thought of it more than you have given me credit for.
E. After you made the first contact with —.
SA. I have not admitted that.
E. After you made the first contact, or before?
SA. I thought of it all along.

For those seven nights running Captain Smith brought the record into my office. He made excuses to stay with me as I read; it looked like a refinement of security, but afterwards he liked to go out with me for a drink, taking his time about it. I discovered that he had a valetudinarian wife, for whom, without letting out a complaint, he had sacrificed his pleasure ever since he was a young man; but even he was not above stealing a pretext for half an hour away from her.

On the eighth night, which was Thursday, September 23rd, he came into my office hand on hip, and, as he gave me the typescript, said:

'Now we shan't be long.'

'What?'

'Our friend is beginning to crack.'

'Is it definite?'

'Once they begin to crack, they never take hold of themselves again.'

He said it in his parsonical tone, without any trace of elation.

I felt – visceral pity; a complex of satisfactions: anxiety that the time was near (I neither wanted to nor could have done it while the issue was not settled) when I must speak to Martin.

'How long will he get?' I asked.

'About the same as the other one.'

He stared at me.

'Ten years, there or thereabouts,' he went on. 'It's a long time for a young man.'

I nodded.

'We've got to do it,' he said, in exactly the same neutral creaking tone. He had not spoken of Sawbridge's sentence with sentimentality, but as a matter of fact; but also I had not heard him condemn Sawbridge. Smith had more moral taste than most persons connected with crime and punishment; the country had a right to guard itself, to make sure that men like Sawbridge were caught; but, in his view, it had no right to insult them.

The next night, the Friday, Smith was late arriving at my office. When he did so, fingering the rolled-up record as though it were a flute, he said:

'Our friend is going to make a complete statement on Monday morning.'

CHAPTER 38

Words in the Open

SMITH decided that we ought to take the news at once to Bevill and Rose. I followed him down the corridor to Rose's room, where, as Smith began a preamble about having a 'confab', I glanced out of the window into the dark and muggy twilight, with the lights already shining (although it was only half past six on a September evening) from windows in Birdcage Walk.

Bland behind his desk, Rose was bringing Smith to the point, but, as he did so, there was a familiar step outside, a step brisk and active, which did not sound like an old man pretending to be young – and Bevill came in, with a flushed happy look. He left the door open, and in a moment Martin entered.

'This is good news for us all,' said Bevill.

With one question, aside to me, Rose grasped what news they brought.

'It's jolly good work,' said Bevill.

'I suppose, in the circumstances, it *is* the best solution,' said Rose, and added, with his customary coolness: 'Of course, it will mean a good many awkward questions.'

'I hope this will encourage the others,' said Bevill.

'There mustn't be any more,' said Martin, speaking for the first time since he came in.

Bevill, who had been congratulating Smith, turned to Martin.

'You needn't think we don't know how much we've got to thank *you* for.' The old man beamed at him.

Martin shook his head.

Rose said: 'It's been a real contribution, and we're very grateful. Many, many congratulations.'

'What I like,' said Bevill, 'is that you've done it without any fuss. Some of your chaps make such a fuss whatever they do, and that's just what we wanted to avoid. I call you a public benefactor.' Bevill was rosy with content.

The party broke up, Smith leaving first. As Martin and I walked away down the corridor, not speaking, I heard the brisk step behind us.

'Just a word,' said Bevill, but waited until we reached my room. 'This is a clever brother you've got, Lewis,' said the old man paternally. 'Look, I want to stand you both a dinner. Let's go to my little club. I didn't ask friend Rose up the passage, because I knew he wouldn't want to come.'

It was completely untrue, and Bevill knew it; Rose would have loved to be taken to Pratt's. But Bevill still refused to introduce his Whitehall acquaintances there. In his heart, though he could get on with all men, he did not like them, especially Rose. It was a fluke that he happened to like me, and now Martin.

The evening was sultry, and it was like a greenhouse in the club kitchen, where the fire blazed in the open grate. The little parlour was empty, when we had dinner at the common table off the check tablecloth, but one or two men were drinking in the kitchen.

That night, as on other occasions when I had watched him there, Bevill was unbuttoned; he stopped being an unobtrusive democrat the instant he passed the porter in the hall. His well-being was so bubbling that I could not resist it, though I had resolved to speak to Martin before the end of the night. Nevertheless, that seemed far away; and I felt light-hearted.

Bevill shouted to his friends through the parlour door. He was too natural to assume that Martin would know them by their Christian names, or alternatively would not be curious about the company he was in. Accordingly, Bevill enunciated a couple of the famous English titles: Martin attended to him. Looking at them, sharing some of the old man's euphoria (the evening was still early), I thought of the young Proust.

Unlike the young Proust, Martin was drinking pints of bitter. He appeared to be enjoying himself without reserve, without any sign of the journey that had brought him there.

Bevill, who still had a taste for a night's drinking, was having our tankards filled before we went on to port. For a time, while we sat alone round the table, he became elated with drink and could not resist a bit of philosophy.

'What do all our concerns matter, you two, when you put them in their proper place? They're just phenomena, taking place in time – what I call false time – and everything essential exists in a different and more wonderful world, doesn't it, right outside of space and time? That's what you ought to think of, Martin, when you're worried about fellows like Sawbridge, or your project. All our real lives happen out of time.'

'That isn't to say,' he said, coming down to earth, 'that it won't be nice when you people at Barford give us a good big bang.'

'Fine words butter no parsnips,' went on Bevill gravely, waving a finger at Martin, who in fact had not spoken. 'You chaps have got to deliver the goods.'

'That's bound to happen. It's cut and dried, and nothing can stop it now,' said Martin.

'I'm glad to hear you say so.' Bevill looked from Martin to me. 'You know, you chaps have got something on your hands.'

'What do you mean?' I said.

'It's not so easy pulling this old country through as it was when I was your age. If chaps like you don't take over pretty soon, it's not a very bright look-out.'

Martin and I both replied to him direct, not talking across to each other. But we agreed. Obviously the major power, which he had known, had gone: the country would have to live by its wits: it could be done: better men had known worse fates.

Bevill gave a cherubic, approving nod.

'You two ought to know, I shouldn't call myself a socialist,' he said, as though making an astonishing but necessary revelation, 'but I don't care all that much what these fellows (the government) do, as long as we keep going.'

It was spoken in drink, but it happened to be true. Half drunk myself, I loved him for it.

Cheerful, naïf (one could forget that he was a cunning old intriguer), he rambled on 'philosophizing' again to his heart's content, until in the kitchen, with sweat pouring down his face and mine, and beads at the roots of Martin's hair, he said:

'I want to say something, Martin, before I get beyond it.'

He said it in a different tone, sharp and businesslike.

Perhaps Martin did not know what I did – that when it came to action, it did not matter what state Bevill was in, or what nonsense he had been talking. On serious matters, like jobs or promises, he would not say a word out of turn or one he did not mean.

Martin listened as though he knew it too.

'You're sitting pretty at Barford, young man,' said Bevill.

'I suppose I am,' said Martin.

'I'm telling you, *you are*. We shan't forget what you've done for us, and it's time we did something for you.'

Bevill went on:

'There are different views on how to run the place – and who's to do it, I needn't tell you that. But I can tell you that whatever arrangement we make, it won't be to your disadvantage. You can just sit back and wait and see.'

'I didn't expect this,' said Martin.

'Didn't you? You must have been working things out,' said Bevill. I thought once more, that in such matters he was no man's fool. He continued: 'Now you can forget everything that I've told you. But a nod's as good as a wink to a blind horse.'

Few men who have longed for success can have known the exact minute when it came; but Martin must have known it, sitting at the side of the baking hearth at Pratt's, with the old man lifting his glass of port, and someone from the foot of the staircase calling out 'Tommy', so that Bevill, flushed, still businesslike, said to Martin, 'That's tipped you the wink,' and turned his head and began talking loudly to his acquaintance at the door.

I looked at Martin, leaning back while Bevill talked across him. One side of his face was tinged by the fire: his mouth was tucked in, in a sarcastic smile: his eyes were lit up.

I wished that the party would stretch on. Anyway, why should I ask him anything? It was not like me, or him either, to speak for the sake of speaking; as soon as one admitted out loud a break in the human relation, one made it wider.

I went on drinking, joining in Bevill's reminiscences of how he saved Barford years before. I told a story of my own which exaggerated Martin's influence and judgement at that time, giving him credit for remarks which Francis Getliffe made, or that I had made myself.

At last the old man said:

'Time for bye-byes!' We helped him up the stairs, found him a taxi, received triumphant good-byes, and watched as the rear lamp climbed the slope of St James's Street up to Piccadilly. Martin and I exchanged a smile, and I said something to the effect that the old man's ancestors must have gone up this street many times, often drunker than that.

'Occasionally soberer,' said Martin.

We looked across the road, where the lights of Boodle's shone on to the moist pavement. After the room we had left, the humid night was sweet. We stood together, and I thought for an instant that Martin expected me to speak.

'Well, then, good night,' he said, and began walking down the street towards the palace. He was staying in Chelsea; I hesitated, before turning in the opposite direction, on my way north of the park.

Martin had gone ten paces along the pavement. I called out:

'No, I want a word with you.'

He turned, not jerkily, and walked with slow steps back. He did not pretend to be puzzled, but said, with an expression open, concerned, as intimate as in the past:

'Don't you think it would be better not to?'

'It's too late for that.'

'I am sure that we shall both regret it.'

Mechanically, for no reason, we dawdled side by side along the pavement, while I waited to reply. We had gone past Brooks's before I said: 'I can't help it.'

It was true, though neither of us at that moment could have defined what drove us on. Yes, I was half sad because of what he had done; but there was hypocrisy in the sadness. In warm blood, listening to Bevill, I should not have repined because a brother had stamped down his finer feelings and done himself well out of it. Success did not come often enough to those one was fond of that one's responses could be so delicate.

It would have been pleasant to have been walking that night as allies, with his name made.

We were further from allies than we had ever been. I was bitter, the bitterness was too strong for me. As we walked by the club windows I could think of nothing else.

Nevertheless, the habits of the human bond stayed deeper than the words one spoke. I was not attempting – as I had attempted on New Year's Day – to end the difference between us. Yet the habit endured, and as I said 'I can't help it' under the St James's Street lights, I had a flash of realization that I was still longing for his success *even then*. And, looking into his face, less closed that it had been for months, I realized with the same certainty that he was still longing for my approval *even then*.

'I think you ought to leave it alone, now,' I said.

'How?'

'You ought to have nothing more to do with the Sawbridge affair.'

'I can't do that,' said Martin.

'It's given you all you expected from it.'

'What did I expect from it?'

'Credit,' I said.

'You think that's all?'

'You would never have done it if you hadn't seen your chance.'

'That may be true.' He was trying to be reasonable, to postpone the quarrel. 'But I think I should also say that I can see the logic of the situation, which others won't recognize. Including you.'

'I distrust seeing the logic of the situation,' I said, 'when it's very much to your own advantage.'

'Are you in a position to speak?'

'I've done bad things,' I said, 'but I don't think I could have done some of the things you've done.'

We were still speaking reasonably. I accepted the 'logic of the situation' about Sawbridge, I said. I asked a question to which I knew the answer: 'I take it the damage he's done is smaller than outsiders will believe?'

'Much smaller,' said Martin.

Led on by his moderation, I repeated:

'I think you should leave it alone now.'

'I don't agree,' said Martin.

'It can only do you harm.'

'What kind of harm?'

'You can't harden yourself by an act of will, and you'll suffer for it.'

On the instant, Martin's control broke down. He cried out: '*You* say that to me?'

Not even in childhood, perhaps because I was so much the older, had we let our tempers loose at each other. They were of the same kind, submerged, suppressed; we could not quarrel pleasurably with anyone, let alone with one another. In the disagreement which had cut us apart, we had not said a hard word. For us both, we knew what a quarrel cost. Now we were in it.

I brought out my sharpest accusation. Climbing on the Sawbridge case was bad enough – but climbing at Luke's expense, foreseeing the mistake that Luke's generous impulse led him into, taking tactical advantage both of that mistake and his illness – I might have done the rest, but if I had done that I could not have lived with myself.

'I never had much feeling for Luke,' he said.

'Then you're colder even than I thought you were.'

'I had an example to warn me off the opposite,' he said.

'You didn't need any warning.'

'I admit that you're a man of strong feeling,' he said. 'Of strong feeling for people, that is. I've had the example of how much harm that's done.'

We were standing still, facing each other, at the corner where the street ran into Piccadilly; for a second an association struck me, it brought back the corner of that other street to which Sawbridge walked in a provincial town. Our voices rose and fell; sometimes the bitterest remark was a whisper, often I heard his voice and mine echo back across the wide road. We shouted in the pain, in the special outrage of a family quarrel, so much an outrage because one is naked to oneself.

Instead of the stretch of Piccadilly, empty except for the last taxis, the traffic lights blinking as we shouted, I might have been plunged back into the pain of some forgotten disaster in the dark little 'front room' of our childhood, with the dying laburnum outside the windows. Pain, outrage, the special insight of those who wish to hurt and who know the nerve to touch. In the accusations we made against each other, there was the outrage of those bitter reproaches which, when we were at our darkest, we made against ourselves.

He said that I had forgotten how to act. He said that I understood the people round me, and in the process let them carry me along. I had wasted my promise. I had been too self-indulgent – friends, personal relations, I had spent myself over them and now it was all *no use*.

I said that he was so self-centred that no human being mattered to him – not a friend, not his wife, not even his son. He would sacrifice any one of them for his next move. He had been a failure so long that he had not a glimmer of warmth left.

There were lulls, when our voices fell quiet or silent, even one lull where for a moment we exchanged a commonplace remark. Without noticing it we made our way down the street again, near the corner where (less than half an hour before) Martin had said goodnight, in sight of the door out of which we had flanked old Thomas Bevill.

I said: What could he do with his job, after the means by which he had won it? Was he just going to look on human existence as a problem in logistics? He didn't have friends, but he had colleagues; was that going to be true of them all?

I said: In the long run he had no loyalty. In the long run he would turn on anyone above him. As I said those words, I knew they could not be revoked. For, in the flickering light of the quarrel, they exposed me as well as him. With a more painful anger than any I had heard that night, he asked me:

'Who have you expected me to be loyal to?'

I did not answer.

He cried: 'To you?'

I did not answer.

He said: 'You made it too difficult.'

He went on: I appeared to be unselfish, but what I wanted from anyone I was fond of was, in the last resort, my own self-glorification.

'Whether that's true or not,' I cried, 'I shouldn't have chosen for you the way you seemed so pleased with.'

'You never cared for a single moment whether I was pleased or not.'

'I have wanted a good deal for you,' I said.

'No,' he said. 'You have wanted a good deal for yourself.'

PART FIVE

TWO BROTHERS

CHAPTER 39

Technique Behind a High Reward

I DID not attend Sawbridge's trial. Like the others of the series, it was cut as short as English law permitted; Sawbridge said the single word 'Guilty', and the only person who expressed emotion was the judge, in giving him two years longer than Smith had forecast.

The papers were full of it. Hankins wrote two more articles. Bevill said: 'Now we can get back to the grindstone.' I had not spoken to Martin since the night in St James's Street, although I knew that several times he had walked down the corridor, on his way to private talks with Bevill.

It was the middle of October, and I had to arrange a programme of committees on the future of Barford. Outside the windows, after the wet summer the leaves were turning late. Rarely, a plane leaf floated down, in an autumnal air that was at the same time exhilarating and sad.

One morning, as I was consulting Rose, he said:

'Your brother has been colloguing with Bevill a little.'

'Yes,' I said.

'I wondered if you happened to know.' Rose was looking at me with what for him was a quizzical and mischievous glance.

'Know what?'

'My dear chap, it's all perfectly proper, nothing could possibly have been done more according to the rules. I rather reproach myself I hadn't started the ball rolling, but of course there was no conceivable chance of our forgetting you – '

'Forgetting me?' I said.

'I shouldn't have allowed that to happen, believe me, my dear Eliot.'

I said: 'I know nothing about this, whatever it is.'

'On these occasions,' Rose was almost coy, the first time I had seen him so, 'it's always better not to know too much.'

I had to persuade him that I knew nothing at all. For some time he was unusually obtuse, preferring to put it down to discretion or delicacy on my part. At last he half believed me. He said:

'Well, it's a matter of reckoning your deserts, my dear Eliot. The old gentleman is insisting – and I don't think there will be anyone to gainsay him – that it's high time you had a decoration.'

He paused, with a punctilious smile. 'The only real question is exactly what decoration we should go for.'

This was what Martin had been prompting the old man about. I was not touched.

It might have appeared a piece of kindness. But he was being kind to himself, not to me. It was the sort of kindness which, when there is a gash in a close relationship, one performs to ease one's conscience, to push any intimate responsibility away.

Meanwhile Martin's own reward was coming near. The committee sat in Rose's room, and on those autumn mornings of sun-through-mist, I went through the minutes that by this time I knew by heart. These men were fairer, and most of them a great deal abler, than the average: but you heard the same ripples below the words, as when any group of men chose anyone for any job. Put your ear to those meetings and you heard the intricate labyrinthine and unassuageable rapacity, even in the best of men, of the love of power. If you have heard it once – say, in electing the chairman of a tiny dramatic society, it does not matter where – you have heard it in colleges, in bishoprics, in ministries, in cabinets: men do not alter because the issues they decide are bigger scale.

The issues before Bevill and his committee were large enough, by the standards of this world. Barford: the production plant: a new whisper of what Bevill called the hydrogen bomb: many millions of pounds. 'The people who run this place are going to have plenty on their plate,' said Bevill. 'Sometimes I can't help wondering – is one Top Man enough? I'm not sure we ought to put it all under one hat.' Then they (Bevill, Rose, Getliffe, Mounteney, and three other scientists) got down to it. Drawbell must go.

'That can be done,' said Hector Rose, meaning that Drawbell would be slid into another job.

Next there was a proposal that Mounteney and another scientist did not like, but which would have gone straight through: it was that Francis Getliffe should go to Barford and also become what Bevill kept calling Top Man of atomic energy. It would have been a good appointment, but Francis did not want it; he hesitated; the more he dickered, the more desirable to the others the appointment seemed, but in the end he said No.

That left two possibilities: one, that Luke, who appeared to have partially recovered, though the doctors would not make a certain prognosis either way, should be given Barford, which he was known to want.

The other possibility had been privately 'ventilated' by Bevill and Rose ever since Rose mentioned it to me in the summer: assuming that there was a doubt about Luke, couldn't one set up a supervisory committee and then put M. F. Eliot in as acting superintendent?

They were too capable to have brought up this scheme in the committee room, unless they had found support outside. But Rose mentioned it – 'I'm just thinking aloud,' he said – on a shining autumn morning.

For once Francis Getliffe spoke too soon.

'I'm not happy about that idea,' he said immediately.

'This is just what we want to hear,' said Bevill.

'I know Luke has his faults.' said Francis, 'but he's a splendid scientist.'

Mounteney put in:

'Even if you're right about Luke – '

'You know I'm right,' said Getliffe, forgetting to be judicious, a vein swelling angrily in his forehead.

'He's *pretty* good,' said Mounteney, in the tone of one who is prepared to concede that Sir Isaac Newton had a modest talent, 'but there's no more real scientific thinking to be done at Barford now, it's just a question of making it run smooth.'

'That's a dangerous argument. It's always dangerous to be frightened of the first rate.'

I had seldom seen Francis so angry. He was putting the others off, and he tried to collect himself. 'I'm saying nothing against M. F. Eliot. He's a very shrewd and able man, and if you want a competent administrator I expect he's as good as they come.'

'Administrators, of course, being a very lowly form of life,' said Rose politely.

Francis flushed: somehow he, as a rule so effective in committee, could not put a foot right.

There was some technical argument among the scientists, taking up Mounteney's point: weren't the problems of Barford, from this time on, just engineering and administrative ones? Someone said that Martin, despite his calendar youth, was mentally the older of the two.

When we broke off for luncheon, Francis and I walked across the park together. For a time he strode on, in embarrassed silence, and then said:

'Lewis, I'm very sorry I had to come out against Martin.'

'Never mind,' I said.

'I couldn't have done anything else,' he said.

'I know that,' I said.

'Do you agree with me?'

By good luck, what I thought did not count. I said:

'He'd do better than you'd give him credit for.'

'But between him and Luke?'

'Luke,' I said.

Nevertheless, Francis had mishandled his case, and that afternoon and at the next meeting, it was Luke against whom opinion began to swell. Against Luke rather than for Martin, but in such a choice it was likely to be the antis who prevailed. They had, of course, a practical doubt, in Luke's state of health. I was thinking, if you wanted a job, don't be ill: for it had an almost superstitious effect, even on men as hard-headed as these; somehow, if you were ill, your *mana* was reduced.

'Is it in Luke's own best interests to ask him to take a strain like this?' someone said.

It was not a close thing. Getliffe, who was a stubborn man, kept the committee arguing through several meetings, but in truth they had made up their minds long before. He twisted some concessions out of them: yes, Luke was to become a chief adviser, with a seat on the supervisory committee: yes, Luke would get 'suitable recognition' when his turn came round (Sir Walter Luke: Sir Francis Getliffe: Sir Arthur Mounteney: in five years' time, those would be the styles).

But the others would not give way any further. It was time a new arrangement was drawn up, and Bevill and Rose undertook, as a matter of form, to get Martin's views.

On an afternoon in November, Martin came into Rose's room. Bevill did not waste any words on flummery.

'We've got a big job for you, young man,' he burst out.

Martin sat still, his glance not deflecting for an instant towards me, as Bevill explained the scheme.

'It's an honour,' said Martin. Neither his eyes nor mouth were smiling. He said: 'May I have a few days to think it over?'

'What do you want to think over?' said Bevill. But he and Rose were both used to men pulling every string to get a job and then deliberating whether they could take it.

'We should all be very, very delighted to see you installed there,' said Rose. Martin thanked him and said:

'If I could give an answer next week?'

CHAPTER 40

Visit to a Prisoner

THE day after Bevill offered Martin the appointment, Captain Smith came into my office and unravelled one of his Henry James-like invitations, which turned out to be, would I go with him to Wandsworth Gaol and have a chat to Sawbridge? I tried to get out of it, but Smith was persistent. He was sensitive enough to feel that I did not like it; but after all, I was an official, I had to live with official duty, just as he did himself.

In the taxi, he told me that he was clearing up a point about the Puchweins. It was worth 'having another try' at Sawbridge, who occasionally talked, not giving anything away, more for the sake of company than because he was softening. As we drove through the south London streets in the November sunshine, he told me more of Sawbridge. He had not recanted; others of the scientific spies gave up their communism in prison, but not Sawbridge. For a few days, sitting opposite to Martin, he had been 'rattled'. During that time he made his confession. He had blamed himself ever since.

'He's quite a lad, is our young friend. He doesn't make any bones about it,' said Smith with proprietorial pride, stiff on his seat while we rocked over the tram-lines, through the down-at-heel streets scurfy in the sun.

At the prison, Smith took me to an assistant-governor's room, which in his view gave a 'better atmosphere' for his talks with Saw-bridge. For myself, I should have preferred the dark and the wire screen. This room was bright, like a housemaster's study, with a fire in the grate, photographs of children on the desk, and on the walls Medici prints. The smell of tobacco rested in the bright air. Outside the grated window, the morning was brighter still.

When a warder brought Sawbridge in, he gave a smile as he saw Smith and me standing by the window, a smile not specially truculent but knowing, assertive, and at the same time candid. Above his prison suit his face looked no paler than in the past, and he seemed to have put on a little weight.

Smith had arranged for the warder to leave us alone. We heard him close the door, but there were no steps down the passage. Sawbridge, who was listening, cocked his thumb, as though at the warder waiting behind the door, and repeated his smile.

Smith smiled back. With me, with his colleagues, he was never quite at ease; but he was far less put off inside that room than I was.

'Here we are again,' he said.

'Yes,' said Sawbridge.

Smith made him take the easy chair by the fire, while Smith sat at the desk and I brought up a hard-backed chair.

'Have a gasper?' said Smith.

'I still don't smoke,' Sawbridge replied, with his curious rude substitute for humour.

Smith began inquiring into his welfare. Was he getting enough reading material? Would he like Smith to inquire if he could be allowed more?

'I don't mind if you do,' said Sawbridge.

Was he getting any scientific books?

'I could do with more. Thanks,' said Sawbridge.

Smith made a note; for once, Sawbridge was allowing himself to let slip a request.

Then Smith remarked that we had come down for a 'spot of talk'.

'What are you after?'

'We should like to have a spot of talk about Puchwein,' said Smith, surprisingly direct.

'I've not got anything to say about him.'

'You knew him and his wife, didn't you?'

'I knew them at Barford, like everybody else. I've not got anything to say.'

'Never mind about that, old man,' said Smith. 'Let's just talk round things a bit.'

As Smith foretold, Sawbridge was willing, and even mildly pleased, to chat. He had no objection to going over his story for yet another time. It occurred to me that he was simply lonely. He missed the company of his intellectual equals, and even talking to us was better than nothing. Methodically he went over the dates of his spying. As in each statement he had made, he would mention no name but his own: he had inculpated no one, and maintained all along that he was alone.

'People remember seeing you at Mrs Puchwein's,' said Smith.

'I shouldn't be surprised,' said Sawbridge.

'Don't you think you ought to be surprised?'

'I don't see why.'

'I can't think of anything obvious you've got in common.'

'Why should we have anything obvious in common?'

'Why were you there?'

'Social reasons.'

'Did you ever pay any other social calls of any kind?' Smith asked.

'Not that you'd know of.'

'Why were you there?'

'As far as that goes,' said Sawbridge, turning on me with his kind of stolid insolence,' why were *you*?'

Smith gave a hearty, creaking laugh. He went on questioning Sawbridge about Puchwein – where had he met him first?

'You soon found out that he was left wing?' said Smith.

'I tell you, I haven't anything to say about him.'

Smith persisted.

'When did you first hear that he was left wing?'

All of a sudden, Sawbridge broke into sullen anger.

'I shouldn't call him left wing.'

'What would you call him?' I said.

'He's no better,' said Sawbridge, 'than you are.'

His voice was louder, at the same time impersonal and rancorous, as he let fly at Francis Getliffe, Luke, me, all liberal-minded men. People who had sold out to the enemy: people who would topple over at the first whistle of danger, that was what he thought of liberal men.

'That chap Puchwein isn't any better than your brother,' said Sawbridge. Impersonally, he lumped Martin in with the rest of us, only different in that he was more effective. 'I'm not sure he isn't worse. All Puchwein knows is when it's time to sit on the fence.'

'I thought you'd nothing to tell us about him,' said Smith.

'Well, I've told you something, haven't I?' said Sawbridge. 'We've got no use for chaps like that.'

Back in a café in Westminster, Smith, sipping China tea with his masquerade of preciousness, went over Sawbridge's replies.

'We didn't get over much change out of our young friend,' he said.

'Very little,' I replied.

'No, I wouldn't say that, old son,' said Smith. But, as he argued, I was thinking of Sawbridge – and it was a proof of his spirit that, neither in his presence nor out of it, did I think of him with pity. Faith, hope, and hate: that was the troika which rushed him on: it was uncomfortable to remember that, for the point of action, hate was a virtue – but so also, which many of us were forgetting in those years, was hope.

Could one confront the Sawbridges without the same three forces? He was a man of almost flawless courage, moral and physical. Not many men would have bent as little. Then, against my will, for I was suppressing any comparison with Martin, I was teased by a thought in my brother's favour, the first for long enough. It was difficult to imagine him taking Sawbridge's risk; but, if he had had to pay Sawbridge's penalty, his courage would have been as stoical and his will as hard to crack.

CHAPTER 41

Lights Twinkling in the Cold

Two nights later (it was Sunday) I was walking up Wigmore Street towards Portman Square, hurrying because of the extreme cold. The weather had hardened, the lights twinkled frigidly across the square, I was paying attention to nothing except the minutes before I could get back to a warm room. There were few people in the square, and I did not notice the faces as I hurried past.

I did not notice the couple standing near the corner, in the half-shadow. Without knowing why, I looked over my shoulder. They were standing oblivious of the cold, the man's overcoat drooping open, flapping round his knees. They were Irene and Hankins.

At once I turned my head and started down the side-street, out of sight. A voice followed me, Irene's – 'What are you running away for?'

I had to go back. As they came towards me under the lamp, they both looked pinched, tired, smiling.

'Why haven't I seen you all these months?' said Hankins. We went into an hotel close by and sat drinking in the lounge, among the palms and the sucking noise from the revolving door.

Hankins was quieter than usual, and when he spoke the words seemed dredged up through other thoughts. We asked about each other's careers. He had just got a good job; he had made a reputation before, but now, for the first time in his life, he was free from worry about his next year's rent. I congratulated him, but his thoughts absented themselves again.

Soon he looked at Irene with an odd expression. His face, like that of many with a quickly changing inner life, was emotional but hard to read. 'I think I must be going now,' he said. Her eyes sharpened.

'Goodbye,' said Hankins, and the revolving door sucked round behind him, sucking empty air.

He had gone so quickly that they might have arranged to meet again, when I was disposed of.

Irene stared at me with full eyes.

'I had to see him,' she said. 'I couldn't sit down under things any longer.'

'What are you going to do?'

She did not reply, but continued to stare at me as though I knew. Just for a second, on her mouth there appeared a tart smile. She settled herself against the arm of her chair, and I noticed that her shoulders were getting rounder. In the last year she had thickened both in the throat and the upper arm. It was easy to imagine her in middle age, lolling in her dressing-gown.

'Fancy the old thing pulling in a regular salary at last,' she said.

'Both of them have done pretty well for themselves,' I replied.

She looked puzzled. I had to explain that 'both of them' meant Hankins and Martin, the two men who had meant most to her. They were coming to the top of their professions at the same time.

'The top?' she said.

'The head of Barford,' I replied.

'Oh.' She fixed me with a glance which seemed malicious, regretful, sympathetic.

'And as for Hankins,' I said, 'so far as there is anything left of literary London, this job will put him in the middle of it.'

'He'll dote on that!' she cried. Quietly she added:

'And so should I.'

She spoke straight out:

'It would suit me better than anything I have ever had with Martin, or anything that I could ever have.'

Once more she gave me a glance edged with fellow-feeling. Without explanation, with her expression malicious and ominous, she went on:

'I'm not cut out for it. I can see Martin going on patiently and getting a bit drier every year. What sort of life do you think that means for me?'

We looked at each other, without speaking for some moments. I said: 'But you're going to live it, aren't you?'

'You don't think I'm going off with E.H.?'

'No,' I said.

'I could stop his marriage. I could have everything I wanted ten years ago. Why shouldn't I now?'

'You won't,' I said.

'You're positive?' Suddenly she slumped down, her hand fell on her breast, her tone no longer brittle, but flat, lazily flat, as she said:

'You're right.'

She went on:

'I never knew where I was with E.H. I never even knew if he needed me. While Martin doesn't need me – he could get on without me or anyone else, but he wants me! He always has! I never had much faith that anyone would, until he came along.'

So at last, under the palm trees of that aseptic lounge, preoccupied by the suspicion, which she had provoked, of a crucial turn in Martin's life, I was given a glimpse of what bound Irene to him. In the past I had speculated often. Why should she, in the ultimate run, be anchored to Martin instead of Hankins? I had looked for qualities in Martin which could make some women love him, rather than another man. They were present, but they did not count.

It was true that Martin was the stronger: it was true also that Martin was, if these cant terms mean anything, the more masculine. Hankins was one of those men, and they are not uncommon, who invest much emotion in the pursuit of women without having the nature for it; he thought he was searching for the body's rapture, but his profoundest need was something less direct, the ambience of love, its meshes of unhappiness, its unfulfilled dreams, its tears for the past and its images of desire. Many women found it too delicate, but not Irene.

With her, there was a hypnotic charm about his capacity for feeling; he could feel as she did, he had the power to enter into, as all important, each emotion of love. It was that which she first loved in him, and which held her fascinated for years, her whom other women obtusely thought was searching only for a partner in bed. Against that emotional versatility Martin could not compete. Yet never once, if she had been faced with the choice, would she have left Martin.

The real reason which delivered her to Martin lay not in him, but in herself.

She had just told it to me, so simply that it was difficult to believe. In fact, Irene had suffered all her life from a diffidence which seemed at a first glance, the last one would expect in her. In her childhood, even more totally than with other girls, love and marriage filled her daydreams: those daydreams had not left her alone all her life; yet they had never been accompanied by the certainty of the fibres, that she had it in her to draw the love she coveted. More than most she studied herself in the looking-glass, but not with narcissistic pleasure; only with a mixture of contemptuous liking and nervousness that such a face, such a body, might never bring what she craved.

In the hotel lounge, hearing the revolving doors swing round, I thought of another woman so different from Irene that any resemblance seemed like a joke. Nora Luke, dowdy, professionally striving, in the home a scolding faithful housewife – Irene, once notorious for her love affairs, the most reckless of women – yet in secret they had found life difficult in the same manner. At the root of their nature they were sisters.

Irene had spoken simply, and maybe it was as simple as she said. Hankins, so tentative and undecided himself, she had never had the confidence to reach for; while Martin, all else forgotten, was the one man who wanted enough to stay with her at any cost, to give the assurance, so far as she was capable of accepting it, that he would stay steady, that he would be there to make her feel that she was as lovable as, her nerves twitching under the adventuress's skin, she had never since she was a child been able to believe.

That night, she had sent Hankins away. It was only after he had gone that I realized this was the end between them, that under the lamps of Portman Square they had spoken the last words. Hankins pushing round the door might have been leaving her for half an hour; in fact, they would not meet again: it was curious that he, at any other time so eloquent, had gone in silence.

Irene smiled at me, as though, sitting before her looking-glass, she was putting on her dashing face.

'He will have me on his hands,' she said. She was speaking of Martin.

She added:

'I shall be a drag on him in this new game.'

She was keeping me in the dark, she was obscurely triumphant.

'What are you telling me?' I asked.

'You knew, of course you knew, about this offer that Martin had last week?'

I said yes.

'You knew he expected it before it came?'

'He must have expected it for weeks.'

'I guessed as much.'

She went on, not knowing the break between Martin and me, but knowing something I did not. For days (it must have been during the first sittings of the Committee, and he might have had inside information, probably from Mounteney) he was excited that the job was coming his way. She said that he was lively, active, restless with high spirits; she remembered how he had talked to his son one evening, talked to the three-year-old-boy as though they were both adults and he was letting himself boast.

'Well, Lewis,' Martin had said to the child, 'now I'm going further than anyone in the family's ever gone. It will give you a good start. You'll be able to build on it, won't you?'

In the next few days Irene felt a change. She could not ask him; with her, in his own home, he let his moods run more than I had seen him, but she dared not to try to penetrate them. It was still several days before the offer was made. For the only time she could remember, Martin stayed away from the laboratory without a reason. The weather had turned foggy; he sat silent by the fire. He diid not ask her advice, but occasionally spoke of the advantages of beng the Barford superintendent, of the entertaining she could do there. Occasionally also he spoke of some disadvantages, as though laughing them off.

'He wouldn't talk about them,' Irene flared out. 'But I didn't need him to. I hadn't forgotten the letter he didn't send.'

One foggy afternoon, he suddenly said:

'The head of Barford is just as much part of the machine as any of the others.'

He went on:

'If I take the job, I shan't have the trouble of thinking for myself again.'

Irene said to me, simply and quietly:

'Then I knew that he would never take it.'

That had happened the previous Saturday, three days before the offer came. I asked how he had behaved when he actually had the offer in his hand.

'He was shaken,' said Irene. 'He was terribly shaken.'

With the fog outside the windows, he had sat by the fire so absent that he let it go out. Then she made it up, and I imagined the firelight reflected into the room from the fog-backed window. Martin only roused himself from that paralysis of the nerves to play again with the little boy – the two of them under the window, young Lewis shouting, Martin patiently rolling a ball, and still silent.

Both Irene and I, through our different kinds of knowledge of him, took it for granted that he would not alter his resolve.

'I don't pretend to understand it,' she said to me. 'Do you?'

I shook my head, and, as lost and open as she was, I asked:

'What do you think he intends to do?'

'I don't think, I know,' she replied.

During the past weeks, so as to be ready, he had been making inquiries, unknown to me, of our college. If he decided to give up his work at Barford and return to pure science, could they find a niche for him?

'It'll be funny for him, not having any power,' she said.

She added:

'He's going into dimness, isn't he? He won't make much of a go of it?'

She went on asking, what were his chances in pure science? Would he do enough to console himself?

'They all say he hasn't got quite the talent,' I replied. He would publish a few respectable papers, he would not get into the Royal Society. For a man as realistic as Martin, it would be failure.

'He's got a real talent for his present job,' I said.

'It'll be difficult for him to lead a dim life,' she said, 'having had a taste of something different.'

She said it in a matter-of-fact tone, without any sign of tenderness. I broke out:

'And I suppose you're glad about it?'

'What do you mean?'

'You wanted him to make his protest. I suppose this is the next best thing?'

Irene was flushing down the neckline of her dress. With difficult honesty she turned her eyes away, and said:

'No. I'm not cut out for this.'

'Why aren't you?'

'I'm a sprinter. I could have stood a major row, it would have been something to live through. I should have been more use to him than any of you.'

I said: 'I believe you would.'

She flashed out:

'It isn't often you pay me a compliment.'

'It was meant,' I said.

'But you mustn't give me too much credit. I'm not highminded. I shouldn't have worried if Martin had become the boss at Barford. I should have enjoyed the flah-flah.'

Then she asked:

'Why ever is he doing it? I wish you'd tell me that.'

I was confused.

'Do you think,' she said, 'he's just trying to be a good man?'

'I should like to believe it,' I said.

'You think he's got another motive, do you?'

'We usually have.'

To my astonishment, she burst out laughing, with her high-pitched yelps of glee.

'I believe you think,' she cried, 'that he's doing it to take it out of me. Just to show me that things have changed since he married me, and that he holds the whip hand now.'

It had not even crossed my mind.

'You're wrong!' she shouted. 'If he's reacting against anyone, it isn't me!'

Her eyes glinted triumphant, good natured, malicious at my expense. She said: 'You won't be able to influence him now, will you?'

CHAPTER 42

A Place to Stand?

MARTIN did not give his answer to Bevill until the last day of his period of grace. He called in my office first, just as he used to – but we were both constrained. On the window the frost, coming early that winter, masked the buses in Whitehall. Martin swept a pane with his sleeve, saying that after he had had the interview with Bevill and Rose, he would like to talk to me.

He assumed that I knew what his answer was going to be. When he actually delivered it, he spent (so I learned later) much skill in saving his supporters' credit. He did not once suggest a moral choice; he just used the pretext that, unless he did some real science soon, he never would; in which case his usefulness would be finished in ten years.

The scientists took the explanation at its face value. It was only Bevill who smelt that there was something wrong. In his experience men did not turn down good jobs unless by doing so they got a better. So he fell back on what was always his last resource, and put the blame on to Martin's wife.

Bevill and Rose had been too long at their craft not to recognize the inevitable; that morning, while Martin was on his way back to my office, they had already decided that now, well or ill, wild man or not, it had to be Luke. Rose's sense of justice made him insist that they could not even attempt to put Luke in leading strings, as they had Martin. Thus it was to be Luke in full power.

Meanwhile Martin had returned to my room. His gestures were relaxed, as though to light a cigarette were a pleasure to be taken slowly; yet we could not speak to each other with ease. With anyone else, I felt, he would be smiling with jubilation, with a trace of sadness too.

With me, he could not be so natural.

'That's settled,' he said.

He asked if he could waste the rest of the afternoon for me and I said:

'Of course.' I added, meaninglessly: 'Can you spare the time?'

'Very soon,' said Martin, with a sarcastic grin, 'I shall have plenty of time.'

For many minutes we sat there, looking down over Whitehall, saying nothing to the point, often falling into silence. It was not until we took a walk in the icy park that Martin made his first effort.

'I'm happy about this,' he said, as we trod along the path where, on the verges, each blade of grass stood out separated by the frost.

He added:

'It's a change from the last time.'

He meant the last time we had walked there, the day after the bomb had dropped. It had been sixteen months before. The leaves had been

226

thick then; now we looked past the bare trees, into the mist fuming above the leaden water.

'Since then,' said Martin, 'I haven't found a place to stand.'

He spoke slowly, as though with the phrase he recalled that afternoon when, in the Dolphin Square bathroom, he saw the scientific way ahead.

He went on: 'Up till now.'

In return I made my effort.

'I hope,' I said, 'that I haven't made it harder for you to find it.'

There seemed a long interval before Martin replied. Our steps rang in the frost. We were both evasive, reticent men, who used irony to cheat out of its importance the moment in which we breathed: each of us that afternoon had set ourselves to speak without easing the moment away. That was why we stumbled so.

'You can see too much in personal causes,' he said.

'They exist,' I said.

'Without them,' said Martin, 'I *think* I should have done the same.'

'I should like to be sure,' I said.

'Motives aren't as important to me as they are to you,' he said. 'I'm more concerned with what one does.'

'You have done some contradictory things,' I said.

'I can tell you this. That night we went to Pratt's – it hasn't affected me one way or the other. As far as I can answer for myself at all, I tell you that.'

He groped less when he spoke of his Sawbridge policy. He did not have to stumble; there we understood each other. We both knew the temptations of action, and how even clear-sighted men did not inquire what their left hand was doing. It was nonsense to think that Martin had been dissimulating all the time and that he had always intended to retire. Men were not clever enough to dissimulate for long.

He had, of course, been after the top job. Until quite recently he consciously intended to take it. For months he had been acting, as many men were acting on both sides of the great divide, out of the cynicism of self-preservation. Many men, delicate in their personal relations, had come to behave, and even to think, with that kind of cynicism, even though we concealed it from ourselves.

'Some of us have been too delicate about personal relations,' said

Martin, back in my office, sitting by the window in the murky afternoon. 'People matter; relations between them don't matter much.'

I stood looking out of the window, where the lights scintillated under a sky ochreous and full of snow.

'Lewis!' His voice was quiet; it was rare, when we were alone, for us to use each other's name.

'That night after old Bevill left you said some true things,' he said.

'You also,' I said.

'I am colder hearted than you are. I care much less for the people round me.'

'Why are you saying this?'

'If it weren't so, I couldn't have made this choice.'

For any of us who had been concerned with the bomb, he repeated Luke's earlier comment, there was no clear-cut way out. Unless you were a Sawbridge. For the rest of us, said Martin, there were just two conceivable ways. One was the way he had just taken: the other, to struggle on, as Luke was doing, and take our share of what had been done and what might still be done, and hope that we might come out at the end of the tunnel. Being well meaning all the time, and thinking of nothing worse than our own safety.

'For a warm-hearted man who's affected by the people round him,' said Martin, 'perhaps it's the only way. It's the way you're going, though you're more far-sighted than they are.'

'It wouldn't be easy for me,' I said after a pause, 'to break right away.'

'If you do choose their way,' he said with sudden energy, 'I've shown you how to do it.'

He meant that you could not compromise. If you accepted the bomb, the burnings alive, the secrets, the fighting point of power, you must take the consequences. You must face Sawbridge with an equal will. You were living in a power equilibrium, and you must not pretend; the relics of liberal humanism had no place there.

'I completely disagree,' I said.

'You can't find a compromise. But your personal ties keep you making them,' said Martin. 'That's why you leave it to worse men to take the other way.' He went on:

'Sometimes it's only the cold who can be useful.'

It had taken him a long time to be positive about what he must do:

but now he spoke as though he had it in the palm of his hand. Previously he had wondered about leaving science altogether. He had contemplated 'doing a Charles March' (a friend of mine who, years before, had given up society and career in order to become a doctor) – but Martin decided that for him it was too 'artificial', too much out of his line. For him, there was only one course, to go back to pure science.

Most unusually for him, he showed a flicker of bravado.

'I shall be just a little better than those pundits say,' he said.

He had not many illusions, though perhaps, just as he contrived to see Irene both with realistic observation and also surrounded with a romantic aura, he could still feel, in the depth of his heart, a tremor of the magic that science had once evoked there.

He told me in so many words that he had not lost faith that science – though maybe not in his lifetime – would turn out for good. From some, after his history, it would have sounded a piece of facile scientists' optimism. From him it had a different note. For to Martin it was jet-clear that, despite its emollients and its joys, individual life was tragic: a man was ineluctably alone, and it was a short way to the grave. But, believing that with stoical acceptance, Martin saw no reason why social life should also be tragic: social life lay within one's power, as human loneliness and death did not, and it was the most contemptible of the false-profound to confuse the two.

'As long as the worst things don't happen –' said Martin. 'That's why some of us must get clear of office and friends and anything that ties our hands.'

'Is that what you thought of most?'

'I hope they'll leave me alone,' he said. 'But there may come a time when people like me have to make a nuisance of themselves.'

He went on:

'I'm the last man for the job. It may be dangerous and I'm not cut out for that.'

It might not be necessary, I said. In my view, the danger was over-rated and the betting was against it.

'All the better,' said Martin. 'All the more reason for having a few sensible men who aren't committed.'

He meant, good could happen as well as evil; men might run into a little luck; if we were too much hypnotized by the violence we had lived through, if each man of good will was mobilized, paid and silenced, we might let the luck slip.

'That, may be the best reason of all for getting outside the machine,' said Martin. 'If a few of us are waiting for the chance, we might do a little good.'

He turned in his chair. In the tenebrous afternoon, the room had gone dark outside the zone of the desk light; and past the window flakes of snow were dawdling down on to the Whitehall pavement. He was looking at me. Suddenly, with no explanation necessary between us, he said:

'You know, I shall never have the success you wanted me to have.'

Again we were speaking without ease, as though each word had to be searched for.

'If I had not wanted it for you, would you have liked it more?'

'I said before, you can see too much in personal causes.'

'Have they made it harder for you?'

'That doesn't matter,' he replied. 'In the end, I should have done what I am doing now.'

Our intimacy had not returned, but we were speaking of ourselves more deeply than we had done before.

That afternoon, at last, Martin was answerable to no one. Speaking of his future, he had lost the final residue of a younger brother's tone, and took on that of equal to equal, contemporary to contemporary, self-made to self-made.

CHAPTER 43

A New Empire

MARTIN left Barford at the end of the year: Luke became Chief Superintendent the following May. A few weeks later, I went down to do some business with him on my way to Cambridge, where Martin had invited me to a college feast.

The Drawbells had not yet finished moving house, although Drawbell's own new appointment had been announced. It was a come-down. Perhaps that was why, more bullyingly even than in the past, he insisted that I should stay my night at Barford with them, not with the Lukes. I could not say no: in his decline he was hard to resist, partly because his personality was one of those that swell, become more menacing, the more he saw his expectations fade away.

He and his wife had waited for each post the preceding November, looking for a letter about the New Year's honours list; and they were doing it again before the birthday list. There was nothing for them. They still pretended to expect it. At breakfast, in a room with covers on some of the chairs, ready to move that week, Drawbell made believe to threaten me, fixing me with his sound eye.

'My patience is exhausted,' he said, as though making a public speech – but it was the kind of joke which is not a joke. 'It's high time the Government did its duty.'

He may have suspected that I knew his chances. I did. But, for the last time with Drawbell, I had to follow his lead, do my best to be hearty and say nothing.

For his chances were nil. I had heard Hector Rose rule him out. It was the only time I had known Rose be, by his own standards, less than just. By Rose's standards, Drawbell had done enough for a knighthood: Barford had 'made its contribution', as Rose said, and Drawbell had been in charge for five years. According to the rules, the top man got the top decoration; but for once Rose would not have it so. He asked cold questions about who had done the work; with the methodicalness of a recording angel, he put down to Drawbell's credit the occasions when he had backed the right horse – and then turned to the other side of the sheet. The final account, in Rose's mind, did not add up to a knighthood.

At the breakfast table, Drawbell, still ignorant of that decision, hoping against hope, put on his jocular act, and threatened me. His wife regarded me, monumental, impassive; she was looking forward to getting Mr Thomas Bevill down to the new establishment. Between her and her husband, I had never seen more than a thread of that friendliness-cum-dislike which comes in lifelong marriages that are wrong at the core: yet she remained his loyal and heavy-footed ally. She was no more defeated than he was. And when finally his last hope wilted, they would, without knowing it, be supports to each other.

That morning, Drawbell gave just one open sign of recognition that he was on the way down. He refused to come with me to his old office, which Luke was already occupying. He could not face the sight of someone who had passed him, who had – in Drawbell's eyes and the world's – arrived.

Yet Luke himself would have had his doubts, I thought, sitting beside his desk, behind which, in his shirt-sleeves, he tilted back in his chair – in that room where he had made his first proposal about the pile. He would have had his doubts about his arrival, if ever he had spared time to consider it, which – as he remained a humble and an immediate man – he was most unlikely to.

He knew that he would not now leave much of a scientific memorial behind him. You could not do real scientific work and become a 'stuffed shirt', as he used to argue rudely in the past. Ironically, he, so richly endowed for the pure scientific life, had, unlike Martin, put it behind him. There were times when he felt his greatest gift was rusting. His corpus of work would not stand a chance of competing with Mounteney's.

Nevertheless, Luke was enjoying himself. His chair tilted back against the wall, he gave the answer I had come for. Gave it with the crispness of one, who in reveries, had imagined himself as a tycoon. Once or twice he shot a response out of the side of his mouth.

'Curtains,' he said once, indicating that the discussion was at an end.

'Come off it, Walter,' I said.

Luke looked startled. As always, he had got into the skin of his part. Then he gave a huge cracked grin.

I had come to clear up one or two administrative tangles, which in Martin's time would have been dealt with at Barford, and we were talking of getting Luke a second-in-command to tidy up after him. Luke was determined to appoint Rudd, who had, as soon as Drawbell was superseded, transferred his devotion to the new boss.

'He's a snurge,' said Luke. 'But he can be a very useful snurge.'

Was he the man that Luke wanted? In my view, Luke needed someone to stand up to him.

'No,' said Luke. 'I can make something of him. I can make a difference to that chap.'

Already, I thought, Luke was showing just a trace of how power corrodes. As we walked round the establishment, in the drizzling rain, I teased him, bringing up against him his old ribald curses at 'stuffed shirts'.

'If ever you think I'm becoming one, Lewis,' said Luke, 'you come and kick my behind.'

He was limping as he walked. His knee was still giving him pain, and at the back of his mind there was the ache of not knowing whether he had recovered. Nevertheless, limping, grey at the temples, not disguising his fear of whether his life was going to be cut short, he seemed physically to expand as he took me into bay after bay of the new buildings. By this time they stretched for many acres on both sides of the river: in and out of the rain we dodged, as he took me to see the new piles being built, where the floors were busy with scientists and artisans. Then he took me to the two piles already working, working in the humanless space. The building looked less crude now; above was a large chimney, and there hummed the faint noise of fans. This had become Luke's empire.

Like any sentient man, he had had his hesitations about this project (for my benefit, he was reckoning up, as we stood beside the working pile, just how many such machines existed in the world). He had given his reasons why he went on with it, and why he believed all might turn out well. But now he had shut both doubts and justifications within him. He was not one of those who can work and at the same time remain detached about whether or not they are doing good. This was Luke's empire, and as he looked over it he thought of nothing but how best to make it run.

CHAPTER 44

Two Brothers

THAT evening, in Martin's rooms in Cambridge, which by a touch of college sentiment were those I had lived in before the war, I described that talk with Luke. Martin and I were alone, and there was an hour before dinner; only the first fringe of rain had reached Cambridge, and the sun was shining, after a shower which filled the room with a smell of wistaria from the court beneath.

There, in the high room, which the sunlight did not reach, Martin questioned me about Luke: how was his régime turning out? How were the latest plans working? For Martin, although he had changed

his life, did not pretend that he could will away his interest, and liked
to talk of the place where he had had an influence which would not
come to him again.

He disagreed with one of Luke's arrangements and gave his reason,
which sounded sensible.

'Why doesn't someone tell him so?' he said.

'Some people are going to get more than they bargained for,' I said.

'It's not necessary,' Martin was not displeased to find fault. I said
that, though Luke's methods might be rough and ready, under him
Barford would be a success.

'Poor old Walter!' Martin said, with a smile, with an edge of envy.

Martin had not gone back on his choice, although by this time he
knew, what one can never imagine until one lives it, the wear and
tear, hour by hour and day by day, as one tries to reshape a life. He
knew precisely what it was like to work in the same laboratory as his
juniors, and realize that they were outclassing him. He came to them
as a man with a big outside reputation, and felt a nobody. At colloquia
and laboratory teas he became nervous in front of young men whose
confidence, unlike his own, was absolute.

He believed now that his critics were right: from every practical
point of view, his choice had been stupid: he would stay there, doing
his college teaching, without a realistic chance of achievement for the
rest of his life.

He had always been quiet, but in the days of his power it had been
the quietness, trained and confident, of a high functionary, the quietness of Hector Rose. Now it had changed; it had the special quality
that you see in one who has learned something from life and who has
lost his high spirits during the lesson. His interest had become passive.
Sitting in the darkness of his room, looking out of the window at the
court brilliant in the rain-clear sunlight, he had none of the authority
of action that men like Luke carried on their brow.

But he was happy. It was a curious kind of happiness that had come
upon him almost without his knowing it. It occurred to me that I
had seen others make renunciations similar in kind to his: in each case
they gained happiness. It might have been otherwise, it might have
been one of the ironies of the human condition that, when you throw
away the game with a chance of winning it, you regret it ever after:
but, in the cases I had seen, it proved the contrary.

I was glad that he should be happy. Suddenly I thought that, hoping so much for him, with the fraternal concern that identified myself in him, I had worried little about his happiness. Even now – in the room where he had first mentioned the proof of fission, which had led us both to the fringe of such events as had darkened our consciences and given him the chance of secret power – he could not, now that he had resigned the power and found his happiness, share any part of it with me.

My concern for him had, in the midst of those convulsions, shown the flaw which exists in any of its kind, which, if we had been luckier, might not have come out so clear.

If we had been luckier, if events had not taken hold of us, there might have been no occasion for him to tell me, as he had done in St James's Street, when I said that I had wanted much for him:

'No. You have wanted a good deal for yourself.'

It was the truth; it was the reason why the most sacrificial of human affections twist into the most selfseeking of all. It can cripple those who receive it, and those who give can never find anything of what they seek.

I had looked to him to go the way I chose for him. In the Sawbridge affair, he had done the opposite, and, whichever of us was right in the abstract, that was why I had felt it like a betrayal. It was clear now. As men went, we were sensible and did not expect over much from human beings: but events had taken hold of us, and had shown up the nature of my concern.

As Irene perceived, with the insight of jealousy, the time came when he had to cut himself quite free.

If you identify yourself in another, however tough the tie between you, he cannot feel as you do, and then you go through (you who have been living your life in another) a state for which the old Japanese found a name, which they used to describe the sadness of a parent's love: a darkness of the heart.

I ought to have known it, for my mother had tried to relive her life in me; and I had not been able to return that kind of love. I too had been compelled to cut myself quite free.

It was a little thing, the human price that Martin and I had paid, as a result of those events which Hector Rose called 'too big for men' – and yet that was what I thought of, sitting in that dark room, the sky brilliant over the roofs opposite, waiting for the college bell. Through being forced together in our corner of those events, I had out of the nature of my affection done him harm. I had brought some sadness on myself. We were both too realistic to expect that our intimacy could be complete again.

The dinner bell began to toll. Martin gave an indrawn, sarcastic smile. As we stood up I was thinking that, though we had paid our modest price, we had regained most of the ease of old habit in each other's company. We were on our way to repairing something of what had happened between us. Of the human relations I had so far known, I had found, despite our mistakes, none more steady and comforting than that with my brother; I hoped that in time he would feel the same.

MORE ABOUT PENGUINS

If you have enjoyed reading this book you may wish to know that *Penguin Book News* appears every month. It is an attractively illustrated magazine containing a complete list of books published by Penguins and still in print, together with details of the month's new books. A specimen copy will be sent free on request.

Penguin Book News is obtainable from most bookshops; but you may prefer to become a regular subscriber at 3s. for twelve issues. Just write to Dept EP, Penguin Books Ltd, Harmondsworth, Middlesex, enclosing a cheque or postal order, and you will be put on the mailing list.

Some other books published by Penguins are described on the following pages.

Note: *Penguin Book News* is not available in the U.S.A., Canada or Australia

ANGUS WILSON

—

Anglo-Saxon Attitudes

'This brilliant and ambitious novel is about the conscience as it worries two generations of a middle-class family' – *New Statesman*

Hemlock and After

'It establishes him immediately as the most important novelist to come forward since the last war' – *Listener*

Such Darling Dodos

A frighteningly vivid picture of decaying gentlepeople and out-moded idealists, and of the ambitious 'new-look' young intelligentsia of the late 1940s.

The Wrong Set

His first published work, these twelve stories contain some of his most perfectly observed characters.

Also available

THE OLD MEN AT THE ZOO

NOT FOR SALE IN THE U.S.A.

C. P. SNOW

C. P. Snow has firmly established his reputation as a novelist with his ambitious sequence of books, *Strangers and Brothers*. These novels, each of which is complete in itself, relate the experience of one man – the narrator, Lewis Eliot. Sometimes he describes his direct experience, as in *Time of Hope* and *Homecomings;* sometimes the experience is gained through viewing the lives of others, as in *The Masters* and *The Conscience of the Rich*. Altogether the sequence is forming an impressive study of both the great public issues and the private problems of our age.

STRANGERS AND BROTHERS

The story of George Passant, a Midland solicitor's clerk. (1925–33)

TIME OF HOPE

Lewis Eliot's early life, in the Midlands and at the Bar. (1914–33)

THE CONSCIENCE OF THE RICH

The story of Charles March, scion of an Anglo-Jewish banking family. (1927–36)

THE LIGHT AND THE DARK

The story of Roy Calvert, a brilliant young Cambridge linguist. (1935–43)

THE MASTERS

The struggle for the mastership of a Cambridge college. (1937)

HOMECOMINGS

The middle life of Lewis Eliot and his second marriage. (1938–51)

THE AFFAIR

The story of a miscarriage of justice in a Cambridge college. (1953–4)

Also available:

CORRIDORS OF POWER

NOT FOR SALE IN THE U.S.A.